THE FIENDS IN THE FURROWS II

More Tales of Folk Horror

THE
FIENDS
IN THE
FURROWS II

More Tales of Folk Horror

FOREWORD BY
ANDREW MICHAEL HURLEY

Edited by David T. Neal & Christine M. Scott

NOSETOUCH PRESS

CHICAGO | PITTSBURGH

The Fiends in the Furrows II: More Tales of Folk Horror

© 2020 by David T. Neal and Christine M. Scott
All Rights Reserved.

ISBN-13: 978-1-944286-20-0
Paperback Edition

Published by Nosetouch Press
www.nosetouchpress.com

Cataloging-in-Publication Data

Names: Neal, David T., editor. / Scott, Christine M., editor.
Title: The Fiends in the Furrows II: More Tales of Folk Horror
Description: Chicago, IL : Nosetouch Press [2020]
Identifiers: ISBN: 9781944286200 (paperback)
Subjects: LCSH: Horror—Fiction. | Paranormal—Fiction. |
Fairy tales—Fiction. | Folk tales—Fiction.
GSAFD: Horror fiction. | BISAC: FICTION / Horror.

Components of the figures on the cover by:
© xunantunich at AdobeStock.com

Cover & Interior Designed by Christine M. Scott
www.clevercrow.com

For the Bees

CONTENTS

FOREWORD

ANDREW MICHAEL HURLEY

It seems entirely fitting that the origins of the term "Folk Horror" are mysterious. Some attribute the popularisation of the label to Piers Haggard, the director of *Blood on Satan's Claw*, others to Mark Gatiss, who used it in his 2010 documentary series, *A History of Horror*, as a way of connecting Haggard's film with *Witchfinder General* and *The Wicker Man*.

Yet, wherever it comes from, whatever it means, it's a genre that encompasses far more than a handful of films from at most a half century ago. Folk Horror continues to evolve into an eclectic mix of cinema, television, art and music from across the world. Recent additions to the stable include the Austrian film, *Goodnight Mommy* (2014), for instance, and South Korean director Na Hong-jin's *The Wailing* (2016).

It's become of interest to writers, too, and the last decade or so has seen an increase in literary Folk Horror—for example *Harbour* by John Adjvide Lindquivst; Benjamin Myers', *The Gallows Pole*; *Water Shall Refuse Them*, by Lucie McKnight Hardy; Jenn Ashworth's, *Fell*; Adam Nevill's *The Ritual; Such Small Hands*, by the Spanish writer Andrés Barba; as well as the anthologies, *This Dreaming Isle*, the first volume of *The*

Fiends in the Furrows, and the second, which you're about to read.

There's perhaps no better way to get a sense of Folk Horror's contemporary diversity than to type the words into YouTube. The well-known examples that Gatiss cites naturally turn up at the top of the list, along with reviews of Ari Aster's *Midsommar,* it being such a recent release. But then we tumble down the rabbit hole and find the 1922 Swedish film, *Häxan: Witchcraft Through the Ages,* the "10 Scariest Japanese Legends", a playlist called "Harvest Hymns"; another entitled "60s-70s Folk Horror & Occult Psychedelia". Keep going and you'll come across the podcast, "Terrorised by Gnomes— Horror of the Hidden Folk" and a wealth of cult British television programmes from the 1970s, such as *Penda's Fen, The Stone Tape* and *The Owl Service.*

Apart from a vague threat of the "supernatural", it's not immediately obvious what binds all these examples together. What is it that links "harvest" with "witchcraft"? What is specifically "Folk Horror" about the era of the counterculture?

In part, the complexity of accounting for these associations lies in the fact that we are not experiencing a Folk Horror *revival*—which would come with pre-existing analysis and interpretation—but viewing many texts as "Folk Horror" for the first time. The term might have been circulating for a while, but it's perhaps only in the last ten or fifteen years that it has become a recognisable *genre* that filmmakers, writers and musicians are able to consciously explore as a context for their work.

Effectively, any "Folk Horror" made before the twenty-first century was not necessarily conceived *as* "Folk Horror", and so because we're retro-fitting the label to a large extent it's only now that we're considering the relationships between these older texts, their aesthetic patterns and how they've influenced the Folk Horror of today. It's a "prism of a term", as the writer, Adam Scovell, puts it.

And yet, in his book, *Hours Dreadful and Things Strange* (2017), he does attempt to establish a framework and proposes the idea of a Folk Horror "chain" that links works that might belong to that category by four essentials. The first—a landscape, "where elements within its topography have adverse effects on the social and moral identity of its inhabitants"—often goes on to inform the others, namely: "isolation", "skewed belief systems and morality" and a "happening/summoning" (usually of something malevolent).

It's a useful way of connecting up a mass of seemingly miscellaneous material, but thankfully stops short of any concrete definitions of what constitutes "Folk Horror", which—as the YouTube hits reveal—is largely a subjective conclusion. As Andy Paciorek says in *Folk Horror Revival: Field Notes* (2018), "There is frequently an indefinable 'certain something' that makes a work appear more or less Folk Horror". In other words, you know it when you see it.

None of that makes things any clearer, of course, but as with the study of any genre, it's generally less interesting to fret over the shape of its edges than it is to value what the genre produces and when. So perhaps a better question to ask is why Folk Horror is of interest to us *now?*

Part of its appeal lies in our proclivity for nostalgia. The films and television programmes from the 1960s to the 1980s that we might now think of as "Folk Horror" have acquired a kind of kitsch value. In our digital age, there's something intriguing and attractive about the lo-fi and the analogue.

But for those of us in our forties and fifties who were children then, these texts resonate more deeply when we recall childhoods spent in a world where, rightly or wrongly, there was more freedom to encounter danger.

This is reflected in the Public Information Films of that period, some of which have now found themselves part of the "Folk Horror" canon. That they existed at all says a lot about how we spent our time as children then—mostly outdoors, mostly away from adults. Left to our own devices, the world could be a lethal place, but the prevailing attitude was that "authority" was not there to protect us by quarantine or through gentle discussion but to educate with directness, even if that directness was upsetting.

The man meant to frighten us.

And so in these films there is a great anxiety about safety and good behaviour but—paradoxically—not about the graphic manner in which it is encouraged.

Some examples have become notorious. In the 1973 film, *Lonely Water,* a black-hooded spirit of death (voiced by Donald Pleasance) haunts ditches and rivers to catch out "the unwary, the show-off, the fool". In *Apaches,* from 1977, a gang of kids playing on a farm is gradually depleted as they fall foul of various nasty accidents. One is crushed under the wheels of a trailer, another drowns in slurry, a girl is poisoned, her friend flattened by a heavy gate and then the last of them is trapped on a moving tractor as it crashes down a steep hillside.

Other films were even more controversial, such as *The Finishing Line,* in which a boy fantasises about what a school sports day might be like if it were to take place on a railway track. In dreamlike sequences, the various events—breaking down a perimeter fence, dashing across the line—are treated by the teachers as innocuously as if the children were competing in the relay or the sack race. Points are deducted from teams who lose members under the wheels of the trains, but can be gained, for instance, in the "Twelve-and-Under Stone Throwing" competition which rewards the amount of damage or injury the children cause as they hurl rocks at a passing express. Smashing a window scores two; blinding the driver is worth six.

The culmination of the gala is The Great Tunnel Walk, where all the children who are still alive file into the dark to race the three miles to the other end. After a train speeds through, a few eventually stagger into the light, bloodied and bruised. The rest are carried out by parents and medics. The final shots in which dozens of dead children are laid side by side on the tracks is, like the whole twenty minutes of the film, genuinely disturbing. Which was the point.

Modern sensitivities may leave us astonished that anything so gruesome was ever thought appropriate for children in any context, but what is it that makes these films specifically "Folk Horror"? What connection do they have with any other examples?

If we go back to Scovell's "chain", then we can see how in all three, the "landscape" plays a role and certainly the children in *Lonely Water* and *Apaches* are "isolated"—both geographically and from parental help. Perhaps the naivety of the children accounts for a kind of "skewed belief system" and there is many a grisly "happening".

But for me, they're "Folk Horror" because of the way they were made—not as mere pedagogy, but as films in their own right by directors who interpreted the brief by drawing on and reimagining the tropes of horror cinema. As the BFI website says, John Mackenzie (who went on to make *The Long Good Friday*) generates much of *Apache*'s power by using the narrative structures of the slasher movie.

Similarly, many children's television dramas of that period (though less gory) come out of the traditions of science fiction, fantasy and horror and—crucially—retain what makes those kinds of stories unsettling. A few that come to mind include *Doctor Who, The Box of Delights, The Tripods, The Boy From Space, Chocky* and *Moondial*.

Put next to children's programmes today, they seem much stranger and edgier. In comparison to modern CGI, the special effects seem low-budget, even when many weren't, and it's easy to dismiss them as dated. But it's the hand-made feel of these programmes that makes them eerie. There's something uncanny about suspending disbelief and at the same time seeing the puppet's strings.

But Folk Horror isn't only the preserve of the nostalgic, the middle aged or even the British and so there must be other reasons why it is becoming an increasingly globalised genre.

One explanation may be our collective human desire to 're-turn' to a less complicated existence. For there seems to be an inverse law which says that the more we 'advance' as a species, the deeper the yearning for what we've left behind. Or as H.H. Symonds, one of the founders of the Friends of the Lake District puts it: "As man civilises, his desire for wild and primitive beauty becomes greater: we guard ourselves in this way against insanity, and remain what we must in part always be, earth-born".

These sound like the words of a New-Age mystic, but Symonds was writing in the 1930s and in fact the fantasy of retreating to the wilds and reconnecting with the rhythms of the natural world goes back further still. For hundreds if not thousands of years, we've been seduced by the idea that in the rural we will find the authentic life that has been eluding us or which we have been denied.

At certain times in our history, this need to 'go back' becomes more pressing, a means of survival, a defence against madness, as Symonds says.

For many who adopted the values of the late-1960s counter-culture the regression to communal, agrarian subsistence and rejecting organised religion for older beliefs was the best—perhaps the only—sane response to the growth of post-war materialism and its facility for withering the soul.

And for us now, re-thinking what we consume, what we produce, what relationship we have with the planet has a similar urgency, which is perhaps why the "Folk Horror" of the 1960s and 1970s is meaningful to us. In both eras there is a similar sense that the structures in which we are obliged to live are not fit for purpose.

For all its sophistication, technology does not inherently make us any happier or better off. The Industrial Revolution that shaped the modern world generated as many horrors as benefits—pollution, overcrowding, slavery, inequality—and has brought us to where we are today with the earth stripped of its resources and wildlife.

The Digital Revolution, too, has not been wholly benevolent. Social media has the means to keep us in touch with one another but has engendered new strains of depression and neuroses. We have the luxury of acquiring what we want at the click of a button, but online shopping has killed the high street and our personal details have become commodities to be harvested and sold. The Internet might be the greatest repository of information we've ever known, but it also enables the dissemination of hate and the spread of fake news, making fact and truth elusive when we need it most. Never more so than now, of course, as we try to find a way through the Covid-19 pandemic, which has brought out the best and, inevitably, the worst in humanity, and rendered the future even more unstable and uncertain.

How tempting it is, then, to want to take refuge in the old ways, to find simplicity and order again in the pre-industrial past.

Communities which offer such a possibility appear frequently in Folk Horror. In *Midsommar,* the heroine, Dani, finds a balm for her grief in the (initial) serenity of the Hårga, and in *The Wicker Man,* even though Howie is prickly with the locals as soon as he gets off his plane, the opening shots show him flying into what looks like paradise. It's true that the beliefs of the island folk are at odds with his stern Protestantism, but he finds a well-established communal structure nonetheless. Summerisle is a utopia, in fact, until the harvest fails.

And it's at moments of crisis like this, at the precarious junctures of a community's history, where we see the methods the inhabitants must employ in response and the "horror" of Folk Horror ensues.

The close relationship that these isolated country-dwellers have with the natural world demands that they adopt a different set of morals and practices that are bent towards survival rather than any metropolitan notion of rationality. Relying on 'the land' for sustenance is to have life shaped by powerful forces that must be endured or appeased in ways that, to the outsider, seem strange and atavistic, and nearly always horrific. It's this that Folk Horror obviously exploits for dramatic purposes, but the sacrifices—however vicious—are always purposeful to those who perform them. What underpins these rituals is an understanding that the land must be nurtured; that we live *with* nature, not off it. Folk Horror chimes with our anxieties about climate change and ecological collapse, anxieties which are rooted in how powerless we feel, how limited our influence as individuals can be. If 'going back to the land' is such a traumatic experience for outsiders in Folk Horror, then it is only an expression of how estranged we've become from the natural world, with the blood offerings to the soil acting as a metaphor for an intimacy most of us have forgotten.

Sometimes in Folk Horror that intimacy is forced upon the characters and takes them by surprise. In Peter Weir's film of *Picnic at Hanging Rock* (1975) the schoolgirls and teachers of Appleyard College succumb to the latent energy that seems to haunt the spot in the outback chosen for their Valentine's Day outing. Their watches stop, they become drowsy, and of the four girls who venture into the upper reaches of the hill two are never seen again. Where they go is never revealed, nor do we ever see the 'force' that apparently spirits them away, only its effect. Similarly, in Ben Wheatley's film, *A Field in England* (2013), there is an invisible 'something' in the soil that appears to slur time and reality. But these two films are quite unique, as the "monster" in Folk Horror tends not to be the spiritus loci itself but the effect of it on us. So we get communities who worship the deities they perceive around them (*The Wicker Man, The VVitch*), people perverted by isolation (*Straw Dogs, The Texas Chainsaw Massacre, Deliverance*) and the folkloric figures we've invented to try and give shape to the sense of danger the natural world creates in us—the ghosts and demons that we conjure up to haunt the dark woods and the lonely lanes.

The Folk Horror countryside is rife with superstitions that never quite dissipate but slowly layer the landscape, infusing it with an otherworldliness that festers just beneath the surface—hence the title of this anthology.

Returning to the rural not only unearths ancient demonic fiends but our own violent history, too. As such, Folk Horror can steer away from the supernatural in favour of politics and tackle the "horror" of oppression. In this way, bucolic landscapes become a place of conflict between the rich and the poor, the powerful and the powerless.

It's this polemic strand of Folk Horror which grants films like *Witchfinder General* admittance into the genre, along with Kevin Brownlow's *Winstanley* (1975), which follows the real-life battle of Gerard Winstanley to establish a commune for his fellow Diggers in Cromwell's England. His egalitarian call for an earth that "shall be made a common treasury of livelihood to all mankind" is systematically thwarted by the landowners and eventually put down by thuggish force.

There's an equivalent brutality in Peter Watkins' 1964 film *Culloden*—a documentary-style recount of the eponymous 1746 battle in which the Jacobites were first slaughtered on the field and then in the glens as they and their families retreated and were hunted down by the Duke of Cumberland's soldiers.

Unlike the elemental forces that in *The Wicker Man*, say, might be at least partially apprehended through accumulated mutual knowledge and ritual, the "horror" here comes from the ruthlessness of a human power that cannot be reasoned with.

A gentler, but no less visually arresting, study of the fruitless fight against power can be found in David Gladwell's, *Requiem for a Village* (1976). The film opens by contrasting images of a field being bulldozed to make way for new housing and an elderly man cycling to a country churchyard in order to tend the grass around the graves. As a response to the encroachment of modernity, the old man's memories become more and more vivid, the dead appear to rise from their sleep and the old routines of village life are re-enacted alongside shots of marauding motorbike gangs and industrial machinery ravaging the landscape in the name of progress.

There is no simple polarisation here of urban=bad/rural=good. As in so much Folk Horror, the countryside has its strangeness and darkness and violence, too; it's not wholly safe. Yet, the message in *Requiem for a Village* seems to be that concrete can never be preferable to meadowland, commercialisation never advantages anyone but the already advantaged, and that no good can ever come of stripping an individual of the power to control their own environment.

Folk Horror often articulates the frustrations of the marginalised and the downtrodden, and has a timely and important radical voice in an era of ever-growing disparity between the affluent and the impoverished.

Fiona Mozley's Booker-shortlisted, *Elmet* (2017) tackles class struggle, and questions the ethics of land ownership in a similar way to *Winstanley*. And Mark Jenkin's 2019 film, *Bait*, (which lingers on the edgelands of Folk Horror) examines the effects of gentrification on a Cornish fishing village. In both, the "horror" comes from the economically disenfranchised being pushed to the edge.

What we also see in *Bait* is a romanticising of the past. The fisherman's cottage that the family of wealthy Londoners have bought to rent out to other wealthy holidaymakers has been 'modernised' by making it look old. The place is strung with fishing nets and buoys, the materials of industry now merely twee decorations.

But there is a bigger and more worrying appropriation of history occurring as populist politicians seek to distil our heritage into sentimental images of yesteryear; a 'golden age' in which everything was timeless and settled—usually in favour of the privileged minority. If such people could recreate Britain, for instance, it would look very much like the Britain in the opening sequence of Paul Wright's film essay, *Arcadia* (2018) with its thatched cottages, haymaking, and the farmer scattering his seeds by hand, all to the strains of *Jerusalem*. And it would be characterised by the conservative social and sexual hierarchies of the past in which everyone "knew their place".

But, in the film, this chocolate box Britain is soon intercut by the real countryside—a place of eccentricity, ancient knowledge and cryptic traditions. It's the place of the 'Obby

'Oss, the May Queen, the water diviner, the Morris dancer, the raver, magicians, witches and wanderers. In contrast to the urban, there is, in the rural, at least the *potential* for liberty. One passage splices the carefree dancing of happy naturists with dark-suited crowds moving herd-like down a city street in a manner reminiscent of *The Wasteland:*

> Under the brown fog of a winter dawn,
> A crowd flowed over London Bridge, so many,
> I had not thought death had undone so many.

Again, *Arcadia* doesn't suggest that the countryside is an easy cure for urban woes, only that if we are to change as a people then we need to re-find the magic and miracle that's there in natural world. And that, at least, might begin to restore our freedom to wonder and imagine.

As musician, Julian Holloway, of the "Haunted Electronics" group, Flange Circus, says, "Too much of our lives are given order by routines, authorities and forces mostly beyond our control. So if we can revel in the unknown and enchanting we might be able to see the world a little differently. From this, hopefully progressive change might be summoned."

The conclusions that *Arcadia* comes to about our future are fairly bleak. As the film draws to a close with a montage of urban squalor, glue-sniffing teenagers and the homogenous boxes of 'ideal homes', the message is that we, the "folk", the common people, have been systematically cheated out of the right to shape our societies by the forces of commerce and compelled to live in a way that brings out our worst excesses. We've become greedy, paranoid, aggressive and above all, fearful. We've been driven to ruin the natural world and, more disturbingly still, become indifferent to its fate. This is true not just in Britain, but across the globe.

But hopefully this can be altered, and Folk Horror, with its rear-view mirror, has an important role to play in enabling us to see what we've lost and what we're losing. And while there might be no possibility of reversing time and living once again in small rural communities, if we put aside the clichés of the pagan robes and burning effigies, those places can stand as emblems of how best to live together—through common endeavour and respect for the land we share.

As we move forward, looking back might just be our salvation.

Preston, England. May 2020.

INTRODUCTION

DAVID T. NEAL

What a difference a couple of years makes. From the lingering terrors of yesteryear to a world held spellbound in the grip of a global pandemic and the accompanying madness it inflicts on people unaccustomed to the haunting, lingering spectacle of pestilence.

In 2020, it's impossible to not think of the coronavirus pandemic, which marks a fault line between the world that was and the world that will be (or could be). Whether safely quarantined or ignorantly and angrily defying lockdown, to fiery protests in the street against police brutality met with still more violence and choking clouds of tear gas, the newfound prominence of masks in our daily lives echoes the ghastly, macabre masquerade of Folk Horror. Dark times deliver darker horrors, and for anyone living today, the shadow of dread looms larger now than ever.

Still a specter stalking at the margins of Horror, Folk Horror has made some great strides in the pre-pandemic pop culture. Most noteworthy, of course, is the sunny, sinfully cinematic *Midsommar* (2019) and its brooding older sibling, *Hereditary* (2018), both directed and written by Ari Aster. These have left an indelible stamp on the Folk Horror consciousness.

And they also speak to the boundaries and even limitations of Folk Horror, in terms of imagery, motifs, themes, and the terrors and horrors they can inflict on unsuspecting viewers.

In the realm of fiction, with this sequel anthology, Nosetouch Press continues to test the waters of what can be credibly presented as meaningful Folk Horror, above and beyond the ground it's traveled already. We sought stories that evocatively presented Folk Horror in a variety of settings and contexts, in hopes of homesteading new areas for future writers to develop.

In "Yan" by Alys Hobbs, an eccentric shepherdess struggles with the consequences of a horrifying vision haunting her out on the pasture. Coy Hall's "Hour of the Cat's Eye" takes us back in time to the Thirty Years' War, where a wounded and feverish mercenary encounters eldritch adversaries.

Elizabeth Twist's "The Complete Compleat Gardener" serves up an arcane tome to a Scottish gardener who puts it to ready and fateful use. Neil McRobert's "A Well-Fed Man" chases a starving and desperate boy in a deadly game of cat-and-mouse with a relentless cannibal.

"The Binding Tide" by Shawn Wallace, pits a brazen, Boston-based real estate developer and his jet-set team against a group of Rhode Island locals in the seaside town of Skraeling. Jack Lothian's "A Deed Without a Name" places wandering sibling witches in a war-torn and horrifying world.

Hazel King's "The Hanging Tree and the Old Tom Pit" documents a town's annual ritual to cheat Death running into more than a few snags. In "The Death of a Drop of Water" Sara Century explores a grieving woman's harrowing haunting by a waterborne legion of dark spirits.

"A Ritual for Pleasure and Atonement" by Kristi De-Meester portrays a young man struggling with his demons, bedeviled by carnal and other appetites. Tim Major's "The Slow King" offers up a young actor sacrificing everything for the role of a lifetime.

Finally, Tracy Fahey's "Daerg-an-Daol" conjures a mournful young man braving an old folk tradition to honor his dying uncle's last wish.

Nosetouch Press thanks Andrew Michael Hurley for his excellent Foreword, and hopes that readers will enjoy the Folk Horror presented in this anthology, in a time when the very real horror of the world has rarely been more in evidence. We're confident that the Folk Horror aesthetic will germinate in the fertile imaginations of creators, and lead fans further afield.

Chicago, Illinois. June 2020.

ALYS HOBBS

YAN

THE flock spills out from the gate and scatters sleetlike into the field. It is steep here and the ground is frozen hard so they skitter as they go, slipping their hooves, pouring out their alarm in long ribbons of steam. Their wooly bodies clump together, and beating her crook on the track comes Molly Brock with stones in her hands.

She stops, spits, squints over the land. Her cracked lips move as she starts to count; yan, tan, tether. A sheep splits from its huddle, staggers off a little way before thinking better of it and returning to the group. Mether, pip, azer. All the way to jigget Molly counts, and then she drops a stone into her pocket and begins again. Her small streaming eyes flick over the bumping, bustling flock. They shift like drifts of sand in water, each speck followed by all the rest in a cloud. Yan, tan, tether. When three stones clack at her hip Molly stops. She is one sheep short.

The heather is brown and the loam is black and the sky is thick as milk. It will snow tonight; Molly can smell it on the air, clean and clear as a fresh-filled pail. She must get back to the cottage before it comes, must split her kindling for the fire. How she hates to sit all night in the dark, with no sound but the wind knocking on the walls and her own muttering voice for company. Sometimes she lies for hours in her bed, waiting for the call of the hunting owl. She thinks that after all these years it ought to sound familiar, like a friend calling over the distance. But every time it comes—that quivering shriek, that high hunting note—then Molly's blood runs cold through her body. Then she thinks of her one-room cottage squatting darkly in its dip, how small it is—a pin's prick. A snail's shell. And she thinks of herself within, even smaller, and of the owl with its keen yellow eye. She is the shrew, the vole, the tiniest field mouse, and if she moves it will surely see her. Down it will swoop in a beat of jagged talon and knife-sharp beak and the last thing she'll know will be agony. So Molly stays very still all night long with her eyes shut tight, and she counts until daylight comes through the window. Yan, tan, tether.

She must be home before the snow arrives.

A mile Molly walks, then two, retracing the steps of her driven flock. Their hooves have made thousands of half-moons in the hard packed track. All the way back to the crest she goes, to the rise where the stones are so huge and flat they look like fallen-down walls of giants' houses. The wind settles here. It mutters rather than moans.

Here she spies the lone sheep. It has wandered a long way off, finding footholds among the ankle-cracking crevices of the stones where its fellows don't dare to go. On seeing her it lifts its long head, totters away a little further, bleats defiance into the frozen air. Molly spits and rubs her split lips with the back of her hand. She uses her crook for balance to pick her way across the rocks, and the sheep knows the game is up; it allows her to take it by its scruff without too much protest. Molly hauls it back in the direction of its brethren. Turns to follow. Hesitates. Looks back over the ridge.

The land slopes down and away to rugged heath and for-lorn fields of blanket bog. Molly can see for many miles from where she's standing, down over threads of stream and clumps of crowberry and shivering trees grown crooked in the gales.

And something is moving across that empty country, that low running field where the yellow gorse grows bright against the bleakness. Something staggering. Heaving. Running.

At first Molly thinks: wild horse, broken-legged and falling again and again to the ground. Then she thinks: birds squab-bling, rising up in great flurries of wing. But then she sees that it is a person. It is a man. It is a man dressed darkly, wearing a wide-brimmed hat. He hauls a white thing over the heather.

It is not a bird or a lamb—it is too long, too limbed—and it rises and bucks and it pulls from him, and its skirts fill with wind, like a sail.

The man stops and throws the white thing to the ground. He shouts—it carries, ebbing, getting to Molly's ear several seconds after his mouth has closed. Then the man raises his arm and brings it down. He raises his arm then brings it down. He has something in his fist—a stone, a brick, a hammer. He raises his arm and then he brings it down. The sound floats across the moor; meat beaten flat at the butcher. A boot on a stray cur's back. A bubbling scream with no hope in it. The white turns red. The red turns black. The man raises his arm and brings it down, and down, and down.

It goes on for so long Molly thinks she has fallen asleep, thinks she is dozing by a stream, listening to a kingfisher hitting a fish against a rock over and over again. The fish is still squirming. The kingfisher swallows it whole. The river runs red, runs black, runs white as milk frothing.

By the time Molly comes back the man is gone, and the day is almost done. Molly gets home in time to split an armful of kindling before the snow arrives.

Molly goes out to mend wall. Molly goes out to count sheep; yan, tan, tether. She drops stones in her pockets, drives the wandering ewe back to its fellows. Molly roams pasture and ridge, watches clouds skudding over the skies. A hare dashes over the low field. The snowmelt comes down from the mountain, swelling the stream. Little by little, the clotted red heap in the heather rots away.

Dainty nose and cheeks once-rosy are ripped off and carried away by foxes. Slim pretty fingers are taken by rats. Molly finds long yellow hairs snared in fences, caught in fleeces, trapped between her teeth. Not a spot of white is left on the dress. Every bit is russet red, except those parts which are so red they are black. A beetle crawls out from the cavern where an eye should be.

Molly goes out to count sheep. Molly splits kindling for the fire. She thinks now and then of going into town, of finding an ear and whispering into it. *I seen a terrible thing,* she thinks of saying. *A man in a wide-brimmed hat. A white dress reddening.*

But the way into town is long. The people there turn up their noses and away their shoulders; they step back when Molly comes close. She'd never get to an elbow, let alone an ear. And anyway there is work to do, so Molly beats her crook on the track and bends double in the squalls. Molly picks ticks out of fleeces and tips sheep on their rears to check their teeth, their hooves, their noses. She stops going by the low field where the yellow gorse grows, stops visiting that tattering red heap.

And then it begins to visit her.

She glimpses it first on the ridge, wading down, gone in the time it takes Molly to lift her head. It moves in the corner of her eye; a blink of red, a flicker of rags. Through an afternoon's mizzle its bulk wanders. In a dawn's mist. on the long track to town she turns and it is there, far behind but following, the red thing whose skirts rise and fill and whip in the wind. Whose yellow hair lifts from a gaping white scalp. Whose ruined face tilts down at the ground but whose splintering legs walk on after Molly, wherever she goes.

At night she hears the flap of its soaked garments outside her cottage. By the stream's edge she sees its red reflection. When the flock lift their heads and roll back their eyes, she knows they have seen it behind her. The sheep lurch away, spilling down the field, but Molly doesn't run or turn around. Her heart is a thrashing fish but she stays very still, like when the hunting owl comes. And no one touches her. No voice speaks. Only the wind yowls and groans and beats against her back.

It does not follow her to town, where the air is milder and the cobbles are slick with steam. It is market day so Molly buys the burned loaf and the day-old rabbit and the nugget of cheese to see her through the week. All the people smell sheep on her. They smell the dung and the rain. They smell the wetness of her days and they breathe with their mouths open, taking her pennies and dashing them into their lock-boxes before turning quickly away.

The inn feels too hot with its stove boiling and its people all sweating and close. Molly's face soon flushes and her nose runs over her lip. She mops it up with her sleeve, orders a cup of beer, stands in a corner supping it. She is thinking of her cottage many miles away—how still and empty it will be. There the only light will be the thin afternoon, coming in at the narrow window. There the only sound will be the wind at the walls and the far-off bleat of sheep. How strange it is, to think of that silent unmoving room, to think of her table and chair and bed standing in their places, while she is here in this heat with all these voices and comings-and-goings around her. "A white dress," she hears, coming back. A white dress. A white dress.

Molly turns her face toward the group gathered at the near-by table. She tips her head. Listens.

There sits Sam Bethel, the innkeeper, with his shirtsleeves rolled up to his elbows. With him is a man called John Bishop and another man who Molly does not know. John is speaking. He is tapping his stubby finger on the table to punctuate his point, beer frothing at the corners of his mouth. "That's—what—she—were wearing. A white dress. And I says I seen old Lew Linnet bundling something white into his cart 'end of last week. Thas' all I's saying."

"Lew Linnet," Sam Bethel says, "Lew 'ant never crossed path with Lady Hale in his life. And if he did, he'd be more like to have a fit and die at her feet himself."

"Well I says someone knows more'n they're letting slip," John says, changing tack. "And that it's a right shame, that lass being gone all these weeks and not s'much as a peep out of no-one. Someone must've seen summat."

"Ah," their companion puts in, "judge'll get t'bottom of it."

John snorts.

"I'll be buggered if Judge Green'd find more than 'bottom of his pint on a fair day," he says, but he mumbles it and all three men glance around afterwards. Then, "Oh 'eck," John says as Molly shifts over to their table. "What's this now."

"Pardon," Molly rattles. Her hands are slippery and her head is sweating under her bonnet. "I did hear thee all talking." she says. Her voice cracks and quivers—it has been too long since she used it last.

"Oh aye," says the man she does not know.

"And so?" says John Bishop.

"Pardon," Molly says again. "But I was hearing and I was wondering—and I was wanting to ask what did happen to the lady. To Lady Hale, that is."

The men click their tongues and shake their heads at each other.

"Well we don't know, do we," says John. "Ain't nobody knows. Thas' what I's saying, if you was listening."

"Ah but," says Sam Bethel slowly, "maybe thar's someone that does."

John and his companion fall still. All three look up at Molly. Then at once she is aware of herself—of her scabbed lips and her cracked hands, her knotted grey hair, her weak streaming eyes, her blotched and rough complexion. A prickling heat washes over her and she steps back, spilling her cup of beer down her legs and onto the flagstones. The spell is broken; John and his friend laugh, turning away.

"The idiot don't know nothing," John concludes, tapping his finger against his head.

Molly retreats to the fireside, poking her tongue into the bottom of the cup where some dregs of beer still remain. Her legs are damp and the day is seeping away outside, and she knows she must be off. There is kindling to be cut and the dark to beat home, and work still to do. But she waits, waits, waits until Sam Bethel finally gets up from the table, leaves John and his fellow behind, and goes back to the bar. Then mouse-quick Molly scurries to him, leans over, scrabbles her fingers on the bartop until he looks up at her. "I's something to say," she hisses.

Sam's face slackens. "What's that?"

"'Appen I's seen something," Molly says, but the nerve is already leaving her. She feels Sam's soft blue eyes upon her flat, wide face, feels his gaze roving in the creases round her mouth, prying into the filth of her collar and the grit in her ears. And she is backing away across the floor, shaking her head. The door bumps open behind her and the cold cloaks her back. Sam is moving out from behind the bar, coming toward her, and so she starts off up the street at a lurching, loping run. Some children in the square laugh at her, the lumbering old shepherdess fleeing up the hill.

The shops are shutting. The sturdy houses with their warm-glowing windows fall away on either side. The road out of town is steep and Molly's legs are already stiff and aching from the sudden running, and it is almost evening proper. She has left it so late. This light will not see her home.

But Molly has no choice; there is no other way except the long walk over the moors. She must cross the bridges and clamber the stiles, must march across the low field where the red thing wastes away. She wishes she had brought her crook with her to rest on, to beat on the ground as she goes. Ahead of her the wind is squealing. The rain is spitting into her eyes.

And up the track, it is waiting.

At first she thinks: tree. Strayed cow. Fence-post. But she hears the wind in its skirts and in the grey gloom she can just about pick out the red. The red. The red. Below the wind there is a thin shivering wail—no words, after all, could come from that throat's ragged ruin. *Tell them what you seen,* the sound says. *Tell them where my body does lie, Molly Brock. Tell them what he did to me. How his arm rose and it fell. How it rose and it fell. How my white dress all turned red.*

Molly squeezes her eyes shut tight. She stands very still. She is the vole, she is the tiniest mouse in the long grass. She counts, waits, counts. Her heart is the shiver of rain on the stream but she waits and nothing touches her.

And when she looks again the track before her is empty, and she walks on into the night's thickness, meeting no-one. She will not return to town.

In the night she wakes with a start. Her eyes fly open before she can stop them, and she sees that a red light is flooding her room. The floors are stained with it. The walls are russet and pink are the sheets she lies on, and someone is standing at her window, looking in, seeing her in all her nakedness; her neck, her breasts, her face, her legs. The room is red and someone stands at her window.

Molly rolls from her straw-stuffed mattress and smacks onto the flagstones. There she scrabbles into the shadows beneath the bed, low though it is, wedging herself beneath. The straw scratches and pokes her. Here she can't be seen, can't be seen, can't be seen. She waits. She waits.

There is no sound. Not even the wind is shifting outside. The silence goes on and Molly lies panting under the bed, staring wide-eyed at the red-slopped floor.

Then a great scrabbling and scratching, a rattling and beating across the room. It is at her door. Fingernails around the frame, at all the edges, picking and clawing, gouging the wood. Molly whines in fear, pressing herself further under the bed. The hammering at the door goes on—there's a shadow coming in from beneath, a blackness cutting through the red, and it paces to-and-fro looking for a way inside. It knows she was in town. It knows she did not tell Sam what she saw.

Molly bites her tongue to stop herself crying out. She holds her breath, stays still, presses her eyes shut tight. She counts the seconds as they pass; yan, tan, tether.

Molly drives the flock up the track.

Molly picks her way over the stones. She frees a sheep from a snare of fence, picks a tick from another's back. On the ridge she smells snow. Hesitates. Turns back to look again, for there is something moving below, something lumbering over the heath. Coming up the slope are two men dressed darkly. Molly feels ice slither into her belly, a flush rises up in her face.

Sam Bethel is puffing. His cheeks are ruddy with the wind, but he lifts a hand to her as they approach. Behind Sam comes the man who must be Judge Green, wearing an important hat and a billowing coat. His boots look expensive, but they are slicked with mud from his trek to her.

Molly ignores their cries hallo; she turns and pretends not to have seen them, so they almost have to run to catch her. "Miss Brock!" the Judge is bellowing as she wanders away across the flat stones. "Miss Molly Brock!"

She makes her face the moon, turning serenely toward the two men. She lets her mouth hang open. Nothing here but a glass-eyed sheep. Nothing here but a cow chewing cud. "Wassat," she says.

"Now then," the Judge says, wiping his nose on a handkerchief. His face is broad and whiskered but his mouth is oddly pursed, his top lip protruding beaklike. "Do you know who I am?"

"'appen thou's the judge," Molly says, taking a good amount of time to say each word.

"That's right."

Sam Bethel looks relieved. He puts his hands on his waist and bends over, still catching his breath. Judge Green casts an eye over the land beyond, at the sheep picking among the stones.

"Mighty view you've got up here, Miss Brock," says the Judge. Molly doesn't reply to this. She picks at the buttons on her shirt, pulls an unravelling thread. The Judge clears his throat.

"Sam here tells me you've something to say about our Lady Hale's disappearance," he says. "That right?"

Molly does not speak. The wind rises from a low moan to a sudden piercing shriek, and the men clutch their hats onto their heads.

"D'you hear me, Molly Brock?" the Judge says. "This is very important. I said we're here to ask about Lady Hale. A young lady she is, with yellow hair. Sam here says you've seen something. Says you told him so yesterday, at the inn."

Molly lifts her chin to look at the sky. A spot of rain has fallen.

"Miss Brock, do you hear me?"

Still Molly says nothing. She is thinking about the hunting owl. She is thinking of it soaring high over the moor, its white body borne by the late afternoon. Over heather and grass and bog and rock it flies and sees no-one on its way. The world below is brown and grey and it stretches on, on, on. White spots of sheep speckle the land. Tracks run out. Paths are grown over or washed away and bridges crumble into streams, leading no-where. And she sees herself far below—Molly Brock beating her crook on the track, counting yan, tan, tether. Molly walks with a lurch, bow-legged, the stones in her pockets clacking. The country spreads out ahead, behind, in all directions, and the only sound is the raw, blowing wind. Even under Molly's feet there is nothing, nothing but rock and dirt and echoing chambers in the earth.

But following her many miles behind is a figure.

Red and billowing are its skirts and its face has rotted all away. Its long hair lifts in the gust. Its legs bow and buckle and its back heaves, cracks, splinters with every step. And still it comes on.

If Molly looked over her shoulder she'd see it. Steady, red, flapping, coming on. And if she ran she'd not outrun it, if she hid she'd not be hidden. And on the high ridge too it'd be, and at the stream's edge, and at her window and her door, filling the room of her cottage with its terrible light. The red thing, the dead thing, the beat-up caved-in knowing thing. *Tell them what he did to me, Molly,* it says. *Or I'll follow you forever.*

The owl watches Molly and the figure drift across the moor, two flags caught on the same current. Where Molly goes, so does her red companion. On cold pale days and in thick black nights, when the land rolls out as far as the eye can see and even the flock is nowhere to be found, Molly need only look behind her. And on the ridge she'll see. And on the track she'll see.

By the time Molly comes back, the Judge's temper has left him altogether. "Molly Brock!" he is saying, waving a flat square hand in front of her face. Sam Bethel is flushed a different colour altogether. He speaks now, his blue eyes narrowed. He raises his voice to be heard over the wind, slow and deliberate. "Molly Brock! Tell us now, lass. No need to be afraid. Tell us now. What—did—you—see?"

Molly lets her face go. Her mouth slackens into a wide dripping smile. Her eyes mist over, her chin presses back to her neck. "Oh," she sings, "I sees all sorts!"

Sam steps back. The Judge raises his thick eyebrows.

"I sees my sheep up in 'sky and clouds down here on 'moor," Molly says. "I sees the river all white and the snow all black. I sees owls and hares and peewits and adders."

"But—what about Lady Hale?" the Judge barks. "What of her have you seen? Did you see anyone out here? Was she being harmed? Who was she with?"

"I sees trees all bent by the wind and the track leading long up to the moon," Molly goes on. "And the rabbit in my pot jumping and the crust of my bread buttering itself for my supper!"

The Judge's lip curls back. He is the horse before it bites, the snarling dog in the yard. He rounds on Sam. "All this way," he says, "for a damned idiot!"

"She said she's seen summat," Sam protests, purpling. He gives Molly a look like she's a rat on a rubbish heap. But she will not meet his eye. She sways on the spot and claps her hands together. She hums a merry tune and is about to start speaking more nonsense, but the men have given up. They are leaving, turning their backs on her. Their dark coats ripple on their shoulders. Their heads bow into the wind.

They've miles to walk back, Molly knows. Down the track, through the gorse. They must clamber the stiles and cross the ditches, pick between the rock slabs and trample the heather turning spongy in the thaw. Maybe they'll spit on the ground as they go and curse Molly Brock for the wasting of their time. And in town, sooner or later, they'll give Lady Hale up for gone. Perhaps they'll put up a memorial—a statue or a carving on a stone plaque in the cemetery. The brute who bashed her body in will walk free down the lanes, his thumbs crooked in his pockets, whistling. He'll sit at his supper and eat 'til he's full. In the evenings he'll cross the square to the inn, and he'll sit with Sam and John and Judge Green, and he'll laugh as loud as the rest of them.

And far out of town, where the stone road has long since turned to hard-packed mud, where the wind yawps and gibbers, will come Molly, beating her crook on the track. The land will stretch out ahead of her, behind, above, below. The heather will green and the clouds will run and beneath her feet the world will turn. She'll not look over her shoulder. At night she'll not answer the knock at the door. But she'll know it is there, just over the ridge. Or beyond the wall. A mile behind down the track, staggering, falling, rising up again. Far away, but coming on. And with the stones in her pocket clacking, Molly will start to count. Yan, she'll count. Tan.

COY HALL

HOUR
OF THE
CAT'S EYE

THE woman uttered a word that, to most villagers in Brandenburg, had become a repugnant curse. *"Landsknecht,"* she said, which meant mercenary. She paused then, and the noises surrounding her—"scraping armor, the din of a wagon, birds in the trees, horses—became clearer. With no objections forthcoming, the woman continued praying in a pidgin of German and Latin. *Landsknecht* pulled Tristram from a delirious fugue. Opening his eyes, a moment of clarity blessed him. To his bewilderment, he was on his back, stripped of breastplate and buff coat, riding in an open cart. Sunlight and shade, sunlight and shade: a sensation as the cart passed beneath trees. His arms and legs were heavy as stone, immobile.

In a hasty withdrawal, Lieutenant Groza must have counted Tristram among the dead. He had, he presumed, been lifted from the battlefield by scavengers (the war rats flourished in devastated regions of the empire).

The woman, who clutched a wooden cross, ceased her prayer and watched Tristram. Wary lines formed at the corners of her mouth. She turned and looked at someone Tristram could not see.

A man's voice then, in German of the lower sort: "He's weak as a foundling," he said. "Look at his leg. What can he do to you?"

Tristram did not protest. He doubted he had strength to speak, let alone lift his hand against a villager. He'd lost too much blood to be a threat to anyone. Groza had not been unwise to leave him for dead. He looked it. He remembered the initial shock of the wound, the sound of it, and marveled that he'd survived this long.

"*Landsknecht*," the woman repeated. She mustered disdain and looked into Tristram's eyes.

Before fading, Tristram took in another sight. The cart was fairly empty, returning from a journey rather than embarking, it appeared. A heap of armor (his blade and harquebus were nowhere in sight) lay in one corner, while a pile of wooden figurines rested in another. Save for passengers, this was the only cargo. Tristram concentrated, which was imprudent with so little strength, in order to make out details of the carvings. He looked upon a hoard of wooden cats—toys to hock at a fair, he supposed, but fine work. Delicate faces and lifelike eyes. One of the cats seemed to look back at him, the way the eyes of a portrait can follow a viewer. He matched the stare for a moment. The cat squinted. *Delirium again.*

The woman began her prayer anew. It then occurred to Tristram that the words interspersed with German were not Latin but, rather, a tongue he didn't recognize. She seemed to be invoking names.

A prayer for what? Tristram wondered, because it was surely not for the sake of his recovery alone, not when peppered with vitriol. A few blistered, incoherent thoughts came between him and unconsciousness, a shock of agony then in his crushed leg, and all was mercifully dark.

It was night when Tristram awoke. Gentle straw prodded his back rather than the splintered planks of a cart. For a moment, the stillness was peaceful, the darkness calming. There were no candles around him, but an open window allowed moonlight into the room. A breeze, too, entered the window, cooling sweat on his face. It was summer and the night was warm. The scent of wood smoke in the air irritated his swollen throat. He wondered if the discomfort had awakened him. *No*, he realized quickly. *It's the leg.* He attempted to slow his rapid breathing. It felt as though a torch prodded the muscle and bone. The agony was maddening. Nausea moved his stomach.

In a testament of will, he tried to gather himself and look about the room. The sight of anything would be grounding. He tilted his neck, careful not to see the leg, and gazed about. A figure near the window, silvered by moonlight, caught him by surprise. He had thought himself alone in the room. The shape, which was that of a man, sat on a ledge protruding from the wall. The man clutched the edge and tilted forward. He was either so high or so short that his legs dangled without touching the floor. Shadows obscured his face.

Tristram greeted the man inelegantly. A simple *"Who's there?"*, graveled by pain, escaped him.

A beat of silence followed. The figure offered no response. It remained very still.

It was then that Tristram became aware of similar figures that ringed the room in which he lay. A ledge extended around the wall, ceasing only for the window and an open doorway. He did not have the strength to rise and look behind him, but, from the continuity of shapes he could see, he assumed these men filled every space of the bench. In the dark it felt like a clandestine tribunal. Or watchmen noosing their quarry.

Nothing moved. Despite his effort, he could not make out faces.

Tristram then remembered the feline statues in the cart. *Carvings*, he thought, amazed. He returned to the first figure, perched at the window and swathed with more light than the others. He tried to deny his unease, imagining the skill it took to do such work, but a movement in the silvered man obliterated the effort. The knuckled joints of the hand creaked, as if gripping, and the wooden man leaned forward slightly. It was a subtle but perceptible alteration, enough to bring the head into moonlight, like bas-relief from shadow.

Whereas the cat had possessed lifelike eyes, this figure had no eyes at all. Rather, a mask of crisscrossed limbs and vines caged the head. With masked face in view, the figure stopped moving. The hands loosened and relaxed.

For several beats of silence, Tristram watched and waited. His heart was fast, and the movement of blood weakened him.

Footsteps then.

In terror, as light spread into the room, he looked towards the open doorway. The woman who had prayed over him in the cart stood there, framed in the soft light of a candle, puzzled. Her face had imprinted on his fevered mind. He recognized her immediately.

The flame trembled in her grip. "Did you speak?" she asked. Her voice, too, lived in his mind.

Tristram reclined his head, relieved that she had come. He nodded.

The woman brought the candle forward and light touched the wooden statues. Each carving had jointed arms and legs and hands and each wore a mask of limb and vine. They lined the walls like marionettes in the shop of a puppeteer, but these were not toys. He wondered if these were funeral effigies. He had seen such work, complete with garments and a plaster death mask, in the funeral processions of the rich. Tristram's own father had such an effigy as an eternal guardian in his tomb. It was a common practice, but he'd never encountered craftsmen of such things.

The woman stood at his side. There was something Gaelic in her appearance, an ancestry that belied her accent and home in Brandenburg. Her hair was auburn and her skin pale, touched with freckles across a delicate nose. Her eyes, too, were pale. "You are not German," she said. "What language were you speaking? Dutch?"

"English," Tristram said, in German that had become precise from two years fighting in the Catholic League. "I come from Scotland."

She stood just out of arm's reach. Scotland meant little to this woman. It was a world away.

"In your prayer," Tristram said, "you also spoke another tongue. Was it Latin?"

"No," she said. "Much older than Roman words." She extended the flame and looked into his eyes. After a moment, she said, "You're frightened. Why?"

"Where should I begin?" he started. He approximated a smile, which, coupled with his death's head pallor and slovenly beard, must've been ghastly.

The woman did not find him amusing. She waited.

"One of the figures moved," he admitted, and then, less secure in his assertion, "or so it appeared in the dark."

Now the woman smiled. The grin was inadvertent, telling.

"The one by the window," he said, eager to have his fears dashed.

She stepped towards the shelf. The carvings did not seem as large as they had before. The one by the window was little more than four feet tall. The ledge was not high. "This one?" she asked, growing more amused.

Or pleased, he wondered. Although he didn't want it to be there, he detected a touch of cruelty. "Don't ridicule a fevered mind," Tristram said.

"This one here?" She pushed the wooden man back into place, pressing his back and head against the wall. The joints creaked. "Did he lean forward?"

"So it seemed," Tristram said.

"Ah but the wind will do that. God forbid a gust drop him to the ground." She laughed then, and it was a nice laugh despite the intention, pleasing as a windchime. "What's your name, *landsknecht*? You carried no papers. And the ranting you do in your sleep is mad."

"Tristram Carew," he said. He wondered what other information he'd divulged in his sleep. He did not admit that he fought for Groza and the Catholics. He did not, despite her correct assumption, admit his status as a mercenary. "What's yours?"

"Liliana," she said, simply. She thought a moment. "Tristram is a knight's name. A knight's name for a *landsknecht* is very funny. Did you give yourself the name? Is it good for business?"

Tristram was too weak to counter the ribbing. His father, a martial soul, had named him after a figure of Arthurian romance. Tristram's brother was named Percival Carew. He was impressed she knew of Arthur. He offered the ghastly smile again.

"How is your leg feeling?" Liliana asked now, with less levity. Her face, in shadows thrown by the candlelight, grew appropriately grave.

You're dangerously bright, he thought. Maybe it was a fever dream but, like a sudden dash of color in his mind, he intuited, *You're a wonderful imitation of life, Liliana. You perform the role very well. You could make someone love, hate, admire, or fear you, or you could make all of those things true at once.* Looking at her, she left Tristram in a sort of purgatory.

When Tristram did not respond, Liliana fetched him a ladle of water. He drank it greedily, and it ignited sharp pain in his throat. He drank another ladleful before admitting he had not possessed the courage to look at his leg, not since the moment it had been crushed.

With sympathy, Liliana said, "Gird yourself then, and look." She hovered the candle over the end of his straw mattress. The light reached to his neck. She lifted the blanket. "It saved your life," she said.

Tristram found the courage to look. As he did so, he cried, unrestrained like a child. His right leg was severed above the knee, and the wound had been cauterized. Infection discolored the rawness.

Liliana took a seat on the floor at his side. "Be calm," she said. "Be calm. You could not have lived. The infection before this was worse. Your foot was rotten."

He grabbed at her hand and she allowed him to hold on for comfort. She prayed for him then, again mixing in the unfamiliar tongue, and eventually he went unconscious beneath the lilting voice.

"He ain't likely to walk on a crutch, is he?" one man said to the other. The accent was rural, the voice lazily bellicose. "Leg's gettin' rotted again."

The other man shrugged. "Smells that way. Fetch a vegetable cart," he ordered someone unseen, someone standing outside the window. "He's weak as a foundling. I doubt he'd stay awake long enough to walk."

The first man, young with a red peasant face, knelt at Tristram's side. The smell of manure was heavy on his clothes, which were ratty save for an ill-fitting leather jerkin. Tristram wondered if that garment, too, had been salvaged. Ungrateful though the feeling was, a spark of anger made him more aware. He rose to his elbow, as if that signaled strength. He wondered if these villagers were what his fellow harquebusiers called war rats—desperate night-men who descended on battlefields and pillaged the dead for anything of value. War rats were ghoulish scum, despised by Protestant and Catholic alike.

The other man, older but equally undistinguished and poorly bred, stood near the window. It was afternoon and the sun was high. His voice, like Liliana's, was familiar. "Gotta move you from the workshop now," he told Tristram. "I'm certain you won't find the movement agreeable, but we'll cart you rather than have you hop."

Tristram nodded uncertainly. *A workshop*, he thought. In the light of day, he could see that the figures lining the room were, indeed, funeral effigies. Off-putting, certainly, but without magic. The masks protected the smooth surface of the wood until plaster faces could be applied. The faces would be death masks of the deceased. On a shelf above the human figures was a menagerie of small animals: more cats alongside foxes, bears, rabbits, stags, and horses.

The heavy youth, noticing Tristram's interest in the carvings, said, "He saw one of the little men move, he did." He laughed until his body heaved. There was something off about the man, something childish. Great turbulence waited, barely restrained, behind his eyes. All he needed was a reason for violence.

The older man did not laugh. He stepped forward. "Moving is going to hurt," he cautioned. "Nothin' you aren't used to, but it'll hurt just the same." From his coat he drew a hank of leather. He handed it to Tristram. "Best bite down on that," he said with sympathy. "My name's Ambrus. The lad there slobbering on you is Rowland."

Tristram offered his name and then clenched the leather between his teeth.

Ambrus nodded. "At least you're not talkin' nonsense now. Maybe your fever will lighten." The words were meant to distract, because at that moment Ambrus and Rowland lifted Tristram from the ground. The jostling of the severed limb brought a cold sweat to his brow. A wave of nausea passed through him. The agony was consuming. Splotches of color glossed his eyes. He wavered and came close to succumbing.

"You gonna be sick?" Ambrus asked.

Tightly, Tristram shook his head. The focus made him sicker.

"Quickly," Ambrus ordered Rowland.

The men carried him from the workshop into the adjoining room. The space was small and tightly packed, living quarters with a hearth and workbenches and tools and cords of oak. There was a cramped loft with personal belongings, and at least one bed of rope and straw. The space reeked of smoke and sulfur. Ambrus and Rowland hurried out the door. Another young man, thin as bones would allow, stood beside a vegetable cart that had two wheels and a pair of handles. He did not speak. Like a child, he sprinted off when his duty was complete.

"Bite down hard," Ambrus cautioned. With little delicacy, he and Rowland deposited Tristram in the cart. Tristram shifted into place, trying to hide pain from showing on his gaunt face. His left leg hung over the wall while the sawed-off nub remained on the floor. The bone ached and he felt, as he had several times that morning, a phantom pain where the crushed limb had been. He breathed and gathered himself. He prayed and bit down on the leather. His fever was not lightening, as Ambrus suggested, but worsening.

"We've something to show you," Ambrus said. In the full light of day, his advanced age was more apparent. His hair, protruding from a thinly brimmed capotain, was a dirty grey. He wore a mustache of the same shade, large enough to hide his upper lip. Deep lines crossed his brow and underscored his eyes. He turned and looked about, ready to bark an order, but both of his companions had gone. To Tristram, he muttered, "Both of those boys are touched in the head."

Tristram had noticed, at least with Rowland, but he responded as if this were news.

Then, more darkly, Ambrus confided, "A *landsknecht* gave 'em a beatin' when they was boys. He beat their heads in. Just awful. He left 'em for dead. You could beat on Rowland all day but it wouldn't do anything but bloody him. The other, Kaspar, he hasn't said a word since. That happened in Magdeburg."

Tristram stirred uneasily beneath Ambrus's glare. One never mentioned Magdeburg lightly.

"You there when they burned Magdeburg?" he asked. Ambrus grew very distant for a moment, and his eyes wandered. His tone was better suited for discussing weather.

"I wasn't," Tristram said, and it was the truth. Magdeburg burned twelve years prior in 1631. He had not fought with the League then. "Were you?"

Ambrus nodded. He paused, allowing that to sink in, as if to say, *I know what was done there. I saw.* After a moment, he said, "Here comes Rowland."

Tristram craned his neck and looked back towards the squat cottage and workshop. Rowland strode forward, belligerent, wearing the breastplate stripped from Tristram. His stomach and chest protruded on both sides of the metal, dwarfing the armor. Worse still, he wore Tristram's helmet, an heirloom forged by his father. The helmet fit Rowland so poorly that it failed to reach his ears by the width of two fingers. For amusement, he'd ripped out the helmet's white plume of egret feathers. Tristram's father had brought those feathers from North Africa. Their value was sentimental. The breastplate was also damaged. Rowland had beaten large dints into it with a hammer. He gripped a hammer now.

"Humor him," Ambrus whispered. "He'll go off and play and leave us be."

Tristram lowered his eyes in shame, feeling half a man. Rowland approached, stomping over a path of stones. *What would Groza think of you now?* Tristram thought miserably. *Or your father—he not only forged that helmet, he trained you to fight and live the way you lived. What would he say? That you were better dead. I should've died,* he thought. *I should have died that day.* His resentment grew.

When Rowland neared, he laughed grotesquely, sharing spittle. "Maybe I'll treat you like you treated me," he said, flaunting the hammer. "Maybe you're the little boy now. What do you think, father?" he asked Ambrus. "You think maybe I should?"

Calmly, Ambrus shook his head. "Go now," he ordered.

Rowland looked at Tristram and his eyes were nothing but hatred. In a quieter, more level tone, he said, "Maybe I will." He lifted the hammer.

Tristram stared at his hands. A week prior and he would've killed Rowland without thought. He would've ripped his gut open with a dagger. Then Rowland would have burned with the rest of the village. With the League behind him, no one would be left alive. *No,* he thought then. *You wouldn't do such a thing to Liliana. Even if you desired it, you couldn't.*

A week ago, he countered. *A week ago I would've done that very thing to her.*

With Ambrus unwilling to push away his son, Liliana's voice, distant and then closing quickly, cut the tension. Tristram watched her approach. She spoke to Rowland as one would speak to a young boy.

"You're a true knight now, Rowland," she said. Gracefully, she took the hammer from his grip. Glad for her touch, he didn't protest. She looked down at Tristram. "Two knights," she said. "Rowland is the name of a knight, too, isn't it, Ambrus?"

The old man nodded impatiently.

"Rowland and Tristram," Liliana said, "about to engage in a tournament duel." She touched Rowland's begrimed hand again. "Obey your father," she told him. "This man's no match for a knight like you."

Her composure calmed him. Rowland nodded. He turned his back and started off. He lifted the helmet from his head and carried it in his hand. "Maybe I will," he said in a singsong voice. "Maybe I will, maybe I will, maybe I will."

Liliana gave the hammer to Ambrus.

"May I call you Lili?" Tristram asked. Perhaps it was the sun coupling with his fever, but he felt completely bewitched by her presence. With the sunlight behind her red hair, she looked like an angel of mercy. She still wore the wooden cross about her neck.

"You may not," Liliana said. "How do you feel, *landsknecht*?"

Ambrus cut in. "He feels like he looks. Enough time has been wasted. Come now." He lifted the cart by the handles and backed onto a path of crushed stone. "Chew the leather," he advised.

With Liliana at his side, Ambrus wheeled Tristram through the village. Due to the prosperity of their trade, the community was not a huddled mass of dilapidated huts and muddy fields like so many others in the Margraviate of Brandenburg. Rather, aside from the ubiquitous smoke and stench of hogs, things no village could escape, the array of homes was clean and idyllic. A spired church, perhaps the first sight one took in upon approach from the road, stood at one end of the main thoroughfare. Stone rather than mud and excrement lined the footpaths. A great deal of green—canopied trees and private gardens of herbs, nightshade, and laurel—linked proud homes of wood and thatch. Mistletoe nested in the trees. Blackbirds were copious. A few dogs walked about freely. These were well-fed pets, not the miserable, starving jackals usually kept by peasants for security. Children played. A group of women stood around a boiling cauldron and open hearth, suffering the heat, putting together a communal meal.

The village seemed abnormally prosperous. *How could such a place escape notice of the League?* Tristram thought. "Where are all the men?" he asked.

"There are so few men here now." Ambrus admitted the weakness freely. "The war lured some of them away, the romantic ones. Others are in their shops, carving. A few have gone to Strausberg to market our wares. Important and vain men purchase the effigies," Ambrus went on. "For themselves and their wives and children. Barons. A few clergymen. The latter shouldn't be vain, of course." Ambrus shrugged.

"Something you have in common with Ambrus," Liliana said. "You both profit from death. Perchance he's memorialized a child you've killed."

Bruised, Tristram asked, "Why did you save me?" He had wanted to wait for a time to ask the question with more sincerity but anger tripped him. It came out bluntly. "You performed a surgery to do so. That's a great deal of trouble for a man you scorn."

"Ambrus did both of those things," Liliana said. She fought emotion but her eyes betrayed her. She didn't deny her hatred. She wanted to say a great deal more, and none of it kind.

Slowly, Tristram took his eyes off Liliana. He had been staring through her, trying to fathom who she was, why she seemed alone, who had harmed her. Unlike Ambrus's talk of Magdeburg, she offered no answers.

The cart stopped at a small, windowless cottage at the far edge of the village. There was something forlorn and ancient about this home, and it was less well kept than the others. The cottage had weathered many changes. A garden and forest lay beyond this final building.

"This is where you'll stay now," Ambrus said. "It's important to us that you remain here."

Liliana moved to the unpainted oak door. A heavy branch, several inches thick, lay across two brackets, barring the entrance. It was the mark of a prison. Tristram's stomach turned. Liliana removed the branch and leaned it against the wall. She opened the door outward.

Cowed by the thought of being jailed inside the cottage, Tristram barely noticed that a crowd of people started to gather behind him. An event was occurring, he then realized. Even Rowland had returned, still wearing the breastplate. A man, equal to Ambrus in age and greyness but smaller and frailer, separated from the crowd. Ambrus drew Tristram's attention to the man. "This is Matthias Knock," he said. "He'll look after you."

The man, a phlegmatic tinkerer, nodded but said nothing. Swollen joints left his hands gnarled.

Ambrus wheeled Tristram through the door and into the cottage. The floor was dirt with an indentation, a hole, sinking towards the center. A desire to flee could not change the situation: Tristram was unable to stand, let alone run or fight. He was, as Ambrus twice observed, weak as a foundling. The disturbing thought that his leg hadn't needed severing, that the act served the same purpose as clipping bird wings, had occurred to him. He felt very small and vulnerable under the gaze of the villagers.

He confronted the uncertainty. "Is this revenge?" he asked Liliana. *Whom, here, did I wrong?* he thought. It was not Ambrus. Was it Liliana? Or did Tristram, like the effigies fashioned for the dead here, simply stand in representation of that which had wronged them?

Liliana, searching along the wall for a candle, said, "Far from revenge, *landsknecht*." The words, double edged, failed to comfort the feeling of despair that settled over him. Liliana, unconcerned, located a tin cup full of mutton fat.

Outside, the crowd moved closer to the door, held from entry by the brittle form of Matthias Knock.

"It is revenge," Tristram said.

"You're wrong," Ambrus said. "Fever is getting the best of you. You can rest easy tonight. Matthias isn't here to keep you in. He's here to keep everyone out. He'll change your bandage and clean your leg, too. It needs care. You need to sleep and gather your strength."

"For what?" Tristram asked.

Neither Ambrus nor Liliana provided an answer.

When night fell, he lay in the cottage on a clean bed of straw, with a fresh cloth wrapped around the root of his wound. The tallow candle burned at his side, casting a halo of light that reached to the hole in the floor. With the heat of day still in the room a window would've been a blessing, but that was the least of his concerns. Be that as it may, he had not been gawked at or mistreated. Enigmatic Liliana had not returned. Nor had Ambrus and Rowland. Tristram had been fed and given a flagon of wine. Save for a hunk of bread, which he forced down his gullet, food was not agreeable to his stomach. He kept at the wine, though, until he was drunk and morose. When he emptied one flagon, Matthias brought in another. He drank the second flagon and received a third.

He had time to be alone with his thoughts, whether he desired it or not, because Matthias spoke little when he entered the cottage. The old man responded to questions with grunts, deeming nothing curious enough for words. He would walk with his head bowed and then leave quickly. The door would shut. The branch would fall into place.

In need of distraction, Tristram had studied the interior of the cottage thoroughly. It was an odd domicile, neither lived in nor abandoned nor used for storage. Although it stood empty, the structure was maintained. The roof crawled with the normal insects but allowed in no light and, judging from the condition of the walls, no rain. The floor was hard-packed dirt and was empty save for his straw and a small cistern against one wall. The shallow hole in the center of the floor, whatever its purpose once, was now empty. At the bottom of the hole a plank was visible, as if dirt covered an original, lower floor. Tristram had crawled to the hole and peered downward with the candle, and he'd seen a pictogram on the wood—a symbol he neither recognized nor understood. The symbol was a lattice of limbs and vines within a circle, a lattice not unlike the caging that covered the faces of effigies in Ambrus's workshop. Why someone had dug down and uncovered the pictogram made him uneasy. He had, in his travels, witnessed vigilante trials for witchcraft in poorer settlements—when old women were paraded and tortured and throttled and burned for flaunting such icons.

The arcane symbol was not the only feature of the cottage that left him feeling suspicious. The loft above, occupying the right side of the room, held a single occupant, and it was upon this figure that Tristram stared and worried the most. Standing at the edge of the platform, near a crude ladder that descended to the floor, was the wooden statue of a cat. The eyes, vigilant, troubled him deeply. Whether a fevered thought or true, it seemed the eyes had shifted over the preceding hours, hinging steadily until they caught the candlelight and fell upon Tristram.

Unlike the figurines he had seen previously, this cat did not appear coquettish. It was not a toy. Rather, the animal was poised in the form of a predator ready to strike at prey: its front paws extended, its sharp claws gripping the wood, its spine arched downward, torqueing the strong hind legs. The tail held the mischievous curve of a shepherd's crook. There the animal stood, watching, waiting as hours passed.

He hoped the statue was a scarecrow fashioned to ward off rats, because rats appeared at the base of the cottage walls with frequency. These were scrawny rats the color of charcoal, occupants of every home in the countryside. The rodents never remained in sight for long, and any movement by Tristram or Matthias Knock sent them scurrying for shelter, but they were there and they were legion.

As Tristram meditated about revenge and Liliana, the cat and the rat and the little cottage brought a rhyme to his drunken mind. He had heard his brother sing the words when they were young. His brother, more bookish than Tristram, learned it from one of their father's gardeners. He was always collecting such baubles from common folk. In Edinburgh, presumably, Percival still collected. The rhyme went thus:

There was a crooked man and he walked a crooked mile
He found a crooked sixpence upon a crooked stile.
He bought a crooked cat, which caught a crooked mouse,
And they all lived together in a little crooked house.

A fitting ode, Tristram thought, *for a sawed-off man, newly made crooked.* Pitifully, he laughed, and the laugh felt sick and detached. His fever surged. His leg, despite new cloth, grew worse. He felt the squirm of larvae inside the flesh. He could only deny the sensation for so long. The trauma of such a feeling was not the kind to fade. He took a drink of the warm wine.

He prayed Groza and the League would descend on this place. It would be glorious to thwart revenge, whatever its motivation, in its final moment. Soldiers would finish the job on Rowland and his brother, which they had begun in Magdeburg. The image pleased him. Then who would stand and defend this village? Ambrus and Matthias? A slaughter would ensue. What a funny story it would make if Lieutenant Groza were to find Tristram here, crooked, counting rats, and fearful of a cat in the dark. *Maybe he would realize my condition and kill me out of mercy.*

Why hadn't the League come to this village? Tristram wondered again. In his time with Groza, the League pillaged the countryside of Brandenburg thoroughly. And here this village stood, hidden in the open, shielded by nary a hill, wealthy, untouched, brazen, arrogant. *What deal have these people made? If a deal were struck, then why fear a single* landsknecht? *Because we hold no allegiance,* he answered, for he knew the response well. *We're dishonorable men. We fight only for money. All peasants say the same. Never did a peasant love a mercenary. Just as, Liliana would say, a peasant never loved a knight. May she be damned,* he prayed, *and by a hand other than mine.*

In the small hours of the night, after drifting in and out of a drunken, dreamless sleep, movement in the loft made Tristram very sensitive to his surroundings. He lifted his eyes. Although his candle burned low, he could see that the sculpture's tail had shifted—it now dipped and straightened to a point at the end.

"Matthias," Tristram called. An urge to get free of the room seized him.

The old man did not respond and did not enter. The door remained quiet.

Tristram began the rhyme in a futile attempt to calm his nerves, but the first line alone rushed through and then dissipated. *There was a crooked man—*

—The cat parted its mouth, unhinging its jaw.

"Matthias, please! Liliana! Ambrus!" Despite his weakness, Tristram toppled forward from the straw bedding, digging his forearms into the ground. A vision of absurdity, he dragged himself toward the door, using his left leg to push forward. He moved as quickly as he could manage, making his stomach sick with wine and pain. Only a few feet from the straw, he vomited onto the floor, and then he crawled through the slick detritus.

The cat placed a paw on the top rung of the ladder. Tristram could not see the extent to which it had changed, whether its body was still a coating of wood or if the exterior had relaxed into fur, but the statue was animated enough to move without hindrance. It stepped downward twice before leaping the rest of the way to the ground. The cat, which had been frozen art moments before, landed with grace, almost noiselessly. It looked at Tristram, eyes a faint yellow tinged with black, then it looked at the vomit on the floor, and then it sauntered, shoulders rolling like a panther cub, to the cavity in the center of the room. There the darkened thing began to heave—gargling, coughing, until it disgorged a solid lump. The cat, matching Tristram, vomited. Wine and bile didn't escape its stomach, however. The cat spewed forth a charcoal rat, which had not been chewed or rended. The rodent's coat appeared dry. Tristram had the idea then that the rat suffocated inside the wooden statue. The image of encasement was a devastating one.

Tristram called for Matthias again. When he reached the door he hammered his fist against the oak. He grabbed at the handle and shoved. The door did not give. He battered the planks until his hands were bruised. He listened then, but heard nothing on the other side.

He didn't have to wonder long about how the rat became encased within the statue. The cat, ignoring Tristram's presence now, walked towards the farthest wall. One of the rats, either caught unaware or mesmerized, stood idle. A small pool of urine spread beneath it, darkening the ground. The cat unhinged its jaw like a snake, opening its mouth impossibly wide, and ate the rodent. The cat's throat bulged and then regained its original shape. Without struggle, the cat swallowed.

"Matthias," Tristram called through the door, weakly now.

Then, gingerly as it had come, the cat stalked to the ladder and climbed the rungs to the loft. Once it had assumed its original pose, shepherd's crook tail included, the cat ceased movement and grew rigid. Its eyes, their luminescence the last remnant of life to depart, found the straw empty and then drifted over to the door where Tristram lay. There the eyes stopped and remained.

———————————

Liliana removed the bar and opened the cottage door, allowing in morning sunlight. She looked down upon the soiled form of Tristram, pale as death, and she hummed a familiar melody. It was another rhyme from his childhood, another song his brother Percival had collected, about a lascivious, murderous knight. She sang:

> *An arrogant knight came from the highlands*
> *And he came a'wooing of me*
> *He told me he'd take me to the highlands*
> *And there he would marry me*
> *"Lie there, lie there, you false-hearted man,*
> *Lie there instead of me,*
> *For if six pretty maidens thou hast slain*
> *The seventh has slain thee."*

She knelt, red hair untwined and resplendent and falling to her shoulders. Rather than a greeting, she asked, "Did you see it?" Her face was eager.

Tristram struggled to a sitting position. His leg had bled profusely through the cloth, having dragged hard against the dirt. The bandage was soiled and, he feared, full of worms. Vomit had hardened in his beard and crusted his lips. His eyes were ringed and red.

Impatiently, she asked again, "Did you see it?"

He nodded this time. "How do you know that song?" he asked, his mind dreadfully heavy. "My brother would sing it. My brother," he said, "was always singing little songs like that. Did you know him?"

It was a mad question, and the fact that he'd asked it frightened him. Internally and externally, he felt disconnected. He could watch himself slipping away. He tried to draw the question back inside, and that, too, was mad.

"You talk in your sleep," Liliana said. "Sometimes you sing. You saw it, didn't you? Did it perform?"

"The crooked cat?"

Liliana smiled, deeply pleased. That was enough, apparently. "Rowland," she called.

Yes, he thought. *It performed and did quite the trick. The poor rat. The crooked rat. The crooked man. The crooked cat. The crooked house.* The statue came to life and consumed.

Heavy footsteps approached on the gravel. Armor scraped.

Tristram sighed. He had no strength left to do anything else.

"Fetch your father and Matthias," Liliana said. "He's the right one." She touched Tristram's face and said, "Save your strength, *landsknecht*. Tonight you'll see another trick."

"To whom do you pray?" Tristram asked. "I found the symbol on the floor, Lili. You're a sorceress, are you not?"

Liliana proffered the cross she wore at her neck. "Far from it," she said.

"Then why do this?"

Liliana put her mouth to his ear. "To save us," she whispered. Then, as Ambrus and Rowland and Matthias came near, she sang softly into his ear,

> "Lie there, lie there, you false-hearted man,
> Lie there instead of me."

As they had done before, but with less concern for his pain now, Ambrus and Rowland lifted Tristram from the ground and placed him in the vegetable cart. It had become a pitiful ritual. Rowland was wearing the helmet again, and now battered gauntlets covered his forearms, and greaves his shins. He carried a mallet in place of a sword. The dinted breastplate shone in the sun, making him a gross caricature. He lifted the handles of the cart and began to steer it towards the other homes of the village. Liliana, elated, without remorse for the crippled mercenary, led the procession.

"He'll do," she said, as people emerged from their cottages. She spoke with authority. "He was accepted. He'll do."

There were many voices, but one refrain from the throng reached him, a faceless voice, that of a woman: "Praise her and protect us, Lord. Praise this dearest of goddesses. She, too, is your child."

No. You're damning yourselves, he thought. *All of you.*

Infectious merriment spread through the amassing crowd of villagers, but all of this passed in a blur for Tristram. He tried to roll free from the cart but Rowland struck him hard behind the ear, a hammering blow he couldn't withstand in his condition, and he ceased the fight. He was dead weight, barely able to lift a hand. He began to slip under, and he wondered again about whom he had wronged here.

"Bring it forward, Ambrus," Liliana said.

Ambrus moved forward, carrying the large effigy of a man beneath his arm. The figure wore the limb and vine cage over its head. The dangling arms, jointed at the shoulder and elbow and wrist, moved freely. When he reached Liliana, Ambrus unclasped the mask and handed it to her. Fungus soiled the back of the effigy's head, like a stone in the forest. Ambrus carried the wooden man towards the cottage at the end of the lane. He dipped inside, untroubled.

Liliana, carrying the mask, leaned towards Tristram. "Tonight," she said, "you're the rat."

"Groza's army will come through. You can't do this to all of them."

"No," Liliana admitted, "we can't. This will keep him away, though. For a decade it's kept armies away."

ELIZABETH TWIST

THE COMPLETE COMPLEAT GARDENER

If ye wish for fecund land
and plantings that grow strong,
ye must become a Compleat Gardener
by all means and in all ways.

IT WON'T help if I apologize. I know that, but the impulse is still there. The fact is, it's nothing personal. The land needs what it needs and we unlocked the means to save it, and for that I'm not sorry. Still, here and now, on the day after the night after Bealtaine, the part of me that's rational enough to sit down and write this account is a little sorry for knowing that Jake Henderson's last stand in the house next door is almost over, that his sister Landy and the other women from Cutting's Falls, having figured out that they're impervious to the blasts of his shotgun, are just about to break through the door and pull him out of there.

His son Carter was the first to go, of course. I wish I felt worse about that than I do, but I won't miss the boy's constant visits here, or finding him watching me from his bedroom window, shirtless and doing things with his hands that I don't want to think about too much. Before you judge, Carter was twenty-five years old, and definitely ought to have known better.

I can hear the women's howls through the open window. Not much longer for old Jake. It's always been a point of irritation that despite the fact that I bought five whole acres of land so I could be alone, my cottage is practically right next door to his house. There would have been more privacy if only anything would grow.

That problem's been solved too, I guess. As I write this, I'm pausing from time to time to pet the branches of a tree—apple, I think—that've rustled in through the window. The land has come alive overnight, everything growing at an astonishing rate. You can hear it: toadstool heads, big as fists, pushing up through the soil; a hundred different plant species bursting forth, leaves unfurling to the morning sun. Milkweed and borage and black-eyed Susan; sunflower and bachelor's buttons and calendula. The trees were a bit of a shock, the way they revived from dead dry husks, but it feels to me a lot like the beginning of summer, like it should feel, this far north: everything happening at the first opportunity, the moment the days grow warm enough, as if the plants were ready all along, hounds at the gate, waiting only for it to swing back so they could race across the open field, and howl and bark and tear.

I guess that describes us, too.

Understand, this land was dead when I bought it three years ago. The first pH tests I performed on the soil told me that more acid rain had fallen here than down south, where the earth was too poisoned, full of heavy metals, to grow food that was safe to eat. I'd laid my mother to rest before I sold the house I grew up in and moved here, where I thought everything would be better, or at least, more viable.

Mom succumbed to liver cancer. It's funny how people get used to the new reality as fast as they do. Do you remember a time when people didn't expect to get cancer? When it wasn't something people reconciled themselves to? I don't.

Moving north was my answer to everything. I'd read that there were still natural forests up here that hadn't been completely killed off, even though their composition had been altered. When I arrived, I found that the land around those few remaining wild habitats was out of my price range. Anything that could be farmed was far too expensive. I bought what I could afford: a small cottage on five acres of wild grass, packed with thistles.

Jake Henderson came over the day I moved in. I was up on the roof, nailing pressed plastic board over a hole that the previous owner had for some reason not sought to fix, even though it meant rain poured straight down into the bedroom.

"What're you going to do with the place?" Jake asked me, before he said so much as a how do you do. He'd come over to find out, I guess. And to ask after my husband, and look disappointed when I explained I had none.

"Five acres isn't much," he said. "Can't have more than one or two cows. George Wick kept goats here." He'd spat into the buff-coloured sand. "They didn't thrive."

"I'm going to garden," I told him. Like I said, it was my first day. I was full of dewy hope. I'd planned to create a food forest on my patch of land. I would live off what I grew. Market the rest.

Later on that night, I'd laughed at the look on Jake's face that told me he thought I was crazy. I vowed he would see the truth soon enough, and celebrated with a bottle of real wine that I finished on my own. I remember tottering across the land, spilling the dregs from my glass, christening the hard-packed earth with pricey Shiraz.

I'd thought that working the land would be a ritual, a grand ceremony. Instead it was tedium: fruitless planting, trees that wouldn't take, seeds that refused to sprout, and money spent on truckloads of composted manure that washed into the culvert and drained away when the acid rain came down.

The only thing that supported life was the pond, which I paid Bert Ainsley to dig out with his backhoe. That life was exclusively of the insect kind. When the weather got warm enough in May or June, mosquitoes hovered over the mucky water in a thick cloud, and I tithed to the land in my own blood. It didn't pay me back. Not until last night.

I should have known something was coming, but it's a fact you hardly ever do until you admit that magic is real, or that consciousness flows in ways we habitually discount. I'd been having dreams where I was stuck in the pond, where the mud caught my boots and I knew I would never get out. In those dreams, a hand reached for me from the bank, and I caught a flash of red: red cloth, red blood. I chalked the dreams up to anxiety. My land had failed, and there was nowhere else in the world for me. We would go down together.

Today, I'm hearing frog song. I've read the stories about live toads emerging from hunks of coal, mined from deep underground. Maybe they've been underground all this time, dug in beneath the acidic soil, resting in clay until it was time to emerge. Maybe their eggs can dry and remain dormant until just the right moment. It doesn't matter. What I know is that it took magic to bring them back, and we worked that magic.

Nothing else could account for the return of the frogs, or for the fact that, as I sit here, the sun is blazing in the sky, and the air blowing in through the window is warm. Climate change brought wildfires farther north, out west, and in the southern hemisphere, and searing summers to central North America, but the collapse of the jet stream meant that Arctic air has been pouring down over this part of Canada all year round for a decade, bringing cold temperatures and a cloud cover that seldom breaks, or seldom did. That's changed now.

Kirsten found the book in an antique store down in Livermore. Kirsten works at the General Store—worked, I suppose. I'm not sure what she'll do now. As I write this, she's taking an axe to Jake Henderson's front door. I can hardly see her ringing up people's orders of milk and toilet paper tomorrow, or making change and small talk.

Since my arrival in Cutting's Falls, she'd tracked my comings and goings with what I'd guessed was the interest of someone who was bored with the people she'd grown up with. Anytime I went into the store, she would squint at the withered, stale produce I was buying with an eyebrow raised.

"Aren't you growing enough of your own?" she would say, as she poked at the lettuce, its leaves edged in brown.

I would lie, telling her I was just supplementing my own crops. The fact was, I was supplementing my General Store purchases with a trip down south for a bigger grocery run, once every couple of weeks. Kirsten would ring up the lettuce: five dollars; eight dollars sometimes. She would tell me to have a nice day, but we weren't friends. She certainly never came over for a visit. No one did.

Yesterday afternoon, she drove up my laneway in her blue Honda, a car she'd tweaked to run on ethanol. "Hey, hot stuff," she said as she climbed out.

I don't think I managed to say hello from where I sat on the ground, next to the raspberry patch. I'd managed to harvest ten dry, barely sweet berries, even as I discovered that the canes were rotten, the stems pulpy and foul-smelling inside. As Kirsten pushed her aviator sunglasses up onto her forehead and surveyed my barren land like a queen, all I could think about was the fact that she'd finally found me out.

I don't know why I was embarrassed. My land was the same as everyone else's. You know the story already: how the trouble started in the mid-21st century, with the mass collapse of commercial crops. The struggle to maintain the viability of farms that had always worked in the past led to the deregulation of fertilizers and pesticides, which in turn meant a sharp decline in public health: shorter lives, more cancer and heart disease.

The new measures didn't work for long. The late 2060s saw more crop failure, escalating grocery prices, and food scarcity. In a lot of places, the soil was radioactive, a by-product of Fukushima, Belarus, and Monticello: worse and worse for food safety. Farmers began to abandon their work.

My land was no different. Radiation wasn't a problem— at least, nothing was so hot that I couldn't grow food that was mostly safe to eat—but the longer I nurtured it with no success, the more certain I became that the perfect storm of human fuckery, changing temperatures, and insufficient sunlight had made it impossible for anything good to grow, even here in the middle of nowhere.

None of that stopped me from feeling totally ashamed as Kirsten reached out to break a dry twig from a shrivelled plum tree next to the driveway. Her red hair shimmered like fire against the dull landscape; her expression was sharp, like she'd come with a purpose.

I stood. My bottom was soaked from sitting on the ground. That's how the revolution started, with Kirsten standing over me, beautiful and fully aware of the truth of my situation, and me with a pair of muddy jeans clinging to my ass.

"I've got to change," I said.

"I've been saying that for the last three years." She took a long look at me, then gestured at the desolation all around me. "I've known about this for a while, by the way."

A pit opened up inside me, shame at being caught in the lie, and every bad thing I felt about the way my plans had gone. It was the end. If I couldn't get even a few plants to grow with nothing but time to work on them, then what would happen to the world? What would happen to me, now that I'd run out of money?

"How long?"

"Landy Henderson is one of my best friends." She pointed a thumb at Jake Henderson's house. "Jake's sister. She's been telling me what Jake says about you since the day you moved in. It's a small town, Rebecca. Everybody knows."

I laughed. It wasn't the deep belly laugh that would happen later, after I met the Scottish Dancing and Bitching Club, not the deep triumphant howl that's building in me even now, that I have to hold back so I can keep writing, but it was something. A letting go of sorts.

Kirsten carried a book under her arm, something old, with a green cloth cover. "I want to show you something." She eyed the Hendersons' place, then looked at me. "Inside though. Carter's watching us from his bedroom window."

"Yeah," I said. "Okay."

She sat down on my sofa and eyed the books stacked on the coffee table. "*The Ultimate Permaculture Guidebook*," she read. "*Practical Biodynamics*. Someone's been having a party."

There were five or six other books along the same theme: how to rehabilitate land, how to work with the Earth's natural ability to heal. She placed them on the floor along with the notebook I'd used to carefully record my efforts, the first year. I'd given up after that. "I thought you would like this," she said, placing her book on the table. "Now I know I'm right."

It was slender, like a children's storybook. The title, in faded embossed gold letters, was *The Compleat Gardener*. I sat beside Kirsten and touched the cover. The book seemed to vibrate, purring like a friendly cat. "What is it?"

She didn't quite answer. "I found it in a box of romance novels, believe it or not. The store owner was going to chuck them. She let me have it for a song."

"Wow, okay. Is it about gardening?"

It's funny, the moments that turn out to be the most important of your life. Kirsten smiled, and suddenly I realised she was more than a store clerk who'd been, for the past three years, my only reliable source of human interaction. She was a friend, maybe. Maybe a co-conspirator, maybe the guardian of some threshold. She opened the book to the title page: *The Compleat Gardener*, or, *A Method to Renew the Soil, by Merrie Tricks*. No publisher was listed, but under a stylised illustration of cherubs dancing amid mushrooms and flowers it said *Glasgow: 1798*.

I read in silence as Kirsten turned the page. On the left were a few cryptic words. *For good bounty, give the ground excrements of the moon.* The right-hand page displayed a chart or graph: stylised stars connected by flowing lines, or loops like simple Celtic knots. That pattern repeated throughout the book: *Dancing is the cure for troubled grounde*, one page claimed, opposite a drawing that looked like the sign for eternity. *On Bealtaine we celebrate; the night of Bealtaine is for the Gardener to make her offering.*

"When is Bealtaine? I asked.

"May first. Today," Kirsten said. "So tonight's Compleat Gardener's Eve, I guess."

We read on. The book's advice seemed to blend the practical with the completely bonkers. *Plant not the fruits of the dance in the grounde where ye grow turnips or other roots, but elsewhere to bring good harvest.* "How do you plant the fruits of the dance at all?" I asked.

Kirsten didn't reply, but flipped to a page that was folded twice over. She opened it out across the table: here were more diagrams, more knots and curves that each looped and spiralled around a small circle. These drawings had been coloured. The central circle was red, the loops and knots black and gold.

"All right, I have some things to say about this," Kirsten said, after I'd had a good long look. "I think it is about gardening, in a sense. All the advice, at least, seems to be about reinvigorating the land, or performing some kind of ritual for it." She chewed her ripe lower lip as she looked at me, and even though I'd come to Cutting's Falls to be alone, I wondered about rethinking that decision.

"Okay."

"Are you down?"

"For a ritual? Uh. I mean, nothing else has worked so far." I tried my best to speak with a calm, level voice, but my hands were shaking. I was falling down Alice's rabbit hole, and I wanted to fall. I frowned at the page spread out before us. "What do we do? Is this a layout for garden beds or something?"

"No." I could tell from the look in her eye that she was about to deliver a killing blow. "It's a crib diagram for a dance. See, these are the dancers—" She traced her fingers over the stars. "And these lines are the patterns of movement. It's standard format for recording a dance in print. I mean, this is an old timey version of the format we still use. Normally, women are represented by squares, and men by circles. Here there's just the one circle and then these funny stars. But yeah, *The Compleat Gardener* is a dance. The club has done it before, but this version is different."

The illustrations looked like gibberish to me. "How does this tell you what to do?"

"Each panel is a sequence of movements. They change from one verse of the song to the next." Kirsten touched a golden line. The diagram's loops seemed to blur as I looked at them.

"See? This is an ending I haven't seen before, but each dancer moves around this one." She tapped a red circle. "He doesn't appear to move at all. That's very strange. But here—" She pointed to the next panel. "The next dancer does the same thing. And the next, until there's only one left, who dances around him three times." She flipped the page. "Oh, there's a bit more." She frowned at a pattern that looked like a schematic drawing of a flower unfolding its petals. "Yeah, wow, this circle guy really doesn't do much of anything."

She'd invited me to come to her Scottish Country Dancing and Bitching Club a few times, describing what went on there as *really fun exercise and then drinking a lot of wine from a box*. I'd never gone.

"I thought your group was all women."

"It is, but there are usually men in these dances. The traditional mix is fifty-fifty. We just divide our group into pairs, and half of us dance the men's parts, like shirts and skins, you know?"

I laughed. "Who gets to be the skins?"

"Whoever wants to. Not literally. Usually. Theodora likes to take her top off from time to time."

Theodora was seventy-eight years old. "Awesome."

She studied the page, her look turning serious. "This version of the dance is really weird. First of all, it requires an odd number of people. This guy in the middle doesn't have a partner, see?"

I counted eight stars, and one lone circle. "Okay."

"I don't know. Theodora or one of the others will probably have an answer. Anyway, look. I know you're desperate for something to shift, and I'm not saying this will work, but it seems like, true to its name, this dance was originally intended for an actual gardener. That's you. Play along? It'll take your mind off things, even if it doesn't actually *cure your troubled groundee*." She put on a terrible fake accent as she repeated the words of the book. "Besides—"

She flipped the page, revealing one more pairing of text and image. The left page simply said *The Gardener Predominant*. On the right, a woman sat astride a prone man. Above them, a looping pattern, like the pattern of the dance, seemed to glow in the air.

"See? Might as well join us. I guarantee a good time. Maybe not that good, but good."

So help me, I said yes. Or maybe, to tell the truth: to help myself, and maybe help the land, I said yes. I didn't think it would work, but I didn't dare think it wouldn't. I held out hope, held my breath a little, and whispered *please* to the sterile ground.

When I walked Kirsten back out to her car, Carter Henderson was standing in his yard, his broad young chest naked in the cold summer air. He stared at us, clutching a shovel. The day before, he'd turned up at my door, and talked about how hungry he was until I cooked him breakfast. He'd watched me like he wanted to eat me, and talked about all the girls he'd gone out with that spring, like he was trying to hand me his sex resume.

He was just an idiot, really, but he was eighty or ninety pounds heavier than me, and bored, and wanting. I meant to speak to his father about him, but Jake seemed to think that everything I said was nonsense, and I didn't think he would understand what I was driving at.

"Which one of us gets to be the fool?" Theodora Guthrie said, tapping the foldout page with her finger. The women of the Scottish Country Dancing and Bitching Club gathered around a table in the corner of the dance studio in the Rec Centre, studying Kirsten's book. The room was nice—Cutting's Falls had a pair of dedicated dance teachers who excelled at fundraising, so the studio had a sprung floor, mirrors, and a ballet bar. The pot lights glowed a warm yellow. Inviting. Small comforts were all we had left now that the world was falling to pieces.

"This is a strange variation," Kate Olmstead said. It was weird to see her outside the feed store, and away from her kids: she usually had a child balanced on her hip, and another one or two racing around her legs. "Eight dancers, plus—why d'you call it a fool, Theodora?"

"It's an old term for any member of the dance who doesn't move. A central figure who thinks the world revolves around him, and, I suppose, for the duration of the dance, it does. But the purpose of the dance is movement, after all, and if you're not moving, you're a subject of it. Or an object, maybe." She shook her head. "I could never get that right."

There was a cadence to her voice, a musicality that kept us listening. She was a widow, and kept a herd of goats—thriving ones—on a little farm just outside town. I meant to ask her what her secret was, once we finished dancing. "The fool may stand and watch as the dance goes on around him, and he may think he's king, but he's merely inert," she said.

Kirsten nudged my shoulder. "I bet you thought you wouldn't learn anything tonight. Theo's from Dundee. Keeps us honest. And Scots enough."

"Scottish," Theo said with a wink. "This lot wouldn't have a clue without me."

The group surprised me with their seriousness. The promised box of wine stood with eight coffee mugs on the table, but they let it wait as they settled into figuring out *The Weirde Variation on the Compleat Gardener* with intensity. Theo, Kirsten, and Lucy, the town librarian, took one side of the room, along with Landy Henderson, who, despite her connection to my next door neighbour, treated me with kindness. The four of them draped gold sashes over their shoulders so we could remember who was playing the men's part: Theodora claimed she could tell one set of stars from another based on their positions on the crib diagrams. I stood with Char and Greta from the pub, and Kate of the many children.

The fool's role was easy enough to fill: Kirsten dug around in the studio's closet and emerged with a folding yellow sign with the words *Wet Floor* and a picture of a shadow figure slipping and falling on it. She took a baseball cap from a hook by the door—some dance student's castoff—and set it atop the sign. "There we go," she said, patting the sign. "Stand still, then, like a good lad."

The dance proved to be as complex as the diagrams suggested. We walked through it first. Theo was my partner: she helped me weave around the other dancers, then join hands with Char and Kirsten as we all stepped in a circle together. After one pass through the pattern, Kirsten put on some music and the women began to bounce on their toes. The beat was four times as fast as I would have imagined. We no longer walked: we skipped.

At the new pace, the turns were as much about centrifugal force as anything else. We looped and swirled and I was sweating and panting before I knew it. The more we practised, the pattern became clear, soaking into my muscles until my feet found the way for me. We went through it again and again, returning always to the beginning. I eyed the *Wet Floor* sign at our centre, remembering the spiral movements on the foldout page, the way the dance would, when we reached the end, close on the fool.

"Finish!" Theo shouted at long last. The dance changed, and the room's corners filled with thick mist, or maybe I was passing out, or maybe I passed through some gateway along with the others. We coiled around the fool like a pack of jackals circling its prey, and the spirals from the diagrams turned in my bones.

Theo spun me into the middle of the dance. Kirsten caught me and sent me into Landy's arms where she stood next to *Wet Floor*. We hadn't practiced this part, but the women guided me. The studio walls melted away, and the pot lights in the ceiling swung to the rhythm of drum and violin. I threw my head back and laughed while the women sang a high battle cry. I tripped over my feet and crashed into *Wet Floor*, collapsing the sign and kicking it off into the area where the wall should be, but wasn't.

We were out in the parking lot, somehow, and then in the field across from the Rec Center. The box of wine had come with us: or at least, the plastic bag inside that held the wine. Kirsten tore the remains of the cardboard away and sucked wine into her mouth through the plastic nozzle. She tossed the bag at me, where I sprawled on thorny ground.

My face had somehow planted in the grass; when I reached for the wine, I licked my lips and found the dew was sweet, and the air tasted sweet, and the moon that had risen high and swollen in the sky looked sweet. The wine itself was as foul and dilute as cheap wine had been for a great long while, but I knew if we could only get hold of some fruit, we would make much better.

"To the land!" Kate screamed as she tore into the bag with her teeth, letting the wine soak into her shirt and splash out across the ground, a dark red streak.

I thought someone, maybe Kirsten, would call a party foul, but the women roared their approval, and we swept on through the empty fields where woods once stood, feral and strong and whirling in the patterns of the dance. It ran through my blood as I partnered with the brittle bones of last year's thistles, with Greta and with Char, and with one surprised deer, who stood with eyes locked on mine as I spun around it, arms raised, praising it for surviving as long as it had.

White stars and green twisting shapes glowed in my vision as we burst through fences and the wreckage of tree lines. Phosphenes bloomed behind my closed eyelids, and my partners in the dance panted and ran until we were back on my land, crowded into the little space between my cottage and Jake Henderson's house.

The thump of the Earth's heart came up through my bare feet, scratched and bleeding from contact with the rocks, with the thistles, with the long years of ache and pain, with the slow, churning need to throw off the scab of humanity, to find renewal again, to burst forth with new life. I was the Gardener the land needed; I would guard.

"Carter Henderson!" I yelled, my voice like a bull's bellow. "Carter Henderson! Come over."

"Carter! Carter!" Even his Aunt Landy added her voice to the chorus. "Come over! Come over."

It took him only a moment to come. As always, he'd been waiting. He walked over the stile that stood between our properties. His father's bedroom window was dark. Jake went to bed early, rose early to tend his cattle, leaving Carter to watch television all night long, to watch me.

Carter stared at me. "What're you ladies all about?"

"Dancing," Theo said. "All you have to do is stand in the middle."

The Compleat Gardener was different under the moon, with our bare feet on the ground. Carter was just as cooperative as *Wet Floor,* or maybe, like a mouse who has been selected by a cat, he knew to be still until the end.

Understand, I don't think it was his fault, the fact that the world was utterly fucked, the fact that nothing would grow anymore. Understand: I don't hate men, despite what people will say, about how we spread some kind of murderous rage throughout the county, through the country, or beyond, if it goes that far. The ceremony isn't personal. It's about who can perform it, and who must be sacrificed.

Kirsten told me she'd already taken the liberty of spreading the images from the book online. She would say *The Compleat Gardener* is about reversing a polarity, making a shift from where the world's been at for the past few thousand years, to something new, or something very old.

It isn't personal, but it is satisfying in the way that anything is, if it lets you understand you're part of something bigger. Even now, as the sun shines bright on the greening world, and the apple tree pushes forth its blossoms, I can hear the groaning of Carter Henderson, who I rode into the ground as it moved up to swallow him. I can see his face, if I look out the window. It's tilted up to the sky. Bees sip the nectar of his eyes. He tries to yell, but his mouth is filled with earth. He's well away from the carrots and the turnips, which press their sprouts up into the air, green soldiers in an army of plants that will feed the world.

There's a sound of breaking wood, and Landy Henderson, mighty as a bear, tears her brother's door off its hinges at last. Sparrow song rips into the open air, to join the music of Jake

Henderson's screams. I hope they'll plant him where he lived. His cows deserve better fodder.

NEIL McROBERT

A
WELL-FED
MAN

ARKADY was trying to kill swans when the man arrived. Swan tasted unpleasant but it could feed his family for days. Arkady shivered with pleasure at the thought of the coppery organs, the small explosion of juices on his tongue. He gathered stones, each weighty enough to drop a bird but not too large for his eight-year old hand, then he set to throwing with a determination that permitted nothing of childish play.

He was so weak. His small strength had been devoured by each missed meal. The previous winter had withered his arms to chicken bones and he couldn't throw the stones any distance. When the first splashed harmlessly into the river the swans paddled out of range, casting haughty glances at the skinny boy twisting in frustration on the bank.

Tears came with the last stone, his dreams of carrying a bird home to mama fading to the cruel promise of another hungry evening. The final missile landed mere feet from the bank and, as if recognising the end of a harmless game, the swans took to the air, cracking their wings like unruly angels. Only then did Arkady turn from the river to find the man watching.

He sat on a nearby bench, draped in the shadows of trees. When Arkady turned, the man ducked behind his newspaper, but there was time enough to recognise the thinning blond hair and round, babyish face, the thick neck bubbling up around his collar. Three meetings in as many days was one too many for coincidence.

Arkady felt a dribble of unease. The riverbank was empty. It wasn't yet eight in the morning and everyone was already in the fields or in their beds all day. The village was full of sick people, hungry people, hidden away like soiled linen. More than a few had died in the spring: those already starving or who didn't plan for the lingering cold. A few of the dead came from families like Arkady's. They were people who had plenty until the government came with their trucks and trains and took it away. Papa's friend Nikja was dead. Once he owned goats and pigs and nearly twenty acres. He was dead before the snows melted, and though Arkady hadn't seen the body he'd seen how lightly the coffin sat on papa's shoulder.

He'd asked papa why they hadn't given Nikja and his wife some food.

"Because then we would be dead, too," papa replied.

Now the village felt empty. Only children slinked through the narrow streets, a sharp-cheeked tribe of ungoverned boys and girls, fighting like weasels in shifting allegiances, willing to maim and wound for a single potato or ear of corn. They colonised the parts of the village where the guards didn't go. Strangers were not welcome and adults walked nervously in the quiet. But here the man sat peacefully and at rest, whilst the hush of the riverbank and the gloom of the trees reserved their menace for Arkady alone.

The man's hand scuttled out from behind the newspaper. Arkady gasped. A bar of chocolate, wrapped in green waxed paper.

"Hello, boy," came a voice from the far side of the pages. "Are you hungry?"

Two days earlier Arkady had wandered to the station to beg from the warehouse guards. They looked at him with granite faces and shooed him away. He cried and pleaded and talked about his mama, dancing from foot to foot, always ready to run. Eventually the older of the two threw him a half loaf. It was burned to the black sheen of a beetle's shell. They warned him not to tell anyone. Arkady bowed and smiled and whispered a dozen thank yous, but he knew that this would be the last charity he found there.

He stepped out of the warehouse yard into the street, looking around for boys who would beat him unconscious for the food in his pocket, boys sent by their own mamas on just such a mission.

The man was sitting on a horse trough opposite the yard. His hands were busy at his mouth. Thick digits rubbed and massaged, slipping in and out of the greasy hole in his face. Arkady wondered if he was an idiot. There had been many on the land during the last few summers: helpless men and women who couldn't contribute on the farms, open mouths crying for food but producing nothing. They were set loose to find their way amongst the fields. Back on their old farm Papa had given food for a day's work. Now, when wanderers came to the door, papa just pointed to the gate and watched until they were far down the lane.

The man had the same vacant face and slumped posture as those roaming fools, but he didn't share their starved expressions. Clearly he had found a kinder family than Arkady's somewhere along the way. He looked hungry now, though. The rubbing fingers were slicked with saliva. It glistened between his knuckles. The sight of it roused Arkady's disgust and his pity. Hunger bred compulsion and there were many nights when Arkady had sucked his own fingers, searching for the ghost of a meal eaten three days before. He thought about the bread in his pocket and wondered if he could give just a little to the man. Then he pictured his sister's concave face and hardened his heart.

He looked back once and his stomach dropped. The man was looking straight at him. His slackness had been replaced with scrutiny. Man and boy stared at each other and Arkady was reminded of foxes caught amongst the hens, the way that a creature paused, suspended in the moment of its own discovery.

Arkady looked down at the bulge in his pocket and wondered what a hungry person would be willing to do for a loaf of bread. The thought broke his paralysis and he hurried away, ducking through backyards and alleyways rather than taking the obvious lanes. When he finally reached the farm he thrust the loaf into mama's hands. She kissed his forehead until laughter banished the terror of imagined pursuit. The pleasure of bread overwrote everything that night.

———————————

The following day Arkady and Evgenyi were searching for bird eggs in the trees behind the Sobal farm. Evgenyi asked whether he would eat a baby rat if they found one and Arkady said of course not. In his inner places, though, something churned at the thought of such pliant meat.

Whilst his brother beat the tall grass with a stick, Arkady scanned the trees. There were rumours of a pair of collared doves nesting nearby. Arkady doubted the story; the farm seemed a sad place for such pretty birds. But still he let his eyes linger over the branches, alert for a flash of white amongst the green.

Evgenyi suddenly stopped.

"*Blyat.*" The curse was more breath than sound.

"What? What is it Evi?"

"Over there, by the house."

Arkady looked. The big man stood with his back to the house, staring out across the field in their direction. When he saw them looking he turned as if to examine the boarding.

It was a silly charade. The Sobal farm had been empty for two years and the only people who came here were children daring the ghosts. Arkady wasn't sure whose ghosts they would be. No one had died in the house as far as he knew. The Sobals had just left. One day Sveta and her sister hadn't turned up for class and Arkady had never seen them again. Word got around that their house was empty and soon the boys came to break the windows. Someone painted messages on the walls that Arkady didn't understand. *Our soil is ours* said one. Jagged paint-strokes shouted *Slava Ukrayini*. It was faded from two winters of frost but still legible.

He asked papa once about what had happened to the Sobals. Papa had been drinking that night and he looked at Arkady strangely.

"They did too well Arki, owned too much."

"What do you mean, papa?"

"Their farm. Twenty-two acres. Too much for one man."

"Did they sell the farm, papa? Do they live somewhere all together like us now?"

Papa laughed: a single bullet of air. "Ha. No, Arki. They tried though, once they saw the way the wind was blowing. But *Moskva* doesn't buy when it can just take."

Mama had shushed them both then and shooed Arkady off to bed. The day after, papa refused to talk about it, so Arkady never understood where the Sobal sisters went or what it had to do with the wind. He was left with the unsettling image of the girls being picked up and fanned from their house like kites.

Now the man was lurking at the abandoned house. Arkady wondered if he had followed them from the village.

"Evi," he whispered, "is he police? Is he going to arrest us?"

"No, Arki. I don't think he's anyone. Look at his clothes. Look at the size of him. The OGPU wouldn't have him." Evgenyi sounded as confident as always but he still gripped Arkady's arm, pulling him towards the trees.

Evgenyi was right, he looked nothing like the policemen or soldiers, or even like the men who came to take the harvest. His woollen trousers were threadbare and surprisingly heavy for the summer. His shirt was a dismal white, fading to yellow at the collar and a light pink at the cuffs. There was none of the neatness, the sharp utility that Arkady associated with officials. Moreover, he had a round face, the kind that looked unnatural with a scowl. His hair was neatly cut and his cheeks clean-shaven, but there was a softness to his features that

Arkady couldn't reconcile with authority's stony face. Above all there was the obvious oddity of the man.

He was fat. Not like the cartoons Evgenyi showed him of foreigners drawn like pigs, or the posters of the *kulaks* with their swollen faces and greedy hands that made papa so angry. No, just fat compared with everybody else Arkady knew. His cheekbones didn't saw at the skin of his face like papa's. His shoulders reached all the way to the edges of his shirt. He looked well fed.

"Come away, Arki, let's go home."

"Who is he, Evi?"

"I don't know, it doesn't matter. But let's go."

"But we haven't found anything yet. Mama will be mad if we go home this early and we don't have anything."

"She won't be mad, I promise." His brother spoke almost kindly and it was this that alerted Arkady to something he had never expected: Evgenyi was scared.

"Come now or I'll tell mama that we found some eggs and you ate them."

As Evgenyi dragged him through the trees Arkady saw the man lift a plump hand to his mouth. He was still rubbing his lips when Arkady lost sight of him amongst the leaves.

That evening, whilst Evgenyi and their eldest brother Misha helped papa move the grain, mama spoke to Arkady and his sister. Summer had only just passed but the evenings were already cold. The wood and clay of the walls sucked heat from the room but Arkady knew the real problem was their hunger. Cold breached skin and chipped away at the shallowly buried bone. It had always been Misha's job to chop firewood but these days he was so thin and tired that the axe looked fit to topple him. Arkady felt the fire at his back and wondered what it would be like to be without both food and warmth through the winter.

Marta was so skinny that it made Arkady sick to look at her. Her beautiful hair had turned as thin and brittle as a forest after a fire. Arkady tried not to see the way her mouth gaped for air or food or some other lifeblood. She reached for his hand, but he brushed her away. Her fingers felt like bones wrapped in unwashed cotton.

"Evi says you saw a man today," mama said. "Out near the Sobal's?"

"Yes, mama."

"And you had seen this man before?"

"Yes, mama. I saw him outside the railway. Am I in trouble for taking the bread? I'm sorry."

"Oh *lyubov*, you aren't in trouble. But I want to talk about that man. Evi says that he was…" She puffed out her cheeks and held her arms out round her body. Marta chuckled. It was a sad, breathless sound.

"He wasn't that fat, mama," Arkady said.

"But was he skinny like us?" Arkady watched as her eyes flashed to Marta and quickly away.

"He had a little belly and his neck was thick."

Mama's face stilled. She slid from the chair to sit between him and Marta. She put an arm around their shoulders.

"This is important, okay? If you see that man again, Arki, you are to run home right away."

"Yes, mama." He paused. "Why?"

"Because strangers can be dangerous. There are a lot of people now who don't have very much. Think about everyone we work with on the farms. Everyone is working hard, everyone is hungry, yes?"

He nodded.

"Do you know anyone who looks like that man you saw today?"

Arkady thought about the other families on the farm, people who had been their neighbours and friends. He didn't think anyone was ever rich, but since the soldiers came and made everyone work together it had gotten bad. A year ago some of the families still had a cow or a few chickens, but they had all been eaten now. No one shared anymore. No one smiled. And no one played. People finished their work and went back to their cabins and closed the doors. They all looked the same, like papa and Misha, thin and tired and rubbed raw by a new life that they didn't recognise.

"No, mama." Arkady said. "He looked different from us."

"Did he look hungry?" she asked.

"No, mama."

She nodded. "Exactly. And we don't trust strangers. Especially well-fed ones. Both of you promise me, if you ever see a well-fed man, even if he looks kind, even if you think you know him, promise me you'll run away."

"I promise, mama," Marta wheezed.

"Arki?"

"Yes, mama, I promise."

"Good boy."

"But mama?" he asked.

"Yes?"

"Where does the man get his food from? Maybe we could ask him for some."

Mama paused again. Before she could say anything else the door opened and papa, Misha and Evgenyi stepped into the room. They looked unhappy. In the dim firelight the dark circles under papa's eyes were like hungry mouths. He slammed the door.

Mama stood quickly to her feet.

"What is it, Pavel?"

"Sour news." Papa said. "Pavlovych has gotten word, they are coming for the grain next week."

Mama made a low noise and rubbed a hand across her face.

"Then we will have to work quicker."

Papa scowled. "Quicker? How can we work quicker? Look at him, look at our son." Papa placed a hand on Misha's shoulders. Misha looked as if he could hardly bear the weight of it.

"I don't know but we must" mama said. "We can't let them find it." She looked down at Marta and Arkady. "We need that grain."

Papa let his head drop to his chest.

"That's not all, mama," Evgenyi said.

They waited.

"Ulyana Kolysnik has gone missing."

———————

Now, standing by the river, Arkady heard his promise again. *If you ever see a well-fed man, run away.* Yet he stood unmoving. Arkady had tasted chocolate three times, the last over two years before, on Misha's thirteenth birthday. Today he would have given anything just to run his tongue across the paper wrapping.

The man stayed curtained behind his newspaper, but he edged the chocolate closer.

"Well, little man," he said. "Don't you want it?"

Arkady said nothing.

"Take it. I have plenty." The man's voice was kind. It reached a higher pitch at the edge of words. It was made for laughter.

Silence.

"Fine then, boy. I understand. Mama says take nothing from a stranger. Very wise." Suddenly the paper fell away, revealing the man's grinning face. His round, *full* face.

Run away, Arki, run away . . .

"I am Mr. Vovk," the man said. "What is your name?"

The man's sudden appearance shocked an answer out of the boy.

"Arkady sir. Arkady Hubenka."

"Well, I am pleased to meet you." The man stretched out a hand. Arkady didn't look at it; his attention was still on the chocolate.

"If we shake hands then we're friends, Arkady. And if we are friends then we can't be strangers and you can have some chocolate." His smile widened yet further. "And I'll have another friend."

Arkady began to feel foolish. Mr. Vovk seemed very nice indeed. He hadn't moved from the bench or shown any intention of harm. Arkady wondered why mama would want him not to have chocolate. Surely she would want Marta to have it?

Marta would die this winter, he knew. She would waste away before the fire and die without having tasting sweetness. Arkady was suddenly furious. He raged at the men in *Moskva* who sent the trucks to steal their farm and food, at the men in the trucks who did the stealing, and at this man who tempted him to break his promises. But most of Arkady's fury was for mama. How could she ask him to walk away from such a prize? How could she not want Marta to taste chocolate before she died? She had decided that all the world was bad. But she was wrong, Arkady thought. There could be kindness even amongst the hungry.

"Last chance, Arkady," Mr. Vovk said. He thrust the green wrapper forward again. "There are lots of other hungry boys who want to be friends."

As he broke and took his first step Arkady heard his mother's cry. He crushed the voice. On his second and third step he realised that the chocolate would never reach his sister. He would gobble it down here on the riverside and never tell another person about his good luck. On the fourth step he saw Mr. Vovk raise his thumb to his lips and begin to rub. The gesture shattered Arkady's illusion. Truth rushed in. Mr. Vovk's eyes did not gleam with kindness but with hard good humour. It was the glee of the *krokodil* before the crash of water and the baying of the bitten. Arkady realised all of this and tried to halt but his body was a slave to momentum. He walked forwards, reaching out for his reward even as he realised it was bait. Another step was the last step and his fingers brushed the waxed paper for a heartbreaking moment before Vovk's hand clamped down around his forearm.

Arkady howled, more in disappointment than fear, though terror was an instant behind. Vovk thrust out a hand and his mouth was suddenly full of fingers. They pinned his tongue and suppressed his scream. He felt the heel of the man's hand grip his chin. He tried to bite down and Vovk shook him roughly by the head.

"Stop that," Vovk said. "If you bite, I'll hurt you." With his other hand he took hold of Arkady's ear. "I'll rip this right off your head."

The boy read the man's face and turned boneless. He saw that whatever the man was going to do to him, he had done it before. There was pity in the swollen features, sympathy for Arkady's torment, but also amusement at how well the lure had worked. Arkady saw all of this and his bladder let go. He felt the urine run down his leg and into his shoe.

It broke the tableau. Vovk looked down and scowled.

"Dirty boy," he said. "I'll have to wash you now. Otherwise they will smell it on you."

Still gripping Arkady's head, Vovk dragged the boy towards the trees that fringed the riverbank. Arkady knew that if he passed into those autumnal shadows he would not come back out, or at least not whole.

Papa and Misha and the others had searched for Ulyana Kolysnik until late into the night. They found nothing. She was only eleven, too young to have run away from home. When Misha finally fell into bed he told his brothers that someone must have taken her. Lots of children were going missing these days, Misha said, so better watch out.

Arkady didn't want to be taken. He didn't want to disappear. The thought of his papa and brothers walking the fields, beating aside the long grass in the hope and dread of discovering his body, it made him feel sick to his stomach. The fingers in his mouth fed the nausea. Fat worms full of blood, they wriggled deeper as Vovk reinforced his grip. Most horrific of all, a part of Arkady welcomed the memory of meat.

Beneath the revulsion and paralysing fear, there was a part of him that wanted to bite down, to chew and rend and fill his belly with flesh. It was too much and when a fingernail scratched the back of his throat Arkady convulsed.

Thin vomit sprayed out around the fingers. Vovk squealed and jerked away. He released Arkady's ear but a knuckle caught on the boy's teeth. Arkady bit down and felt his teeth part flesh. Suddenly Vovk was screaming. He danced on the spot, holding one hand with the other whilst blood seeped between his knuckles. Arkady spat out the fingertip. It disappeared in the grass. The boy turned to flee.

He ran away from the trees. Behind him Vovk bawled in pain, but Arkady knew he was already in pursuit. He could feel the thunder of the man's feet. Arkady hadn't run in weeks. Hunger had long-ago reduced everyone to a shuffling walk. For a few fear-fuelled seconds, however, he flew along the path as if he had never missed a meal.

If he followed the river it would lead him to the farm where papa and the others worked. The man wouldn't dare follow him there. But it meant crossing a half mile of unsafe ground. The hunger and the arrests and the deaths had left a lot of homes empty and Arkady didn't know which doors would offer rescue. His speed wouldn't last and he had to make this miracle burst count for something.

He risked a look over his shoulder. Vovk was close. A red flush bloomed in his face and Arkady thought that if he kept running then the big man might tire. After fifty paces he was still there though, beet-faced and gasping, but still coming.

He is getting stronger, Arkady realised. *He will catch me.* Even if they were to meet someone along the path Arkady doubted it would matter. Everyone in the village was weak and Vovk would have no problem overpowering them. Arkady needed papa. Papa was still strong enough to protect him. The food that they had hidden—that they were still hiding—had kept the severest edge of starvation at bay.

Arkady veered away from the river. A narrower path led through the thinning wedge of trees and emerged into an alleyway. The transition from soft earth to cobbles jolted him and he barely kept his feet. He dashed along the alley, his lungs beginning to fray. On either side of him the rough tin-and-board fences were unclimbable and doorless. They made the walls of a death-chute, a slaughterhouse corridor. Ahead the mouth of the alley was a slice of green in a grey world.

He emerged into open space. The cobbles turned sharply right and bridged the river where it snaked out of the trees. Momentum took him forwards, toward a low stone wall. Beyond was a field of feathergrass and in the middle a sway-backed barn. It leaned in the wind like a beaten mule. The river curved around the back of the barn and wended its way to the horizon.

Vovk had fallen behind but he was still coming. He grew larger as he approached, seeming to swell and fill the tight neck of the alley.

"Stop, boy," he growled between breaths.

Arkady vaulted the wall. On the other side the feathergrass reached almost to his shoulders. If he ducked and weaved maybe it would cover his escape. He heard the sound of soft impact and guessed that Vovk had reached the wall. Arkady dropped to his hands and knees, tucked in his head, hoping it was enough to keep him hidden.

"*Peizdets.*"

Vovk's curse made Arkady's heart flutter with hope. *He can't see me.*

He turned toward the barn and the river beyond. Rescue was that way. Papa and Evi and Misha, and all the other men from the farm. They were hiding the harvest in a barn just like this one. They thought he didn't know.

He also knew that it was dangerous and that the men in the trucks would beat papa, or worse, if they found out. But he saw the way that mama and papa looked at him and Marta, felt their hands flinch away from his sharp bones as if scalded. They would risk anything. Because what would you quail at when the only other option was to starve? So, he knew where papa was right at that moment. He just had to get there.

When he had crawled half the distance to the barn he turned and peeked back through the grass. Vovk stood on top of the wall. He was looking around the field, his gaze resting nowhere. The white shirt he wore had turned dark grey with sweat, except at the cuffs where the pink tinge remained.

Suddenly he jumped down from his vantage point. He landed badly, stumbling forwards out of sight, crashing into the feathergrass with a grunt. For a terrifying moment Arkady felt a laugh begin to build. A hysterical bubbling started behind his tongue and he clawed a hand down his face to settle it. His dirty nails broke the skin and he felt blood trickle from his cheek.

Vovk regained his feet and scanned the field again. His breath came in seismic lurches that shook the flesh around his jaw. Sweat poured down his face.

He can't find me, Arkady thought. And then, as if to prove the lie, the man's head snapped in Arkady's direction. The boy felt the attention pin him in place. He thought of hawks and mice and the final moments of small things.

Vovk walked directly toward Arkady, crossing the ground between them without hesitation. For the second time Arkady felt a squirt of urine sting his skin. He was watching death stride towards him and now, at the end, exhaustion swept over him like bad weather. He sank down to his backside.

As Vovk's shadow fell across him Arkady almost screamed out a pointless plea for mercy. Panic stilled his tongue and, to the boy's disbelieving relief, Vovk marched past without pause. He passed less than a body's-length from where Arkady was sitting and headed into the half-light of the barn.

Arkady knew that this was his best chance to escape but it was a struggle to move. The muscles of his legs quivered as he tried to stand, his hands shook as he pushed himself away from the ground. He could hear Vovk moving things around inside. It wasn't a large building and the search wouldn't take long. He had only moments to circle the barn and flee to the river.

He dashed to the side of the structure. It had slumped in its abandonment, leaving gaps between boards through which Arkady could make out movement. Vovk was still searching. He dragged tarpaulins from rusted tools and kick piles of debris aside. As he searched he whispered.

"Come out, Arkady. No point hiding. If they run I always find them." He pushed an old barrow out of the way. "I sniff them out."

Vovk crossed the barn. He stopped feet from the wall they shared. The boy thanked God that the sun was on the other side of the barn. A few hours later and he would have been caught in stark relief against the gapped planking.

Vovk continued. "I can smell children, you see. All I have to do is sniff." He made an exaggerated snuffling noise and then laughed. His hand played at his mouth. "All the little children smell different. Some smell like sugar and some smell like fish and some of the fatter ones smell like butter."

Now he was standing only a few feet away, on the other side of the wall. Arkady held his breath but continued his slow traverse. His foot kicked something solid and he froze, sure the sound would bring Vovk running. The man's maddening voice didn't stop, it only rose in pitch and volume as his excitement grew.

"You smell like bread and potatoes, Arkady. Like what your papa is hiding in the barn. Oh yes, I know about that. And if you don't come out right now, I'll tell the police. Do you know what they'll do to your papa? You'll never see him again."

Arkady looked at what he'd kicked. It was a sliver of plank with two rusted nails sticking up like fangs. If he'd stepped on them it would have been all over. Slowly he bent and picked up the plank. It felt insubstantial in his hand, but the nails still looked sharp.

He was nearly at the rear corner of the barn. From there it was only a few dozen steps to the river. If he could swim across there without being seen then he knew he could lose himself in the trees on the other side. They were only a few hundred yards wide and the farm was right on the other side. Even if Vovk gave chase he would probably assume that Arkady had taken the path that skirted the trees rather than cut into them.

What if Vovk did tell the men in the trucks about the grain and potatoes, though? Arkady had heard the stories the boys told of the *Cheka*, of how they used to skin people alive or drown them in boiling water, how they would come in the night and whole families would disappear. Mama said that the *Cheka* didn't exist anymore, that they were gone before he was even born. But the boys had said that the new police were just the same people with a different name. Arkady thought of mama and papa being dragged away in the back of a black wagon and he slowed his crawl. The plank dangled from his shaking hand.

Only feet away on the other side of the wall Vovk was still searching and talking. His voice had become moist and spit-tle-flecked.

"Your mama and papa will be in such trouble. They'll smell the food on them just like I smell it on you, boy. Bread and potatoes, that's what you smell like. That's your scent. They all smell different at first. But when you're cooked you all smell the same. When you carve a little bit off and give it a sizzle, well then you all smell like bacon."

The truth caved in on Arkady. It pinned him in place.

He hadn't had much time to ponder what Vovk wanted from him. He'd imagined fleeting horrors, words as much as pictures. The things his parents had warned him about, *Cheka*, OGPU, the police, the government. They came along and took children away in their black Volgas. Papa had never said to what end, only warned him to behave lest they come for him. The boys had filled in the gaps though, with stories of experiments, and secret laboratories. Failing that there was always the diffuse threat of what strange men did to young boys in unwatched places, things Arkady only dimly compre-hended. All those thoughts had flickered through his frantic mind. But Vovk's giggling revelation was too horrible to be true, though true it seemed to be. Mama's warning suddenly made sense.

The man on the other side of the boards wanted to eat him.

Arkady stood motionless whilst this sank in. His thoughts flashed to Ulyana Kolysnik. Pretty little Ulyana. She used to bring mama eggs from her grandmother's chickens. Had she ended up as meat on this man's table? Was Vovk's fleshy body stuffed with pieces of children, like some awful fatty sausage. He pictured little arms beneath the man's skin, still curved as if in embrace, or splayed as if warding off a violent end.

A new silence punctured his horrified reverie. Vovk had stopped speaking. There was no sound at all from inside the barn. It was time to dash for safety. Readying himself, he looked once through the boards to check that Vovk was still busy searching. What he saw made his stomach fall to his feet.

Vovk was staring at him.

His face was pushed up against the planking, so close that his cheeks were bubbling through the gaps. A dark brown eye peered out between the wood and held Arkady as firmly as a chain.

"There you are, boy."

Fingers emerged between the boards. Arkady watched the knuckles whiten. Vovk roared and the boards cracked. With a second pull he ripped a hole in the barn. Suddenly there was nothing between the boy and the well-fed man and still Arkady didn't run.

"Good boy," Vovk said. "No use running. If I don't do it they will, anyway. And I know where to cut so it doesn't hurt."

He grabbed hold of Arkady's shirt and pulled. Arkady felt his feet begin to lift as his body was pulled through the hole in the boards. The splintered planking were teeth in a monstrous mouth.

Without conscious thought Arkady swung his arm. The broken plank disintegrated as it connected with Vovk's head. Arkady saw it shatter to dust and thought his last chance was gone. He was released a second before the screaming started. He fell to the ground and watched as Vovk fell forwards through the barn wall. The man rolled on the ground holding his hands to his face. He screamed like a wounded hare.

"Oh, you bastard boy. You *ublyudok*. My face, my face."

Arkady looked with a sickly delight at the nails buried in Vovk's face. One had caught deep in the crease between the man's nose and cheekbone, the other angled upwards just below his eye. Blood dribbled out around them, mixing with the that still seeping from his severed fingertip. Vovk continued to flail and moan as Arkady struggled to his feet.

The river was cold but he plunged into it without hesitation. Within seconds he was chest deep and fighting the current. He half-swam, half-stumbled across to the opposite bank and dragged himself out. The trees were right there and through them, just a few hundred yards away, papa.

Vovk was halfway across the river. The nails still jutted from his face and he looked almost as tired as Arkady felt, but still he came. The water coursed past his hips and complicated his centre of balance, slowing him down, but not enough. He met Arkady's eyes and grinned. Blood had run down his cheek and into his mouth, staining his lips and teeth red. Was that the last thing Ulyana saw before she died, Arkady wondered? Did he take a bite out of her whilst she watched?

"Still coming, boy." Vovk's voice remained light, even laden with pain and effort. "Before it was just business. Now I'm going to make you howl."

For the last time, Arkady turned his back and ran. He cut straight into the trees, hoping to hear voices or the growl of a tractor. If he kept straight he had to come out somewhere on the farm, but straight wasn't easy. The autumn leaves refracted sunlight into strange configurations. They fell in bands of light and shade that confused the eye. Arkady fell more than once and each time it was harder to get up. He thought he could hear Vovk in pursuit but it was difficult to distinguish between footsteps and the thudding of his own heart.

He ran for his life. Exhaustion clenched him, black gloved fingers crept in at the edges of his vision. And then, the trees began to thin.

Stumbling, sobbing, sweat-soaked, Arkady reached the treeline. A short distance across the field, men huddled at a barn door. They had shovels in their hands and their backs to the trees. He saw Misha standing shirtless in the sun. As Arkady watched, Papa stepped out of the shadow of the barn and clapped his brother on the back.

Arkady staggered from the trees, a little boy returning from an ill-written fairy tale. As he opened his mouth to scream he felt something tangle in his hair.

No, he thought. *Please*. Not when he was so close.

Vovk pulled him back towards the woods. He tried to slip his hand across Arkady' mouth but the raw edge of his finger kept him from a sure grip. Arkady wriggled and ground his feet, but he couldn't match the man's remorseless strength. He felt hot breath across the side of his face as Vovk panted. Sour breath. Butter, fish, some other dark aroma underneath.

As the man's thick forearm pressed across Arkady's mouth, he reached up and batted blindly at Vovk's face, trying for his eyes. The edge of his thumb caught something hard and he gripped it in his little fist. With no strength left Arkady let gravity do the work. Unlatching his knees, he fell, still gripping the nail, pulling it down with him so that it ripped lengthways from Vovk's face.

Vovk brayed in fresh agony, a ululating wail that startled birds from the trees.

Collared doves, Arkady thought in the misfire of panic. *The eggs.*

A number of the men had turned towards Vovk's cries. Arkady added his own screams to the cacophony.

"Papa. Misha. Help me."

He watched papa burst from the crowd and sprint across the rutted ground. Misha was only a few paces behind, followed by a dozen others. It took them only seconds to cross the distance and when they reached him Arkady fell forwards into his father's embrace. Behind him Vovk remained on his knees, blood coursing through the hands he held at his face.

"Arki, my god," papa said. "What on earth? What has happened?"

Arkady couldn't find words. He just shook in papa's arms.

"Pavel, look." A man's voice, low and worried.

Arkady felt his father look up. Felt strings of muscle tense beneath his shirt.

"Is that him?" Another deep voice.

"Yeah, that's the bastard."

Everyone began to speak at once. Voices overlapped, some angry, some confused. A few were filled with an odd inflection that Arkady thought might be embarrassment. Vovk's wails were a keening accompaniment to the uproar.

Eventually papa released him and stood. He stepped between Arkady and the kneeling man.

"Get up," his father said.

Vovk sucked in a breath and staggered to his feet. Redness pulsed from the wound beneath his eye. He stared at Arkady with hate and then fixed his attention on papa.

"Your son is a little shit, Hubenka. Look what he did to my face."

"Shut your mouth, Vovk. You will never look at my son again."

Arkady reeled. How did the man know papa? How did papa know Vovk's name? He looked at the men surrounding them. Most gazed at Vovk with sickly recognition. What was going on?

"He wanted to eat me, papa."

Papa looked back. "Misha, take him home."

Misha didn't move. Like the rest of the men he watched the scene unfolding.

"Maybe we should bring the police, Pavel," someone said.

Vovk laughed.

"Yes, bring the police. Once they arrest me they'll help you fill that hole in the barn. I'm sure they won't worry about what's inside it."

The men rustled like agitated birds.

Vovk continued. "Some of those guards are my best customers, you know. You aren't the only people who have been hungry this last year."

"Someone fetch a rope, then," papa said. "We'll hang this *ublyudok* from a tree."

Vovk rubbed his lip, smearing the blood into a clown's grin. He swallowed once and then showed his teeth.

"Yes, you could hang me. But you won't."

"And why is that?" Papa opened and closed his fists. "You are lucky that Ulyana's father isn't here. He'd have ripped your throat out with his teeth."

"Ulyana? Who is Ulyana?" Vovk asked.

"You know who," Misha yelled. "The little girl you took last night."

"She was only seven," another man shouted. "Bastard."

Arkady watched Vovk shake his head. Why were they still talking? Something was wrong here.

"I have taken no child this week, nor last week or the weeks before. Whoever this poor little girl is she is nothing to do with me." He paused. "But I'm sure I'm not the only one who does what I do." Vovk continued to smile. "Maybe even one of you here. Maybe her own mama and papa. Perhaps it was a mercy."

"Get a rope, I said." Papa's voice was raised now.

Vovk's head snapped back to Arkady's father. He was grinning now. Arkady didn't like it.

"Like I said, Hubenka, you won't hang me."

Papa flicked his head. "Misha, a rope."

Misha didn't move.

"You won't hang me because you need me," Vovk continued. "You need me to do the things that you can't do."

He pointed at Arkady.

"Could you take that boy and cut him from belly to throat? Could you carve him, dress him? Could you even hold him down whilst he screamed for you to stop?" You're his father

Hubenka, so you couldn't do it." He chuckled. "Not yet any-way."

Papa turned to the group and raised his hands in disbelief at their inaction. All the while Vovk kept up his high-throated speech.

"But the rest of you. Maybe when you get hungry enough you'll start to look at a neighbour's little one with different eyes. Maybe a nephew or a little sister even. But you'll suf-fer before you get there. Conscience is a terrible curse to the starving man. That's why you need me."

He looked at Arkady and the boy felt his balls climb into his stomach.

"That's why your papa won't hang me, boy."

Vovk backed away into the trees, a wounded wolf slinking back to its lair. Something small came flying from the shad-ows and the group flinched as one. It landed at Arkady's feet. A chocolate bar, still in the waxed green paper. He bent to it but a hand roughly pushed him aside. It was Misha.

"For Marta," his brother said as he slipped the bar into his pocket.

Arkady watched papa diminish. His body shrank as if sud-denly convinced of its own starvation. He took a step for-wards, as if to follow the departing man and then stopped. Turning, he looked at the men of the village.

"He was going to kill my boy."

No one said anything. The men turned and walked back to the barn, leaving Arkady, Misha, and their papa standing alone in the harvested field. From deep inside the trees a bird burst into the air, as if disturbed by something passing by.

The soldiers came three days later. They loaded the harvest into their trucks and ignored the farmers' pleas. When winter came the men dug up the sacks of grain and root vegetables. It was enough to blunt the sharpest edge of hunger and, hud-dled down in their hovels, the families endured. Not all saw the spring come again, however. Some were found dead in their homes, some were discovered frozen in the fields. Some were never found. A handful of these were children and when Marta asked mama and papa where her friends had gone, Arkady saw the look that passed between them.

"Maybe they have gone somewhere warmer, little *holubka*," mama said.

"Lucky them," papa offered.

A few days afterwards there was meat in the evening stew. Grey, gristled and tough, it made Arkady feel sick to look at it.

He ate every mouthful.

SHAWN WALLACE

THE
BINDING
TIDE

SKRAELING ate the afternoon sun, straightjacketing it in clouds. That was the first thing that Martin Thaler noted when his little Thalercon entourage had arrived. The team had booked the flight to the seaside Rhode Island town at the urgent request of Vina Tucci, his marketing director, who'd told him it was essential that he appear. She'd been blazing the marketing campaign trail in Skraeling that summer, ahead of the Strand development project he was spearheading.

Vina had met them personally at Tallmadge Airport, the little airstrip that serviced the beachfront communities of Rhode Island. She'd at least had the courtesy to rent them a pair of limousines, as was expected. She looked harried. Worried, even—her black-haired, New Jersey nativity somehow ill-suited in Rhode Island, although she was impeccably attired in pinstripes. It wasn't enough.

Tall, blandly handsome, lean, and black-clad in a ribbed turtleneck with grey slacks and expensive men's Louboutin loafers, Martin Thaler wore sunglasses even when he didn't have to, and this was another of those occasions, clouds be damned. Martin confronted her in the back of the first limo, with Emma Cavendish, his red-headed attorney and right-hand woman, and a deathly rival of the diminutive, relentless Vina. Educated at Brown, Emma brought brains and an eye for acquisitions.

"What's the goddamned crisis, Tooch?" Thaler asked, leaning back and swigging a bottled water. "You told me you had things handled. Was that, or was that not, where you left it with me in August?"

"It is, Martin," Vina said. "But, you know, things have changed on the ground."

"On the ground?" Thaler asked. "As opposed to where? In the sky? On the sea?"

Emma sat beside Martin, staring green-eyed daggers at Vina, who weathered the Thaler storm with her lieutenant, Thomasina Quintana, sitting beside her. Thomasina had big brown eyes and hair that matched her eyes exactly. She was Vina's spy, but Thaler didn't mind—Vina knew talent, and Thomasina was talented in negotiation. She'd always been able to bring clients to the table, to get them where Thaler needed them. Vina had insisted she come along on the Strand project, because of how dug in the locals were. Thomasina looked like she would have preferred to be anywhere but sitting beside her boss, watching her get dressed down by Thaler.

But Thaler had insisted on her accompanying them on the ride in. Vina, who was known at Thalercon as feisty and formidable, knotted her manicured hands together across her knee, leaned in at Thaler, her black eyes riveted on his shaded visage.

"The sea's the problem, Martin," Vina said. "They saw the plans, they didn't like where the Strand is situated."

Thaler scoffed, glancing at Emma, who grimaced in concert with his displeasure.

"This is what happens when you send a marketer in, Emma," Thaler said. "Maybe your assistant can negotiate a better deal, Tooch. Was that your plan? You clearly worked on your tan this summer. What I want to hear you say is: 'I screwed up, Martin. I need your help.'"

Vina swallowed, maintained her composure, although Thomasina knew it had to be difficult, in such close quarters, with an audience. It wasn't in Vina's nature to stay composed. Thomasina knew for her to hold back, it was literally because her professional life was on the line. She was glad the others weren't here to see this.

The other Thaler staff who'd come along included Jonathan Briggs, the bespectacled, bespoke-suited site architect who had originally sold Thaler on the Strand concept.

Jonathan had brought a handful of others along—his Expensables, Thaler called them. They all rode in the second limo.

The Expensables were: portly, balding Bob Halder (site planner), Wade Ritter (civil engineer), he of the perennial squint, Boyd McAndrews (landscape architect), overly blond and overly fond of his tablet, which he carried around him absolutely everywhere.

"I screwed up, Martin. I need your help," Vina said, all but choking it out. Thaler crunched the empty plastic water bottle and tossed it aside.

"There," Thaler said. "Was *that* so difficult, Tooch?"

Thomasina knew better than to make a move or a sound. Emma studied her silently, while Vina held Thaler's gaze, until he looked out the window, sighing.

"It doesn't matter, anyway," Thaler said. "The calvary's arrived."

Thomasina cleared her throat, took the plunge. It was a crazy play, but she felt she had to be supportive of her boss, however she could. And, to be honest, she couldn't let it stand.

"It's *cavalry*, Mr. Thaler," Thomasina said. "The *cavalry's* arrived. That's us."

Thaler turned away from the window to look directly at her, while Emma's green eyes flashed at Thomasina's presumption. Vina didn't breathe.

"What?" Thaler asked.

"Calvary is associated with the Crucifixion," Thomasina said. "It also means to experience intense mental suffering. Cavalry is what you meant."

"Is it?" Thaler said, glancing at Emma, who smiled back uncomfortably. "Well, *thanks* for the vocabulary lesson, Tomi. Looks like the *calvary's* already here, judging from Tooch's expression. Tooch's definitely experiencing 'intense mental suffering' right now. Right, Tooch?"

Vina managed a nod.

"Piece of professional advice, Tomi," Emma said, patting Thomasina on the knee with her burgundy-painted fingernails. "*Never* correct Mr. Thaler."

"Oh, it's fine, Emma," Thaler said. "This is why Tomi'll have Vina's job someday. She's smart, and she's got moxie. Vina only went to Princeton, after all. Where'd *you* go to school, Tomi?"

"Notre Dame," Thomasina said, prompting a chuckle from Thaler, himself, a Boston native.

"Are you a good Catholic, Tomi?" Thaler asked.

"I'm a lapsed Catholic," Thomasina said.

"It figures," Thaler said, looking back out the window, already bored.

Beyond the berating of Vina, the drive over had been smoothly uneventful, winding through nature preserves and past furtive beachfront dwellings, past the Skraeling Sweet Corn Cooperative (SSCC) building, and the fields of dancing sweet corn that employed most of what was left of the hapless townsfolk.

The SSCC building itself was painted a defiantly cheery pastel shade of blue, which provided a disarming contrast to the green and gold of the swaying sweet corn.

Skraeling had seen far better days. Savaged by Hurricane Irene in 2011, fully two-thirds of the town had been drowned in the storm surge—not literally (although some had died in it), but the damage to the streets and New England charm of the place had been profound. The removal of the ruined buildings had emptied the tourist town's coffers, and the locals were desperate to get back on their feet.

What remained of Skraeling was the curving strip of Conch Street, and a baker's dozen of businesses—Binnacle Bob's Bait & Tackle, Jesse's Joists (a hardware store), the Also-Ran (the sole remaining tavern), the Triple Cross Bakery, the Quayside (a quaintly New England boutique hotel of thirty beds), a weathered WPA-era Town Hall building, as well as a handful of seasonal businesses that were holdovers from Skraeling's better days, when tourists came by with annual regularity.

Conch Street was now beachfront property, post-Irene. That's where Thaler had come into it.

"So, where are we at, Vina?" Thaler asked, having stepped from the limo and into the sea breeze, feeling the salt on the air.

"We're in Skraeling, Martin," Vina said. "It's both where we are, and where we're at."

"Whatever that even means," Thaler said. Emma, Vina, and Thomasina exited in Thaler's wake.

Skraeling had made all kinds of sense to Thaler. With two-thirds of the town effectively underwater, Skraeling was thirsty for investment. It didn't mean something couldn't be done with it. That's what Thaler counted on. The Strand was going to be the answer to their prayers—a proper beachfront resort hotel, just a stone's throw away from Massachusetts.

Thaler surveyed the gentle bend of Conch Street, which, if not quite a boardwalk, at least had a seaside quality to it that was accentuated by the clearly ancient street lamps, which resembled nothing more than spiky crowns around the lantern heads, bearing the corrosive grit and grime of constant seaspray, but fetching, all the same.

"I like those," Thaler said. "*They* can stay."

"Right," Vina said. "That's the thing. It's why I needed you here, Martin. There's a problem, like I said on the phone."

The sound of the sea was overwhelming. It was inescapable, the crash of the waves, the song of seabirds. The scent of it, the sight of it, everything. It was perfect. Idyllic, even. New England beachfronts had their own brand of magic. The Strand would capture this elemental excess and contain it.

"Go on," Thaler said, dragging his eyes down Conch Street, past the weatherworn shops, and the locals, who seemed bemused at their presence in an aloof, pickled, puritanical sort of way.

"The town elders of Skraeling are at odds with our plan. They're waiting to talk to us," Vina said. She brushed an atypically stray wisp of her black hair from her face, while Thomasina stood nearby, watching Thaler's reaction. She saw a white nautical bracelet at Vina's well-tanned wrist, which looked nice against the navy blue of her power suit.

"They approved it," Emma said. "It doesn't matter."

"It's a joint venture," Vina said. "Contingent on their participation and partnership with us."

"Skraelings," Thaler said, scoffing. "I'm not hearing the problem, Vina."

"*That's* the problem," Vina said.

Vina pointed out to sea with her French manicured nails.

Everybody looked, Thaler, most of all.

———————————————

The Swimming Stones of Skraeling, according to local lore, had been raised by lost Vikings who had been blown far off-course by a storm, back in the 10th century.

Whether it was true or not, the Swimming Stones of Skraeling had been a popular attraction as long as the town had been around, since the 17th century, when land grants from the Narragansett tribe had been negotiated.

Skraeling itself had been founded in 1666, largely in honor of the Swimming Stones, themselves. The Swimming Stones featured prominently in the municipal flag of the town—a trio of black rectangles in a white circle on a sea of navy blue.

They were three carved megaliths of black basalt, arranged in a circle on a little island off the shore of Skraeling. When the town was intact, the Swimming Stones were accessible by taking a dinghy or water taxi, although they were known to be navigation hazards, because there was no safe way to moor boats to them, without being dashed by waves.

After Irene, the distance between Skraeling and its Swimming Stones was greater, turning them into something other than what they had been. Like a distant lighthouse, the Swimming Stones assumed a kind of aura of their own—when the sun rose, the Swimming Stones drank in the rays.

When the moon came out, the Swimming Stones basked in the moonlight. Skraelings watched the Swimming Stones when storms came and passed. When Irene had smashed the town, many had thought the Swimming Stones themselves would be toppled into the sea.

But they remained.

"What am I looking at?" Thaler asked. "Rocks."

"The Swimming Stones," Vina said. "That's what the locals call them."

Martin watched the waves pound the rocks, sending great plumes of spray skyward as they smashed the little island upon which they stood.

Boyd took some pictures with his tablet, while the others looked at Thaler, trying to understand the mind of their boss, where he was headed. Thaler was a brilliant businessman, and it paid to heed him.

"So what?" Thaler asked.

"Are they a wildlife sanctuary or something, Vina?" Emma asked.

"No," Vina said. "But they're very special to the Skraelings. Kind of a shrine."

"A shrine?" Thaler said. "You mean, like, worship?"

"That's what a shrine is, yeah," Vina said. "They don't want anything happening to the Stones. They're very concerned about them."

Thomasina took out her phone and did some web-searching about the Swimming Stones of Skraeling. She was often Vina's on-the-spot researcher. They had a good synergy, paired well together at Thalercon. They were the proverbial dream team.

From where they stood, the Stones looked to be about three hundred yards from the shore. Thaler, who had an eye for such things, estimated them as being about 13 to 15 feet tall. The waves that crashed against their island broke beautifully, even on a cloudy day. If anything, the darkness of the churning sea made the white sea spray stand out more. The megaliths themselves appeared free of lichens or moss, with only a hint of sea salt adding a splash of white around their base.

"And this means what, exactly, for the development?" Thaler asked.

"They won't consent to our build unless we make some concessions around the Stones," Vina said. This pricked Emma's ears, who turned her jaded gaze on Vina.

"They won't consent?" Emma asked. "That's nonsense. We have an agreement with them. The town council."

"Pending final approval and recognition of the landmark status of the Swimming Stones," Vina said. "They were *very* insistent."

"I knew *you* should have gone there, Emma," Thaler said. Thaler smiled to himself, could feel Emma's irritation. These kinds of issues always dogged development projects. It didn't mean Emma was any less annoyed by them. Rather, it simply meant that they had to throw more money their way. Money always smoothed municipal wrinkles.

"Rhode Island law stipulates that anything below the mean tide line is public space," Emma said. "The Skraelings don't have the authority to count those stones as part of the town. Not since the hurricane. They are literally offshore."

"Skraelings," Thomasina said, more to herself than anyone. "Fun fact: that's the Viking term for Native Americans."

"Skraelings," Thaler said. "It's what the townies call themselves, is it, Tooch?"

"It is," Vina said. Thaler laughed, and everybody else laughed, too, albeit nervously. Nobody was sure what Thaler was going to do.

"So, let's go meet some Skraelings," Thaler said.

"Already set it up," Vina said, looking at Emma, who was glaring at her. "At the Also-Ran Tavern."

She pointed toward it, redirecting everyone's gaze with her husky voice. Although she was shorter than anyone else at Thalercon, Vina more than made up for it with her boardwalk bravado. It was rumored that she'd been a coxswain for the rowing team at Princeton, once, although nobody had the courage to ever ask her that.

"The Also-Ran Tavern?" Emma said. "The Also-Ran?"

"That's right," Vina said. "Problem?"

Emma raised her eyebrows, shaking her head, looking searchingly at Thaler, who shrugged, laughing.

"Let's go have lunch at the Also-Ran," Thaler said. "My treat."

━━━━━━━

To say that the Also-Ran Tavern was nautical was an understatement. The team felt like *they* were the day's catch, seated at a heavy, dark wooden table, beneath a ceiling festooned with netting. The lights, themselves, appeared to be great blue-green glass globes, which Thomasina explained were glass floats for fishing nets, and cast a positively murky radiance.

"The Norwegians were the first to use them, back in the 19th century," Thomasina said, scanning her phone after they'd placed their orders for drinks from the bartender—a black-mustached man named Jim with rolled flannel sleeves and tattooed forearms that called to mind Popeye, if Popeye had been a Viking. "They've mostly been replaced by other materials, but sometimes wash ashore."

"Fascinating," Thaler said. "Really."

On the walls were old photographs, Thomasina noticed, collected on dingy blue gallery walls around the perimeter. Some of them, terribly old, like tintypes of hardfaced sailors and women in black dresses. There were a few old photos of Skraelings standing dourly with the Swimming Stones. Some of the photos were of ships—sailing ships, sidewheelers, other vessels. Thomasina took some pictures of the pictures, noting some of the dates: 1878. 1902. 1911. 1926. This weight of history hung heavy as the netting at the Also-Ran. Another board listed all the dead at sea, by ship and year. The entries were carved into the wood. At the top was etched something in Norse runes, something she couldn't read—it looked like an R, a lopsided F, and a lazy T.

The Also-Ran Tavern was mostly empty, except for a handful of older townies—identified as Thaddeus Cornwall, Claire Cornwall (sister of Thaddeus), Maude Raines, and Rufus Cornwall (brother of Thaddeus and Claire). They were designated representatives of the Skraeling Town Council, entrusted with the interests of Skraeling as pertained to Thaler's development project.

Thad and Rufus looked like the brothers that they were—Thad, the older of the two, resembling nothing so much as the Gorton's fisherman, with bright blue, sea-bleached eyes. Claire had silver hair she had braided in thick plaits flanking her round, tanned face. Rufus, clearly the baby of the family, was only mostly silver-haired, had industrial-looking glasses and wore a SSCC windbreaker and a blue ballcap that had three black bars on them, enclosed in a silver circle.

Excepting Jim, Maude was the youngest of the Skraelings, had long black hair with a lengthy streak of white that ran from her part down the length of her hair. Her eyes were grey-blue, and her disposition was marooned somewhere between taciturn and reticent.

They'd ordered their round of drinks, some Trinity Anchor Ales and iced teas, while Claire extolled on the virtues of the snail salad.

"Snails?" Emma said. "Ehh, no."

"They're not actually snails, Dear," Claire said. "They're *sea snails.* Not the same as garden snails. Like conchs. You've heard of conchs?"

"Yeah, I've heard," Emma said.

"None for me, thank you," Thaler said.

Claire's smile never faded, just stayed painted on her face.

"It's *real* good," Claire said. "Fresh from the sea."

Thaler was pleased to steer the conversation toward the sea. Even in his brief visit to Skraeling, he was sizing it up, seeing his development there, dominating the beachfront. The Strand would remake Skraeling in his image.

"You harvest them?" Thaler asked. "The snails?"

Mention of the sea seemed to get the locals revved up. They gathered around the visitors, faces animated, eyes alight. They all had blue eyes, except for Jim, who had dark brown.

"We sure do," Thad said. "Locally sourced. Right out there."

"Honest work for honest fisherfolk," Rufus said. "Not like the capital ships you're used to up in Beantown, I'll bet. That's no way to fish. No *real* way."

Thomasina smiled at the others. Emma was prone to condescension in social settings, so she condescended to indulge the townies. After spending months at Skraeling, she was surprised Vina hadn't partaken. Then again, she was from New Jersey, and likely turned her nose up at Rhode Island cuisine. It provided Thomasina a moment to win over the Skraelings.

"I'll try some," Thomasina said. "Sure, why not?"

Claire seemed delighted by it, nodded to Jim, who went in the back. Thaler snorted, while Vina drank her beer without commentary. Of course, after Thomasina had ordered some, Emma decided she would try it. Emma was always about trying things, and always about upstaging everybody at Thalercon.

Jim came out with two plates of snail salad and two knives and forks wrapped in paper napkins, put them on the table in front of Thomasina and Emma, while the others snapped pictures, laughing.

What followed was a momentary, unspoken race, as Thomasina and Emma each tried to graciously dig into the local dish, without appearing to rush. Thomasina managed the first bites ahead of Emma, having grabbed the utensils and speared the snail salad with her fork, to the great delight of the townies.

"Now, she's one of us!" Thad exclaimed. "A proper Skraeling. Almost."

"Almost," Rufus said. "Takes more than a snail salad to make your way in Skraeling. Tourists learned that the hard way, even before Irene."

Conceding nothing to Thomasina, Emma primly undid the napkin and put it on her lap, trying the snail salad with several jabs of her fork, accepting the applause of the Thalercon employees. Emma smiled around her mouthful of snail salad, munching on it.

"It's good," she said. "You sure you guys don't want to try it?"

"I'm good," Boyd said, brandishing his beer.

"See?" Maude said. "She likes it. You can tell she does. Skraeling has the best snail salad in the state."

Boyd watched Thomasina dig into the snail salad, feigned queasiness.

"I'd be grateful never to have to hear 'snail salad' ever again," Boyd said. The others laughed, while Jim took everybody's food orders, which included sweet corn, clam chowder, fish sandwiches, and coleslaw aplenty.

"So, Mr. Cornwall," Thaler said. "Vina tells me that your preference is for nothing to happen to those standing stones out there in the bay."

"It's not a matter of our preference, Mr. Thaler," Thad said. "Those stones are our town's history. They've always been here. Longer than we have. We respect our history in Skraeling."

"That's fair," Thaler said. "What if we made an arrangement? I mean, those stones are in my way."

Thad looked suspicious, glanced at the other Skraelings, who seemed content to follow his lead, except for Claire. Meanwhile, Jim had gone to get the food for the others.

"What sort of arrangement?" Thad asked.

"I only care about the beachfront," Thaler said. "My development is going to revitalize Skraeling in ways you can't even imagine. The Strand will expand Skraeling's profile as *the* seasonal go-to in the region."

"We can't imagine it for a reason," Claire said, prompting a glance from Thaler. "We're not imaginative in Skraeling.

We're a small fishing town. We always have been. *That's* our history. It's our legacy. We fish in Skraeling."

"The Strand sounds like a tourist trap to me," Rufus said. "That's what it is, yeah? A trap? That's what you're talking about, sure as daylight. A trap. Skraeling's a fishing town."

Thaler felt like knew how to speak to townies. These people wanted assurances. They wanted to feel like they were going to profit from his development.

"Claire, Rufus," Thaler said. "You *were* a fishing town. Begging your pardon, but that ship has sailed. I saw maybe three fishing boats left in your harbor. *In your harbor.* Aside from your Conch Street merchant district, the Sweet Corn Cooperative is your biggest employer. Not fishing."

"And who's fault is that?" Rufus asked. "Longliners, factory ships, raping the sea."

Some of the Expensables were digging into their bowls of sweet corn and chowder, while others were tearing into their sandwiches. Thomasina was enjoying the snail salad far more than she thought she would.

Emma was content to let Thaler drive, while Vina looked nervous. But she was a marketer, and marketers were *always* nervous.

Thaler let the words hang out there, before taking a sip of the Trinity Ale. The Skraelings looked at one another a moment, before any of them ventured a reply. The one who spoke up was Maude.

"We're proud of our town's history," Maude said. "There is history, here."

"There's history *everywhere*," Thaler said. "*We* make history. This deal with my company, that's history, too. I'm giving you the opportunity to make history in Skraeling. To turn the page and move past Irene. With me."

"You're trying to rob us," Rufus said. "That's what I see. You stole Drowntown, and you're wanting to build your tourist trap right under our noses."

"Drowntown?" Thomasina asked.

"It's what the Skraelings call the area that the storm surge hit," Vina said quietly.

"It'll mean jobs," Thaler said. "Opportunities for all of you. It'll mean money. More money than you can possibly imagine, I guarantee."

"Thieves," Rufus said. "That's all you are. Thieves. All anybody is. Thieves and robbers. Leastways a robber has an honest go at you. Thieves just come and try to talk you out of what's yours."

"I'm no thief. I *bought* the land," Thaler said. "I'm a *benefactor*. I'm the savior of Skraeling."

"Bought it for a steal," Rufus said, downing a shot of whiskey Jim brought him. Rufus scoffed after his drink, and Thad patted his younger brother's forearm. Thomasina could see they had very weathered sailor's knot bracelets on their right wrists. The women had them, too. They looked they'd worn them for decades, and they probably had.

"What if you and your people slept on it here in Skraeling, Mr. Thaler?" Claire asked. "The Quayside is a lovely hotel, positively charming. Could sure use the business. That's what this is all about, isn't it? Business?"

The Quayside was built like a small wedding cake, with the obligatory widow's walk that seemed to grace all the buildings in Skraeling, with a slate gable roof and a seafoam green hue with white highlights. Irene had torn the face off the Quayside, but they'd done admirable restoration work on it, and were justly proud of it.

"Yes, it *is* all about business," Thaler said.

"Then stay the night," Maude said. "Get to know us. You flew in on a private plane, after all. At Tallmadge?"

"Yes," Thaler said.

"So, you can leave any time you like," Claire said. "Stay the night, I beg you. We beg you."

Thaler thought it might be useful to allow them to extend the negotiations with whatever was chapping the behinds of these Skraelings about their Swimming Stones. Thaler had found, as a developer, it usually paid to be magnanimous when wrangling the riff-raff.

"You know what? Great idea, Claire," Thaler said. "We'll stay at the Quayside."

Emma wasn't happy about that, he could tell. But he wasn't about to have anything—or anyone—spoil the deal with the Skraelings.

"Is there a restaurant at the Quayside?" Emma asked. "Or is the Also-Ran it for food around here?"

"Not the only thing," Thad said, smiling. "The Quayside Grille is open all year, even off-season. I think you'll like it. They also have Shuck Finn's Oyster Bar in there."

"Perfect," Thaler said, glancing at Emma, who was glaring at Vina. Vina smirked back at her. "And I'm dying to ask you—why the hell would anybody name their tavern the Also-Ran? I mean, an also-ran is a loser."

The Skraelings chuckled among themselves, except for Rufus, who glowered at nothing in particular.

"Oh, we know," Maude said. "It's sort of a local joke. People lose things all the time in Skraeling. I mean, we lost Drowntown, don't forget. It was stolen from us by the sea. It's kind of our way of honoring that."

"To Drowntown," Emma said, raising her glass. "Lest we forget."

"We *never* forget," Maude said.

The Quayside staff seemed happy to find the Thalercon team in their lobby. And, despite themselves, Thaler's people were pleased at the cozy little New England hotel, perched as it was at the edge of Conch Street, with the Swimming Stones looming in the distance.

The lobby was a sea of white-painted columns and natural wooden floors, with nautical themes represented in brassy barometers, bowls of sea shells, more old photos of sailors and ships, and comfortable navy blue chairs. The chairs were arrayed around a blue hearth that was, upon closer examination, set with mosaic tiles that depicted a swirling net of grey tiles in the hands of a dark green-haired woman, her hair cascading downward in waves that caught mosaic ships. The woman scowled down toothily at the ships, which were tossed this way and that by the waves of her hair. The Swimming Stones were represented: three black tiles in the churning sea of stones.

"Is that Irene?" Thomasina asked one of the hotel staff, while Thaler and Vina were making arrangements.

"We like to think so," the staffer said. A young woman, well-dressed, with blond hair hanging long and smoothly brushed, and wide-set, sea green eyes.

"But is it?"

"Is it?" the young woman said, wearing a navy blue uniform with a blue and white-striped blouse. Her white nametag identified her as Morgan in white printed letters. "It's a very old mosaic, when Skraeling was a resort town for the rich. A kind of getaway."

"So, it's *not* Irene," Thomasina said. "It predates her."

"It's the goddess of the sea," Morgan said.

"Ah," Thomasina said. The way Morgan said it put her off.

"She sent Irene to Drowntown," Morgan said. "The old St. Andrew's Cathedral, First, Fourth, Fifth, and Third Streets. All drowned."

"Who did?"

"Ran," Morgan said.

"Who ran?" Thomasina asked.

"Nobody ran. *Ran's* Ran," Morgan said, pointing to the hearth mosaic, to the woman with the wavy hair and dark eyes. "*That's* Ran."

"Right," Thomasina said. "She's, what, a goddess?"

"She's *our* goddess," Morgan said. "We honor Her. She protects us."

Boyd and Emma came over, Boyd taking pictures of the fireplace with his tablet, whistling. Morgan excused herself, while Boyd, oblivious, snapped more shots. Emma sized up Thomasina in a glance.

"What do you make of this, Thomasina?" Emma asked Thomasina, her tone prompting Boyd to drag his gaze from his tablet.

"Mosaic," Thomasina said. "Maybe mid 20th century. Doesn't look WPA to me. Probably earlier. Nice workmanship. The hurricane tore this place up, but they did a great job restoring it."

"I don't know what game you and Vina are playing, here," Emma said. "But I don't like it. This is an expensive waste of Martin's time. Marketing should keep their noses out of this. You be sure to deliver that message to Vina, when you get a chance."

Thaler and Vina came over, Vina looking particularly triumphant, for some reason Thomasina couldn't divine.

"What is it?" Emma asked.

"They're thrilled to have us," Vina said. "We each get a suite to ourselves. Martin's paying."

Thaler treated them to a monumentally smug shoulder shrug, motioned for Emma to join him in front of the mosaic hearth. Vina followed along, and Thomasina followed all of them, after snapping some shots of the mosaic.

"Look," Thaler said. "I'm just going through the motions, here. As should we all. We've invested too much time and money in it, already. There's no way I'm letting three old fucking stones derail the Strand."

Emma laughed, prompting a scowl from Vina. Thomasina knew that she and Vina had done a considerable amount of marketing prepwork for the Strand, without even any of the construction commencing. It would be at least a year of construction, and about two years' of marketing around it—before, during, and after.

"Oh, is money a consideration, now, Martin?" Emma asked.

"It always is," Thaler said. "Look, we'll sort out this Swimming Stone business in the morning and get back to civilization."

"I don't even know why you picked this place, Martin," Emma said.

"It's cheap," Thaler said, grinning. "They're desperate. That old coot was right—it was a *steal*."

Even at the Quayside, they could hear the waves. If this was what it was like during good weather, Thomasina could only imagine what it would be like during storm season. Vina talked about how nice it had been in the summer season, despite—or maybe because—of the relative absence of tourist traffic.

"Briggs," Thaler said, bringing the architect over. Jonathan looked at each of them uncertainly.

"What is it, Martin?"

"Have you seen the waves out there, Jon?"

"Hard to miss them," Jonathan said.

"But have you *seen* them?" Thaler asked. "Like really seen them? Have you planned for them? You, and Boyd and Wade? Why do you think I brought you along? I wanted you to see this for yourselves. Properly."

"Architecturally? Of course, I have," Jonathan said. He looked wounded at the implication that he hadn't. "The Strand will be like an oil rig—not in look, but in resilience. It will be built to withstand anything the sea throws at it."

"Nothing can withstand the sea," Vina said. "Not forever."

"The Strand will," Jonathan said. "I give you my word, Martin. I've designed it like the prow of a ship. Again, not in look, but with that in mind. Design. It'll ride the waves and people will love it. They'll feel a part of the sea."

"They'd better, Briggs," Thaler said. "That's all I'm saying: they'd better."

"You'll have to 'Sea' It to Believe It," Thomasina said. It was one of the taglines she'd developed. Emma scoffed, and Thaler laughed. Thomasina cringed, feeling very small, all of a sudden. Vina took that moment to chime in.

"You know, while I was here during season, I was thinking we could set up a race. Right along Conch Street: The Ran Run. Like a 5K. Nothing too crazy. Right along the Conch."

"Ran?" Emma asked. "You heard about that?"

"Yeah," Vina said. "Of course *I* did. It's all people around here talk about, if you actually talk to them, which I did. It's catchy, right? People who're sick of the fuckin' Boston Marathon. Give them a place to go. Navy blue tees. Those three stones. That Ran lady, the Spirit of Skraeling. That kind of thing."

Vina was always coming up with marketing ideas, and it drove Emma crazy, because, more often than not, Martin loved them. An avid runner, he always looked for new races to run. Vina, as ever, knew just how to get him reeled in.

"See, *that's* the kind of idea you should be coming up with, Tooch," Thaler said.

"We can have the proceeds go to hurricane relief or something," Thomasina said.

"Brilliant," Thaler said. "We *have* to sponsor it. The Thalercon Ran Run. Just stupid enough to be memorable—like all the best marketing, right, Tooch?"

Jonathan hung by them, unsure whether he should sit or continue standing. Thomasina could feel the discomfort flowing off him like stink lines. Wade Ritter came in from one of the decks, looking at them, smiling in that feline way he had.

"You guys should check this out," Wade said. "On the deck."

"You mean, like, getting up?" Thaler asked, getting up with an exaggerated sigh. His team followed along. Wade led them to the deck railing, pointing to the beach, where the tide had receded, leaving seaweed along the shore in brownish clusters.

Skraelings had assembled on the beach, gathering the seaweed. They moved in orderly groups—some with hooked poles to grab the seaweed, while others walked with baskets on their backs. They worked efficiently, snagging the fronds and stashing them in the baskets, seawater running down their already wet legs.

"What are they doing?" Thomasina asked.

"Beachcombing?" Jonathan asked. "I've heard that people collect seaweed."

Vina snorted, swatting at Briggs on the shoulder.

"*Losers*, maybe," Emma said.

"Tooch, you're from New Jersey, you're our Skraeling expert," Thaler said. "You tell us."

"They're harvesting seaweed," Vina said, glancing at Thomasina. She looked like she wanted to deck Thaler.

"I see that," Thaler said. "For what?"

"For food," Vina said. "They dry it and eat it. Sometimes, they sell it."

Thaler snorted.

"They *eat* seaweed?" Thaler asked. "Fuck. I didn't see it on the menu at the Also-Ran."

"It's actually good for you," Vina said. When they laughed at her, she got indignant. "I'm serious."

The Skraelings also appeared to be gathering shells.

"Maybe it's community service or something," Thomasina said.

"Whatever it is, I'm bored, already," Thaler said. "I'm going upstairs for a shower and a drink. Don't anybody disturb me unless it's life or death."

———————

The life or death disturbance came around 3:00 a.m.

None of the members of Thaler's team had stayed up past midnight, with the exception of Thomasina, who'd managed to work her way to the widow's walk, to watch the waves by the light of the gibbous moon. Insomnia was her bedfellow more often than not, and when it came around, she walked, rather than tossing and turning.

Up here, she could feel the breeze—a land breeze, now, blowing out from the shores of Skraeling. Unlike in Boston, things appeared to sleep in Skraeling. There was just the wind and the waves, here. Even the old streetlights were turned off.

The crash of the waves was louder, too. Because of the darkness, she couldn't see the waves, but she sure as hell could hear them out there. Endless pounding of the shore.

The Skraelings were jerking them around, she was sure of it. Those three stones were jeopardizing an over $100 million investment that would bring this community back to life again.

Thomasina's phone pinged. It was Vina, texting her:

Where RU?
On the roof.
WTF?
The widow's walk.
K. Don't go anywhere.
Problem?
Just wait.

Thomasina sighed. Vina was prone to slinging after hours texts with urgent project requirements. This was likely one of those moments. Thomasina just listened to the deafening waves, pacing around.

Vina came up minutes later. The marketing director appeared, looking perfect, as ever. She clacked over to the railing, having, for some ungodly reason, decided to wear her heels. Thomasina thought maybe she lived in them.

"What are you doing up here, Tomi?"

"I couldn't sleep," Thomasina said. "What's wrong?"

"Nothing's wrong. Everything's on track. You have my back, right?" Vina asked.

"Yeah, of course," Thomasina said. "Always."

"I mean, you trust me, yeah?"

"Absolutely," Thomasina said. "What's going on? Martin isn't firing you, is he?"

Vina didn't answer, just smiled to herself, shaking her head. "That shit you pulled in the limo—fuckin' cavalry? Hah! That was brilliant, Tomi. And ballsy. I respect that. I want you to know that, no matter what happens."

Thomasina was trying to figure out the angle, here. With Vina, there was an angle. There was always an angle. Vina stood near her, fidgeting, picking at the sailor's knot bracelet at her well-tanned wrist, the bracelet almost luminescent in the moonlight. Never at a loss for words, Vina seemed strangely pensive.

"This job takes a toll on you," Vina said. "What I do, I mean. What *we* do. We're a team, though. Through thick and thin, Tomi. I know you, and I trust you. Right down to the line. And, like, I want to know that you trust me, too."

"Absolutely," Thomasina said, as Vina's phone chirped. She answered. Her New Jersey glower would not be denied, and she clicked her fingernails together while talking on the phone.

"Vina Tucci speaking, who's this?" Vina said, began back-and-forthing with whoever was on the other line. "Yeah, we're here. On the roof."

"Who is it?" Thomasina asked, feeling fear clench at her stomach, while Vina held up a finger to her, hushing her. Was she going to get fired, too? She could imagine Emma whispering in Martin's ear. They were probably sleeping together, which was a total Emma Cavendish sort of move.

"Yeah," Vina said. "I understand. Yes. We'll be down in a sec."

She hung up, pocketing her phone. Thomasina looked petrified, dug out her phone to see if there was something from Thaler.

"Was it Martin?" Thomasina asked. "He's firing us, isn't he?"

Vina put her lacquered nails on the back of Thomasina's hand, patting it three times.

"Trust me."

The door to the widow's walk opened, and a pair of white-robed figures came up, carrying a net between them. They were wearing ghastly masks—which looked to be carved from driftwood. The masks had gaping black eyeholes and toothy grimaces gouged out of the wood and painted white. Brown, carefully braided seaweed hair swung as they moved, as did bunches of shell necklaces wound around their necks.

"Oh my fucking god," Thomasina said. She'd taken more than her share of Krav Maga classes in Boston, but that hadn't trained her to deal with masked maniacs carrying a damned net. She went into a fighting stance, only to be stopped by Vina.

"I would *not* do that, Tomi," Vina said. "Like I said, just trust me."

"*She's* waiting," one of the Skraelings said, to Vina. A man's voice and stature, barely audible over the roar of the waves. "The binding tide is almost upon us."

⸻

Thomasina and Vina were escorted downstairs and out of the Quayside, heading toward the beach, where the other employees of Thalercon had been laid out well below the high tide line. They had been wrapped tight in netting, with only their heads visible. Six old, wooden posts had been driven into the sand. The posts had rusty metal hooks protruding from them, and the nets had been lashed to them.

All along the beachfront were white-robed figures like Thomasina had seen on the rooftop. They wore hand-carved driftwood masks like the ones the others had worn, with the same dreadful expression on them. Thomasina realized they were like the woman on the mosaic. The look was the same, that horrible expression. Some of them carried lit torches. Others carried T-handled metal hooks in fisherfolk-strong arms. Thomasina could see some blood on the sand, what appeared to belong to Wade Ritter, judging from the trail that led to his limp form.

"Vina, why haven't they netted us?" Thomasina asked.

"Let *me* handle this, Tomi," Vina said. "Follow my lead. Not a fucking word."

Thomasina could see a scared Bob, a bleary Boyd, the unconscious Wade Ritter, a terrified Emma, a bewildered Jonathan, and an infuriated Martin.

One of the Skraelings, the one who wore a rusty, three-spiked crown on her head and carried a marlinspike, came forward. She looked like a priestess to Thomasina.

"Thalercon reps," the Priestess said. "We, the people of Skraeling, reject your development proposal as it currently stands."

Martin Thaler glowered at them from his post.

"What the hell is this all about?" Thaler said, his eyes flicking about, trying to find purchase for his rage.

"Mr. Thaler," the Priestess said. "Are you ready to continue our negotiation?"

"What the fuck?" Thaler said. "No. Of course not."

"We are giving you to Ran, as tribute," the Priestess said. "When the tide rolls in, you will all drown. All except Ms. Vina Tucci and her acolyte, Ms. Thomasina Quintana."

This prompted wails and struggling among the Thalercon people, Thomasina among them—although her struggle was internal. There was no escaping the nets. Beyond them all, the waves rolled and crashed, while the Swimming Stones lurked in the distance, like three sentinels, seemingly watching from the moonlit shadows.

"Vina, what in the fuck is this?" Thaler said, trying to strain his head to turn to see them. No sunglasses, now; only his red-rimmed, blue-green eyes.

"I'm sorry, Martin," Vina said. "I told you it was an emergency. *This* is the emergency."

Martin cursed, straining at the netting, to no avail.

"What do you want?" Thaler asked. If they had simply wanted them dead, they would have killed them already, he thought. This was, indeed, a negotiation. What Vina's role in it wasn't entirely clear to him.

"We wanted the Swimming Stones protected in your plan," the Priestess said. "Untouched, unspoiled, and unharmed. You wouldn't listen."

"Sure," Thaler said. "Fine. Whatever."

The Priestess walked over, marlinspike gripped tight in her fist. She let the pointed needle of it hang close to Thaler's eye.

"No," the Priestess said. "You think we are fools, Mr. Thaler. You cannot rob us of our town, our history, our legacy. We will not let you take these things from us."

Thaler glared up at the Priestess, and at the marlinspike, which caught the moonlight and held it fast. It was only inches from his bloodshot eyes.

"I give you my word," Thaler said. "I won't harm the fucking stones."

The words sent a ripple through the ranks of Skraelings.

"Do *not* profane them, Mr. Thaler," the Priestess said. "I have only just begun our negotiations."

"What else do you want?" Thaler asked. "I'm rich. Do you want money?"

The Priestess tapped the marlinspike in her hand a moment, as if considering it.

"We want *all* of you to convert to Ran," the Priestess said.

"Convert? I don't even know who Ran is," Thaler said.

"She's the sea goddess," Thomasina said. "Remember what I said earlier, Martin?"

"Jesus fuck, Tomi," Thaler yelled, squawking. "I'm a little busy negotiating, here."

The Priestess walked over to Thomasina, pulled a shell necklace from around her neck and held it out for Thomasina to take, which she did, unsure what else she should do. It was a leather necklace, from which hung a single seashell.

"Put it on," the Priestess said. Thomasina did, putting it around her neck. "For your first night of the binding tide."

The Priestess walked back to Thaler.

"A forced conversion in this godforsaken town?" Thaler said. "Are you fucking insane? We were trying to *save* you bastards."

"Skraeling *isn't* godforsaken," the Priestess said. "You think Irene broke us? She baptized us. We *wanted* her to come, we *prayed* for her to come. Ran kissed the shores of Skraeling in the hurricane, Mr. Thaler. She came and cleansed our little town of the unbelievers—she stole their livelihoods and drowned them. Irene came and they were gone, and we remained. We took care of the rest, house by house. We knew someone like you would come—a robber-baron, like in the past. We prayed for it. And our prayers were answered, Mr.

138 ℘ SHAWN WALLACE

Thaler. More than you can ever know. A fitting gift for Ran, for all that we have endured."

The surf was rising, and the Skraelings, lined up along the high tide line, their masked faces all bearing the same horrid expression, their seaweed hair hanging limp, their T-handled hooks in hand, at the ready.

"Okay, you want us to convert to Ran," Thaler said. "Fine, fine, fine. Emma? Where's Emma?"

"I'm here," Emma said. She was three nets down, between Thaler and the bloody, still-unconscious Wade Ritter.

"Emma's my attorney, as you know," Thaler said. "She can make the arrangements."

"Not good enough," the Priestess said. "The sun will rise with the sea, and Ran will lay claim to you. Everything above the high tide line belongs to us—your Vina, your Thomasina. Your limousines. Your clothes. Your plans, your phones, your laptops, and all the information they contain. Everything below, well, that belongs to Ran. Our gift to Her, Her people."

The Priestess snapped a finger, and a Skraeling came forward, carrying a sailor's knot bracelet, like the one Vina had been wearing, only pure white.

"This is a bracelet to signify our covenant with you," the Priestess said, to Thomasina. "Once placed, you must *never* remove it, lest the wrath of Ran fall upon you. And it will. Do you accept it? Or do you wish to join your friends below the high tide line?"

Thomasina glanced at Vina, who nodded. She held out her arm, and the Skraeling slipped the bracelet onto her wrist. Another of the Skraelings dipped a brass pitcher into the sea and poured the cool water over the bracelet, soaking it through. When the ritual was complete, the masked Skraelings let out a chorus of whooping cheers.

"You're one of us, now, little fish," the Skraeling said. "Give your thanks to Ran."

"Thank you, Ran," Thomasina said, unsure what else to say. Her knees were weak, her heart thudded in her chest almost

louder than the roaring surf. She could feel the soaked bracelet already contracting to fit snugly around her wrist.

Several of them began to say the name "Ran" over and over
again, and the rest joined in, until they were all saying "Ran"
again and again, swaying and stomping in the sand in time
to the waves that began their inexorable climb up the shore.
Emma cursed out Vina, while Thaler roared and bellowed as
the tide rose, licking coldly at their ankles.

"Don't you know who I am? I'm Martin Thaler! I *own* this
goddamned town," Thaler yelled, trying to kick at the incom-
ing tide with his bare feet, finding the netting constrained his
movements. "I could buy and sell you! What do you want?
Money? I can give you that!"

The Priestess walked over to Thaler, passing a well-veined
hand through his well-tousled hair. She took the rusty crown
from her head and placed it atop Thaler's. He made to shake
his head to remove it, but she held the marlinspike against his
cheek to hold him in place.

"We don't need your money, Mr. Thaler," the Priestess said.
"We have Ran. We have everything we could ever need, right
here, right now."

"Vina!" Thaler said. "What the fuck did you do, for god's
sake?"

"I made a deal of my own, Martin," Vina said. "A way better
deal. The Strand is dead in the water, or will be, once the tide
comes up. Tomi and I are going to work with the Skraelings.
They could use some good marketing. There's a real opportunity here. Quaint is the new modern, as I see it."

"Quaint?" Emma said. "Jesus fucking Christ, Vina!"

"Anything you want!" Thaler said. "I can get you anything
you fucking want! A millions dollars to anybody who lets us
go."

None of the Skraelings moved, only chanted "Ran!" with
each rising wave. The Priestess pressed the marlinspike against
Thaler's cheek, while the waters rose still higher. In the distance, the Swimming Stones caught the first light of day, the

sun peeking over the horizon. Waves splashed against the Stones in great crashes.

"I matter!" Thaler said. "I can't just disappear! People will come for me. They'll find you!"

"No, Mr. Thaler," the Priestess said. "They won't. They won't *ever* find you."

"Claire? It's you, isn't it?" Thaler said. "Claire, goddamn you! I *know* it's you! Take off the mask! Let me look at you! We can make some arrangement! Maude?"

The Priestess did not remove her mask, just gazed down at him through the blackened eyes, like shark's eyes, the very eyes of Ran, boring into him. The grimace of the mask, weathered and worn, downturned, that gouged-out frown. An old mask. The brown seaweed braids danced in the breeze, much like the sweet corn that graced the land that garlanded old Skraeling, itself.

"We have *already* made the necessary arrangements, Mr. Thaler," the Priestess said, watching the waters soaking their legs and waists. "Ran will be pleased to take you."

Thomasina watched the waves come roaring in in, drenching the Expensables, soaking Emma and Jonathan and Martin, who struggled and flailed ineffectually in the netting that held them. Thaler's voice was growing hoarse.

"This is America! People like me don't just disappear!" Thaler said.

"People disappear every day, Mr. Thaler," the Priestess said. "This is *your* day to disappear."

Everyone was screaming, now, while the Skraelings kept chanting "Ran! Ran! Ran!" Thaler sputtered as the water reached his shoulders, and still the Priestess stood by him, the marlinspike mere inches from his eye, dimpling his cheek.

Vina stood by Thomasina, the two of them exchanging glances—Vina mouthed "You. Owe. Me." to her, while their thrashing coworkers coughed and choked on seawater. In that moment, Thomasina understood everything.

Sometimes, negotiation required making sacrifices.

JACK LOTHIAN

A DEED WITHOUT A NAME

RAIN falls. Heath is damp and wretched. My sisters and I shiver as we trudge along the dirt paths. Been walking since morning, but we cannot go home, not yet, not until dark and mother is resting. Nothing else to do but follow the tracks through fields and meadows until our bones ache and our thoughts are finally quiet.

Sow gave birth to a litter just after dawn. All stillborn. Farmer found her with a bloodied snout, and their lifeless bodies torn open, half feasted upon. Farmer sliced sow's throat, dragging the carcass off to be carved and sold at market this afternoon. Yesterday sow was swollen, with child. Now just meat and gristle. I was passing, saw him haul out the body. Farmer caught me looking, muttered something under his breath, that I pretended not to hear.

We trudge on through the dank and drizzle. The men will be returning from war now, Michael among them. I have freckles. A hint of auburn in my hair. Green eyes that Michael said were like a cat.

"They're not green," says middle sister. "They're grey."

I didn't know I was speaking words out loud. Sister smiles at me as if to say maybe I wasn't. We were born within a year of each other. Oldest sister. Middle sister. Then me, with my hint of auburn and eyes of green that might really be grey.

Somewhere, beneath the October sky, men are bleeding and trembling. The rush and excitement of battle replaced by the cold, sharp fear of an end that has come to soon. Stripped of armor and pretense, they cry and beg for their mothers, like children lost amongst the grassland. I pray Michael is safe with every sodden step I take.

Older sister whispers for us to stop. Sliver of alarm in her voice. I look up, understand. Coming down the road that slices through the fields are two soldiers, bearing the king's colors. They walk with a weight and weariness, faces shaded with dirt and fatigue. The one in front has a beard, flecked white like the first drifts of snow in January. Eyes of burnt coal. The man behind is younger, but there's an age upon him, too. These are not good men.

Older sister bows her head to let them pass, and middle sister and I copy her, genuflecting as if we're not worthy to gaze upon such warriors. Perhaps we can vanish from their view. It's a trick I use too much, say my sisters. I am often elsewhere.

I stare down at my bare feet, which look powdered with the cold. A small toe missing on the right from when mother left me out in that winter when I was still just a bairn. Michael says it makes me special. Different from the rest. I focus on the smooth slip of skin as I see the boots of the men come into view, the acidic scent of their sweat hanging in the air. Footsteps come to a halt right in front of us. I can feel their eyes appraising us like the heath is another market, and we are but cattle for sale.

The squeal of the sow as the knife cut across her flabby neck. The desecrated litter scattered behind her. Picture the mother feasting up her young. Wonder what drove her to dig in her snout, to open her mouth, bring those teeth down against barely formed skin and bone. I feel as if I am there, overwhelmed by the smell of the newborn, already rotting as they slid out. Sense the horror and panic in the sow. Stomach lurches, and I think I am going to be sick upon the ground, upon the boots of men.

Middle sister touches my arm, a quiet but firm grip, trying to settle me, and I worry that I have been speaking thoughts aloud again.

The bearded man is speaking, but it takes a second for his words to match up with his mouth as I slip back to the present.

"How now, you black and midnight hags?" he says. He is staring at us with a strange, subdued fury, even though his voice is soft and warm.

The younger man laughs, but it is forced, tinged with fear of his elder. He would laugh no matter what the words had been. These men scare me. They have taken blood today, and satiation is not yet upon them.

"What are these women?" asks the younger as he approaches me. He lays his finger under my chin, to raise my head. "So withered and wild in their attire." He runs his finger down my front, slowly, not minding the dampness of the cloth, the way I shiver not from pleasure.

"They look not like inhabitants of this earth." He presses his hand against my sex, and I try to move back. But older sister gives me a look, and I imagine her voice in my head, telling me to become no-one, to vanish off somewhere inside myself, just like I do on those nights when mother cannot find sleep nor calm.

It only ever takes a breath and a blink of an eye, and there I am. The dark forest. Skeletal black trees as far as the eyes can see. And although some might think the place is carved from nightmares, it feels warm and close to me. It is a place where man is but a memory. A place where no-one else may step.

"I know these sisters," says the younger man.

I do not recognize him. Is he from the village? No. From further away. How does he know of us? His hand is sharp below me, unwanted, not like Michael. He pulls back, bringing his hand to nose, smirking to himself, but it is an unsure smile that fades when the bearded one does not return it.

I can smell the death upon them, just as on the sow this morn. I picture the pale piglets, suddenly springing to life, their stomachs torn open, innards trailing behind them like pennants. They scramble and tumble forward, desperate for their mother's milk even in death. I can hear their frantic shrieking, and the bile rises up in me, bubbling and overflowing. I cannot stop it escaping my mouth where it splatters on the ground, and now the younger one kicks at me, cursing, disgusted. The bearded one reaches for his scabbard, but then older sister speaks, taking his arm.

She is beautiful, even in the rain.

"We were waiting for you," she says, and I almost believe her, the way she holds his eye, her voice low and calm. "We have words."

He lifts his hand to older sister's jaw. Holds it like a skull plucked from the dead fields.

"Speak," he says, and it is as much a threat as it is a command.

"Beware the Thane of Fife."

"More," he says, and those fingers tighten up her skin.

"You will have great glory. You will be named Thane of Cawdor."

He smiles at that. Good words. Good girl.

"And you all have words for me?" he says, looking to middle sister.

I realize this is a game. We all have to speak. We all have to be convincing. If we succeed, then these men will leave us alone. It is a game we play at home when storm falls upon mother, and we have no way out. Trapped with her as she howls at the faces in the walls. We try to calm her, tell her what she needs to hear, hope to bring her back to our world. We are better at this game now, but we don't always win. Thin white scars across arms and legs from all the times we are not so convincing.

Middle sister pushes wet hair from her head. She cannot look at the man. She is shaking. Her voice is barely more than a breeze. "You will be king."

"I will be king," he says, and he laughs, and the younger man joins, but I can tell that these words have sparked some deep fire within him.

And then he looks to me. I try to find words, but they will not fit my mouth. I cannot help it, there is a spark of panic and I slip away, across time and space, to the dark, quiet forest. The safe place. Yet it is not the same now; it is as if these men have infected it. Through the trees, I glimpse a fire. Pale bodies dragged towards it. Like the sow after dawn. Ready for the burning and I cannot help shout out, and then the words come in a tumble, a rush, from some unknown place.

Sisters are looking at me, as are the men. Standing on the heath, aware of my voice, speaking prophecies I could not even imagine. I tell him of his future, of his might, of how no man born of woman could ever harm him.

A brutal crack across my cheek brings me back into this world for sure. The younger one throws a clenched fist, and the sodden earth rushes up to meet me. There is the sour taste of dirt in my mouth.

It is apparent I have said something wrong. I have failed the game.

"These wayward sisters mean to mock you, General," says the young man, staring down at me. But the bearded man hushes his companion. He crouches down as if to talk to a child.

"Is this true…?" he asks me.

There is the iron taste of blood on my lips. I am smiling, but I cannot remember why, and I see the men are somehow afraid of me for a reason they will never quite understand. I widen my bloodied smile and tell him yes, it is true. Every word of it.

I do not know why, but I put my finger to my lips and then place it upon his, a trace of blood passing from me to him. The blackness in his eyes grows small, and his breathing becomes shallow. There is only us in this moment, only his devouring of my words, of a future laid out before him.

Then he is risen and gone, down the road, never looking back. The younger man hurries to keep pace.

Older sister helps me up.

"Where did that come from?" she asks, but I wouldn't answer her, even if I could.

Three sisters, on the damp heath, shivering in the cold, waiting for night to fall, so they can return home once their mother is safely asleep. We think we have done well, said the right things, played the game and won.

Within two months, a hundred men will lie dead, and the blame shall be upon us.

————————————————

Father was taken. That is what mother tells us, night after night. Sometimes she is speaking directly to us, her darling daughters. Other times she is talking to a bottle or a smudged glass. Then there are the nights she hisses at the faces in the walls. Arguing with them. Screaming at them. Striking out until hands are bloody. And then she begins on us.

She tells us the story many times of how we lost our father. A shadow crept into the house and slipped into his mouth while he slept. The shadow would not leave him. Mother never says where this shadow came from or why it chose him; she only reiterates her despair at how nobody in the village noticed the transformation. The idiot townsfolk saw something that walked and breathed and ate and spoke like man, and they never looked any closer. Mother says he was hollow. Something else lived in him. No longer father, no longer husband, no longer even man.

Yet he still puts his seed in her, and from that, I was born forth. For that sin alone, I must take the beatings and whippings, I must not react when she spits at my face and claws at my eyes. Dirty girl. Stupid girl. Wrong to be born.

Then one morning, father awoke, walked out of our failing house, and down the road. He disappeared into nothing. Mother says he vanished into the air in front of her, burning up, ash and dust caught, twisting in the beams of an early sunrise.

One day she will be dead, and I will be free. I will no longer need to hide in the darkened forests of my head. I will no longer have to play the games of saying the words that she needs to hear. Yes, father was taken. Yes, father was changed. Yes, that shadow could return, so we must lock the doors and keep out the light. Without light there can be no shadow. Yes, mother. Yes.

On that day, my face will light up, just like Michael says, and never grow dull again. It starts with my smile, and then the brightness spreads to my eyes and my skin, and I am like an angel. This is what he tells me, in quiet moments we steal together.

Some days he waits around the corner from the marketplace, near the edge of the village. He lets me walk past him and pretends to pay no heed. I feel sparks of fire flicker through me, as I walk the paths, to the woods. Green thick forest, not like the place in my head, but still pleasing to escape to. Still safe.

I walk, and he follows, stalking me like prey. Sometimes I run to make things more difficult for him, but most times, I wait for him to get closer and closer. The beast yearning for the hunter. Those lost afternoons, when he pulls me close, puts himself inside me, whispers my name over and over. Buries himself in my scent, my neck, my skin, my body. Sometimes it hurts, and sometimes I feel like a something rather than a someone, but even on those odd, strange days I grow excited at this power I hold, to start such a burning within him.

He is to be wed to Beatrice, the daughter of a merchant. A woman who gives me looks of pity and vague disgust should she ever have the misfortune to pass me on the road. Aye, I am beneath her, but her man is on top of me, and that gives me a pleasure I cannot describe. Imagine Beatrice naked and watching us. Imagine that cruel curl of her lip trembling as she sees the wild fire he has for me. Sees us bleed together as one, skin on skin, body on body.

He could never be hers like he is mine.

"Things are getting worse," he says as we lie on the forest floor. Curled together, his arms around me, his warm chest behind. He talks of how there is a new King, how the sons of the deceased ruler have taken flight, how there is a rebellion of sorts brewing.

Michael is a good man. He does not believe in this new regent. When men raise arms, he will join them in rebellion.

And then he mentions the name of the king, and I see a man in armor, listening to the mutterings of a shivering girl.

I feel a cold wind pass through me from some unknown place.

I think of the damp heath, and the words we had to say to make the men go away.

I want to talk of something else. I don't want to hear of the new king, with his white-flecked beard and dead, black eyes.

So I tell Michael a secret. The day by the water, six months before. I had spent the morning walking, letting myself become lost in back roads and pathways, old trails and lanes where folk rarely walk anymore. All the way across the hills down to the winding river.

I saw older sister sitting by the bank, with a boy and girl, younger than her, younger than me. They were laughing. I crept closer to see what caused such contentment. Older sister rarely laughs at home. And she has no friends. None of us do. We only have each other.

I heard her call the boy 'brother' and then my foot pressed against loose stone and she turned, saw me, and I fled. Though I had done no wrong, her look was such that it filled me with some odd shame. She came back later and said nothing of it. When I pressed her on who these people were, if our father was dead how dare she call one brother, and she said that I must have seen something else, the way I do sometimes when my eyes go strange, and my body is elsewhere, that this was just imaginations. But no, this was not one of those times.

Michael says nothing. He just breathes deeply, his mouth against the nape of my neck. I feel him stiffen and slowly buck against me.

A man is watching us. For a moment, I think he is not real. Perhaps made of twig and branch, come to life, to try to join this pageantry of humanity. I smile at the sight, imagining the leaves swirling around, forming a foot and then a leg, and the roots winding around like twine, holding in place the bark and the greenery. Then my eyes move to the face, and I see two eyes staring back across the forest floor. I realize that this is a man, this is real, and he seems momentarily shocked. Then he is striding forward, shouting, angry, and Michael is cowering before his father, naked, his manhood still strong but fading fast. I run, still unclothed, through the woods, fear turning to a strange joy. I know Michael is in trouble, but it is good for us. It means things will be forced to change. He cannot wed Beatrice now. And we will be together, the whole world can be our woods.

Then the world changes again. Moon rises and falls, over and over. There are battles fought, and fields of blood. Folk say the false king lies dead. They say the man who killed him was ripped from his mother's womb as an infant. I think of the sow, with her bright red snout, her little ones beneath her as she furrowed away desperately.

Maybe she wanted them back inside. Maybe she wanted them safe.

I have not seen Michael since the day in the forest. I heard he went to fight, and I heard he came home safe, and I hope my prayers guided him in some way, even if I could not remember the right words.

I go to his house, but his father comes out and blocks my way. His eyes look me from head to toe and back for a long time. I think of how long he must have stood in the forest, watching us.

"Do not come here again," he says. His voice is thick, and the warning is clear.

Last night I woke from dreamless slumber to feel someone lying down next to me. For a moment, I thought of Michael, but in the dark, I knew that was not true. It was mother.

She whispered that I had a shadow in me. Then she put her arms around me, and I was scared, for I have never known her touch gentle. I felt like a rabbit in the mouth of a dog. Though I feared the worst, she stroked my hair like a mother should, and her voice stayed soft. She told me how she was sorry she could not protect me, could not guide me to the light. Then she sang a song far older than any of us, and sleep lulled me back into the dark.

And before the dawn, there is the cracking of the door, like a great thunder. Wood splinters. Sisters scream. Men come for us, iron and steel in hands.

They have heard what we told the false king on that day. They say we bewitched his mind. That our foul and dank deeds polluted a once-great man. Michael had cried before them and talked of how I used some enchantment on him, how my filthy body corrupted his pure soul. Beatrice stood behind him, tears rolling down her face at the horrors her man has endured, far worse than any war.

Mother yells and urges us to run and tries to stop them. I see the fear in her, for these men are shadows. She fights for us with a ferocity I could never have imagined, but she is only a woman and has no place in this. They toss her aside like a doll as they drag us outside.

I want to tell her that it is fine as they lead us out through the village, towards the flames that burn and crackle in the dark. I want to let her know that I understand, that there are dark, deserted places in many of these hollow men where shadows can thrive.

Closer and closer to the fire. My sisters are numb with the terror of the flames. I find my voice, and I find the words, and they come out, sharp and clear in the winter air.

"It was only me," I say, and then everyone is quiet as if this is a play, and they have been waiting for my line.

I tell them of the foulness within me. I tell them of consorting with goat-like men and men-like goats. I laugh as I recount the sins I forced Michael to commit upon my defiled skin, and I talk black tales of Beatrice lying with us, too. I boast to the ears of this innocent village about how I drove a good man to murder. How I bewitched him, this kind and good man with the white-flecked beard.

I tell them my sisters are pathetic and have no knowledge of my ways.

I keep talking and talking. Sometimes I am not even using language, only sounds, growls, and barks. I lose myself in the guttural noise. I let them drag me in a rage towards the pyre, as they beat and shove me on, trying to silence this abhorrent tongue of mine, trying to protect themselves from my cracked words and violent phrases. My sisters are sobbing, pleading with me to be silent. Michael can only stare at the ground, but his face is filled with wrath like the others, demanding my burning, my end.

They can do what they want. I am not there anymore. I have slipped away. I am elsewhere.

I am in the dark forest, watching the fire, a moonless clouded sky above me. I see the men force me towards the blaze. I could stay and watch some more, but what is the point?

As the flames rise, I turn my back on them all, looking to these blackened woods, these skeletal trees. I understand there is a freedom here, of a different kind. I run into the darkness, a smile upon my face now, leaving the village behind, the smoke rising in the distance, further and further and until there is no trace of it left.

HAZEL KING

THE HANGING TREE AND THE OLD TOM PIT

CAROLINE'S family always made the effigies on Boxing Day. Once their lunch of Christmas leftovers had been cleared away, Caroline's mother would bring out her sewing kit and spread across the dining table all the scraps of fabric she'd saved over the past year. There was cotton wool stuffing, buttons for the eyes and wool for the hair. Kitchen twine for the rope.

Outside, a soft rain tapped against the windows, and the room was dim enough that they had to switch on the light. An LP of Christmas songs span gently on the record player, and Caroline hummed along under her breath. Caroline's mother was helping David to sew his pieces of old shirts and socks together into a limp figure, although he was ten years old already and Caroline was sure she hadn't needed help when she was ten. Her own effigy was taking shape beneath her practised hands. It was her fifteenth doll, and she had already stitched it and stuffed it, only wishing she could give it a more flattering shape. She carefully painted the face, giving it blue eyes like hers, a narrow nose, and the plump, pink lips she wished she had.

"If you've finished, Caroline, you can make the nooses," Caroline's father said.

David glanced up from his half-stitched doll.

"She made the nooses last year! It's my turn."

But Caroline had already snatched up the twine.

"You wouldn't do it right," she said. "You can't even sew by yourself."

"Yes I can."

He tried to tug the needle out of his mother's hand and she swatted him on the wrist.

"You can make the nooses when you're older," she said. "It's a very important job." She looked at the length of twine in Caroline's hands. "Make sure you knot them tight, poppet."

"I know," Caroline said.

She shot a smug look at her brother and then made a loop in the twine, twisting the rope around and around itself before tucking the end into place. Her father was watching her, but he didn't offer any advice, just let her work on the remaining twine until four miniature hangman nooses were lying on the table before her.

"It's too bad capital punishment is going out of fashion," her father said. "You could have been an executioner."

"Frank!" her mother scolded. "Don't joke about things like that."

"We should make little black hoods," Caroline said, catching her father's eye and grinning. "To put over their heads." She grabbed a piece of black fabric and held it over the face of her doll, and her father chuckled.

"You see, Frank? You're making her morbid."

"Nothing wrong with a good hanging," her father said. "Fine old English tradition, hanging. And where would we be without it?" He gestured to the four dolls lying on the table, made in their family's image, and the four nooses waiting for their necks.

"Next year," David said sulkily, "I want to be the hangman."

On New Year's Eve, Caroline walked the short distance to the churchyard as the sun was setting. It wasn't yet four o'clock, and the ritual wasn't for hours yet, but she hurried through the darkening streets, hugging her coat tightly around her so the chill wouldn't sneak up under the hem.

The town was small, and she kept her head down in the hopes that no one would call out to her, although she barely passed anyone on the road. On either side of her the lights were coming on in the windows of the old stone houses and Christmas trees still twinkled in the front rooms. Smoke drifted from the chimneys, the scent comforting in the frigid air. The temperature had plummeted in the few days since Christmas and the sky was thick with the promise of snow.

The old wooden stocks greeted her at the churchyard gate, and she slipped past them and fumbled the catch with her gloved fingers, leaving the gate ajar behind her. The church itself was squat but traditional, made of stately grey stone with painted glass in the windows. She liked it when the church was lit by candlelight and the figures in the windows seemed almost to move, but today there was no light and the colours were dim.

Caroline followed the crooked gravestones around to the back of the church, and there she found what she was looking for. Judith was standing beneath the yew tree, her dark hair escaping from beneath a hat, stamping her booted feet against the cold. Above her, hanging from the branches of the yew tree, last year's effigies swayed gently in the twilight.

Father Joseph was there, too, patiently watching the last of the light fade from the sky. He noticed Caroline first and beckoned her over.

"You're early, Caroline," he said. "Did you come to help us take down last year's dolls?"

Caroline nodded. She'd known the vicar all her life, but she still felt shy when he spoke to her.

"I asked her to come," Judith said. She was a year older than Caroline, and three inches taller, and she held herself with a confidence that Caroline had always admired. Caroline gravitated to her side. "Dad, can we start yet?"

Father Joseph checked his watch and then looked up at the sky again.

"You know the rules," he said. "Not until night has fallen. But it's almost time."

Judith sighed and grabbed Caroline's arm, dragging her further under the tree and pointing up.

"Look, there's mine."

A ragged, mouldering doll hung from its noose. Once, it had looked like Judith, but after a year in the elements it barely resembled a person at all. Caroline took a few steps back, searching for the right branch, and then pointed at another doll.

"That one's mine."

Judith turned back to her father.

"How many fell down?"

"Four this year."

"And how many of them died?"

She knows the answer, Caroline thought. *When the mine shaft collapsed in the autumn, we all knew who'd be trapped inside.*

"Only two," Father Joseph said.

"So it doesn't really mean you'll die if your doll falls," Judith said. She was looking at Caroline, but she wasn't really speaking to her. "It isn't real, you know. It's all fairytales."

Caroline caught the flicker of annoyance on Father Joseph's face and turned away, hoping they weren't going to have this argument again. She wished Judith wouldn't pick fights when she was around.

Today, to her relief, Father Joseph wasn't in the mood to argue.

"It's time," he said. "Let's get started."

He handed them each an electric torch and a pair of scissors and sent them to stand on chairs and snip the rotting effigies from the lower-hanging branches while he climbed a ladder propped up against the trunk and pruned the higher limbs. Caroline tried not to touch the dolls as she cut them free. They were damp from yesterday's rain, and some were infested with insects. The paint on their faces had run or washed away entirely, so it was impossible to tell one from another. That worried her.

"Do they still work when their faces have gone?" she asked, and then felt herself blush as Judith scoffed. "I mean," she persevered, "how will he recognise them?"

Father Joseph looked down at her and nodded slowly, as though she'd asked a very deep question.

"Death knows us all," he said, and he gestured past her, at the quiet expanse of graves. "Even when your face has gone and your body is food for the worms, Death will know you and come for you."

"Unless, of course," Judith said, snipping through her own effigy's noose and holding it up to the torchlight, "he's fooled by a doll."

It was close to midnight when the villagers started arriving in the churchyard. Caroline had set out lanterns to light their way, each a beacon of shimmering candle flame to guide them around the graves and over to the yew tree. The church was still dark, its doors locked, but there were lanterns hanging from the yew's tiny-leafed branches. They swung gently in the breeze, and Caroline watched them closely and held her breath, afraid that one of them would topple down and the whole tree would go up in flames.

Most of the village had turned up, and the crowd stretched back out of the light. Caroline was standing at the front with Judith, but she knew her parents and David were somewhere nearby. She stood on her tiptoes and scanned for their faces in the throng of chattering people, and when she didn't see them she looked instead at the figures clutched in every hand, each painted face a copy of its maker's, each cloth neck encircled by a hangman's noose.

"Look at mine," Judith said, nudging her arm.

She'd painted the face of her effigy with a dark, round mouth as though caught in a scream. Purple bruises bloomed around the pale polyester of the throat.

"That's horrible," Caroline breathed in awe.

"If I have to kill myself in miniature, I might as well do it realistically. You'd think Dad would be happy, but he said I wasn't taking it seriously." Judith rolled her eyes.

Father Joseph was standing at the foot of the tree, holding his own effigy and quietly waiting for the crowd to settle. Eventually it did, without him saying a word. The murmuring died away and the shuffle of moving bodies became still, until Caroline could hear the quiet creaking of the tree in the breeze and the tinkle of the swaying lanterns.

"I walk through the valley of the shadow of death," Father Joseph said. He didn't raise his voice, but it carried clearly over the silent crowd before him. "We all walk through that valley," he said. "Some of us more frequently than others."

He looked especially at the men, some of whom met his gaze. A young man standing near Caroline, only a few years older than her, looked up into the coal-black sky and clutched his effigy tight enough to crush the bones it didn't have.

"Death comes to us all in the end," Father Joseph said, "and there will come a time when we'll welcome him. But for many of us, that time is not yet here."

He raised his effigy in the air, dangling it from its long noose. It was wearing his black cassock but the white band around its neck was obscured by the rope.

"The tradition of the dolls is old enough that its origins are lost to time, but I have long believed that the Lord God himself showed our forefathers how to cheat Death. Tonight is the one night in the year when Death is not watching us. He's busy tallying the souls he reaped in this past year, and while his thoughts are elsewhere, we will replace last year's effigies with the new."

Father Joseph reached up to one of the lowest branches and tied the end of his effigy's rope around it, knotting it so tight that a flake of bark fell away from the wood. The doll dangled beside him, limp at the end of its twine.

"If Death comes for me this year he shall not find me," Father Joseph intoned, "for he shall see my body rotting in the churchyard and think that I am already his."

"And by the grace of God you will live another year," the crowd murmured.

"And for as long as my effigy hangs in the churchyard, let my faith protect me."

"And by the grace of God you will hang for the whole year long," the crowd replied.

"Let not the storm nor the gale nor the deluge bring my false body down from the tree. Let not the worm eat through the rope nor the lightning strike nor the Devil interfere."

"Amen."

Father Joseph clasped his hands together and lowered his head, and the congregation mimicked him, their effigies caught between their hands as though to infuse them with prayer.

And then Father Joseph raised his head and started speaking with his normal voice, not his vicar's voice, calling out for the children to come first with a parent, who would help them hang their dolls from the branches. The crowd shuffled, and people started talking again. A child laughed and no one shushed him, and the night became easier to breathe.

Judith had stood with folded arms by Caroline's side during the ritual. She hadn't joined in the responses of the crowd and she hadn't put her hands together in prayer. Now she watched the children carefully climbing onto chairs so they could reach the branches and she snorted in disdain.

"Don't believe him, Carrie," she whispered, her breath tickling Caroline's ear. "He cheats, you know."

"You mean Death?"

Judith looked back at the dark church, its windows lightless and empty.

"Him, too."

———

Judith's mother had died a year ago. It had snowed heavily last winter, and her car had skidded on the ice and veered off the road straight into a tree. Caroline had heard people say that her effigy had fallen from its branch that very day. She'd never worked up the nerve to ask Judith if this was true, and Judith had never told her either way.

This year the snow had started in the early hours of New Year's Day, and now, two weeks later, it was still on the ground, most of it now trodden into ice. Every time her father left the house in the morning, the sky still dark and the ice glistening under the beams of his headlights, Caroline thought about Judith's mother and she didn't relax until the evening when his car crawled slowly back again.

This evening, he hadn't come home.

Caroline's mother was standing by the kitchen window, her casserole getting dry in the oven, and staring out into the night. He wasn't an hour late yet, but usually when he was held up he would call from the phone in the mining office. Tonight there'd been no call.

"You could ring the office," Caroline had suggested. "Ask them if something's happened."

"Yes," Caroline's mother had said, but she hadn't taken her eyes off the road. "Yes, I might do that." She hadn't.

Even David had sensed the atmosphere for once and had stopped complaining that he was hungry. Caroline had sent him to his room to do his homework and had felt oddly grown up when he'd obeyed. Now she stood in the kitchen with her mother and wondered if it was the mine or the icy road that had got her father.

"I could go to the yew tree," she suddenly said. "I could check on his doll."

Caroline's mother hesitated again, but Caroline was already tugging on her boots and coat.

"Maybe it's better to wait," her mother said. "Just in case."

"Just in case what?" Caroline snapped as she opened the door, suddenly angry that she had to be the sensible one, the one who had to risk seeing her father's effigy on the ground, but her mother just stood in the hallway, pale and fragile, and didn't answer. Caroline slammed the door and started trudging through the snow and ice as quickly as she dared.

In her frustration she'd forgotten to bring a torch, and as only the main road in their village had streetlights, that meant she had to make her way over the ice in the dark. She'd forgotten her gloves, too, but she didn't dare put her hands in her pockets in case she slipped and needed to catch herself, and so she cupped her hands to her mouth to catch the clouds of warm, damp air she breathed into them. Her fingers ached with cold.

The church was at the end of a narrow road, up a shallow hill, and she slipped and fell when she was almost at the gate, smacking her knees against the ice. Cursing under her breath, she hauled herself upright again and passed through into the churchyard.

There was a faint light misting through the stained glass windows, tempting her inside. It went against everything she'd been taught to resist the temptation of the church, but Caroline knew that if she stopped, she wouldn't carry on. The snow crunched under her feet as she picked her way through the graves, and she thought of all the dead lying under her feet. When she was with Judith, it was easy to convince herself she didn't believe in the ritual, but here in the lonely night without her father, faith was all she had.

A doll lay on the snow beneath the tree.

Caroline stood at the edge of the graves and looked at the small figure lying on the ground. In the darkness, she couldn't tell whose it was. The rest of the small shapes hanging from the branches shivered indistinctly above her, and she could feel their painted eyes on her as she finally crept towards the fallen doll.

It wasn't a death sentence if your effigy fell off the tree. It didn't mean you would die for certain, only that you weren't protected if Death came looking for you. But in their village, where most of the men worked in the mines, Death stalked their borders often.

Caroline picked up the doll. It was cold to the touch, and damp from lying in the snow, but in the darkness she couldn't make out the details of its face or dress. The noose was still looped around its neck, but the twine had snapped or frayed halfway up.

Behind her, a light gleamed, and Caroline turned to see a torch beam coming around the side of the church, flashing briefly over her.

"Caroline?" It was her father's voice.

She didn't know what instinct made her thrust the doll into her pocket, but once she'd done it she couldn't take it out again. She flung her arms around her father and he kissed the top of her head.

"I got home minutes after you'd left," he said. "Had some car trouble on the way, nothing I couldn't fix. Your mum told me you'd come out here without a light."

He shone the torch beam over the ground beneath the tree.

"No fallen dolls?" he asked in a tighter voice.

"None," Caroline said.

"Good. Let's get you home."

They walked back together, and by the time they got home their meal was on the table waiting so Caroline had to leave the effigy in her coat. She was distracted all evening, waiting for her chance to smuggle it into her bedroom, which she finally did by stuffing it up the loose sleeve of her jumper when going up to bed.

As soon as she'd closed her bedroom door behind her she took it out and held it under the lamplight. It wasn't her father. It was wearing a black priest's cassock and a white band under the noose. The end of the twine wasn't frayed, but neatly and deliberately cut.

———————————————

Caroline fretted about the doll for the rest of the week. She hid it at the back of one of her drawers and checked it every day after school, terrified that her mother would find it. She felt that it should have calmed her each time she came home and found it still undiscovered, but the longer it stayed there, the guiltier she felt, as though she'd been the one to cut it down.

That was why she hadn't told anyone, for fear that they'd blame her. She was amazed that no one had noticed yet that the doll was missing from the tree, but Father Joseph was the only person who checked the dolls, and he probably only glanced at the ground for fallen figures. She prayed every night that he wouldn't look up into the branches. The whole village would be in uproar when they learnt their vicar's effigy had vanished, especially if someone realised it had been cut down.

She had to take it back to the tree. It was the only way. Maybe she could even hang it back up. You weren't supposed to replace the fallen dolls—once they'd fallen free, Death knew he'd been tricked—but it seemed so unfair that someone had sabotaged it—and in January! There was a whole year to go before the next New Year's ritual. Maybe Father Joseph wouldn't be safe if she hung it back up, but at least he wouldn't know he was unsafe. Everyone would be happier that way.

She made her decision on Friday night, so she knew she'd have to go through with it on Saturday. On Sunday, everyone would go to church, and there was too much of a risk that someone would notice the missing effigy if she hadn't replaced it by then. So on Saturday morning she set out alone with the doll in her pocket, telling her parents she was going to visit Judith.

Naturally, the lie jinxed her. Father Joseph lived in the vicar's house next door to the church, and as she was walking up to the church gate, Judith came out the front door and saw her. Her face was flushed and she was scowling, and when she saw Caroline she grabbed her by the arm and dragged her back down the street the way she'd come.

"God, he's such a hypocrite," she said, her voice loud in the quiet street. "He's always lecturing me, like he's such a saint. I'm so angry I could scream."

"Please don't," Caroline said. "Where are we going?"

"Somewhere he won't follow!"

Caroline didn't ask what the fight had been about, but as they walked through the village and out into the woods, Judith told her anyway. She'd gone to the cinema in the nearby town to watch *Night of the Demon*, and her father had found the ticket stubs in her room. He thought the film was Satanic, and the ensuing argument had been blandly predictable. Only last week Caroline would have been impressed at Judith's daring, but compared to the secret in her pocket it was nothing. She made distracted noises while Judith ranted and counted down the hours of daylight she had left to take the doll back to the tree.

"Mum never treated me like a child," Judith said. The words rang out through the trees, and although she hadn't spoken any louder, they felt bigger somehow, like black holes that swallowed up all the other words either of them might have said. They carried on walking in the vacuum of silence until they reached the old Tom Pit.

Years ago, long before Caroline had been born, the mines had stretched all the way to the edge of the village, and there were several abandoned mine shafts in the woods. Tom Pit was the closest to the village border, a large round cave cut into the earth, supported with old wooden beams, worm-eaten and rotting now. It had never been blocked off the way some of the other shafts had been, and every child grew up with the warning never to play in the pit. There were stories of children who'd died here, although Caroline wasn't sure if they were true.

The stories the children told was that Death lived here. That if you got too close he'd see you, and he'd know you were alive.

The two girls stood a little way from the mouth of the pit, staring down into the darkness. Above them, the branches of the trees were still and lifeless. No birds sang, no animals scurried through the undergrowth. Even the snow was still pure and soft out here, and the only sound was the quiet crunch of it yielding under their boots.

"Have you ever seen him?" Judith asked, not taking her eyes from the darkness of the cave.

"You mean Death?" Caroline said. The pit made her uneasy and she looked up instead at the grey sky through the branches. "I thought you didn't believe in those stories."

"Death isn't a story," Judith said. "The story is that we can escape him."

She walked slowly up to the mouth of the pit, so close that Caroline thought she was going to disappear inside.

"Hello?" Judith called. "Is anybody down there?"

A faint echo called back to her, but the sound was distorted and the words lost. It didn't sound like Judith's voice. Caroline's skin prickled damply beneath her arms.

"Can I tell you something?" Judith asked. She was still facing into the pit, and Caroline wasn't sure whether she was talking to her or to someone standing just beyond the reach of the light.

"Come back over here and you can tell me anything."

"Last winter my doll fell off the tree."

Caroline stared at her.

"No, it didn't. I would have heard about it. You'd have told me."

Judith slowly shook her head.

"There were only a couple of weeks to go until the New Year," she said. "Dad hung it back up. He'd never done that for any of the others, but he did it for me. And then a few days later, Mum died. Her doll didn't fall, even after her neck snapped at the side of the road. Mine fell, but she died. How is that fair?"

Caroline didn't know what to say.

"Do you know what Dad said?" Judith continued. She was still staring into the black hole in the ground. "He said it was his punishment for saving me. For tying my doll back up. He said Death always takes a bargain, even one made accidentally. So he took Mum instead of me."

They both stood in silence. A breeze whistled through the mouth of the pit like a whisper of breath. Then Caroline dared to follow Judith's footprints and join her at the entrance to the shaft, although she couldn't look directly at the darkness for fear of what might be looking back.

She took the effigy out of her pocket and held it out to Judith, who didn't seem surprised at all to see it.

"Is that why you cut him down?" she asked.

Judith took the doll and fingered the end of the noose.

"I wanted him to admit that it was stupid," she said. "That it doesn't make a difference whether you hang a doll or not. But he hasn't even mentioned it."

She curled her fingers tightly around the doll's chest, and before Caroline could stop her, she wound back her arm and pitched it down into the shaft.

"What are you doing?" Caroline cried, and the echo came back sharp and frightened, a wine-dark voice speaking in tongues.

"Now he'll have to admit it," Judith said, staring fiercely after it, though it had landed out of sight somewhere in the gloom. "When he doesn't die, he'll have to admit that all those dolls are a load of bollocks and it wasn't anyone's fault that Mum died."

Caroline risked a glance directly into the hole and wished she hadn't. The darkness was so deep that it hurt her eyes to look at. She could feel the age of it. It had been sitting there for decades with no light to soften it or noise to waken it. She wished she hadn't shown Judith the doll. She wished they hadn't come here at all.

"Let's go home," she said, taking Judith's arm and tugging her back towards the path. "I'm cold."

They started following their footprints back, but before they were swallowed by the trees again, they both heard a quiet noise behind them. It sounded like a voice echoing back at them from the pit, but neither of them had spoken. Judith half turned to look, but Caroline grabbed her by the wrist and ran, and then both girls were tearing through the woods as though the Devil himself were after them.

That evening, Caroline was waiting when her father came home from the pub. He was always in an affable mood after a few drinks, and when she said she had a question for him, he sat down next to her on the couch and put an arm around her shoulders like she was a little girl again.

"What's up, poppet?"

He was in such a good mood that Caroline hesitated, but in the end the question forced its way out of her lips.

"Have you ever seen Death in the mines?"

The smile slipped off her father's face and he glanced towards the living room door, but no one else was downstairs to overhear them. They could faintly hear David protesting through the ceiling that he wasn't tired yet and his friends didn't have to go to bed until ten. It was such an ordinary noise to be in the backdrop of such airless, underground thoughts.

"No, lass," Caroline's father said. "I haven't seen him. But once I thought I heard his voice."

Caroline was glad the curtains were drawn. She hated the thought that the darkness might see into their lighted bubble of safety.

"What did he say?" she asked.

"My name," her father said.

Caroline pressed closer into his side and he rubbed her arm to comfort her. He was watching the coal fire burning in the grate. That coal had spent a million lifetimes crushed by the weight of the world in a place beyond the reach of the sun, and now it was burning bright for them. A man like Caroline's father had raised it out of the darkness to become the light.

"It was years ago when the shaft flooded," he said. "There was suddenly water up to my knees and the lights went out. And as I was trying to find my way back I heard him somewhere behind me, deeper down the tunnel, calling my name. But I didn't go to him and he didn't find me."

"But how would he know to call your name? We hang the dolls so he'll think we're already dead."

An ember shifted in the grate and the fire sparked and crackled.

"That was the year my doll fell down in a storm," Caroline's father said.

━━━━━━━━━━━━━━━

The next morning, Father Joseph collapsed halfway through Sunday service. The organist had started playing, but before the congregation had uttered the first line of the hymn, Father Joseph raised a hand to his chest and fell to the wooden floor beside the altar. A great cry of alarm had gone up over the swell of the hymn's opening verse, which had carried on for a second line before the organist had heard the shouting and stopped mid-note.

In the clamour that had followed, Caroline hadn't seen much of what happened. Several people from the front rows had run over to see what the matter was, and she'd heard a woman shouting to ask where the telephone was, that someone needed to ring for an ambulance. Then her mother had ushered her and David out of the pew and down the crowded aisle until they spilled out into the churchyard with a host of other anxious parishioners.

It was then that Caroline knew the truth of the yew tree. It was a solid, heavy truth, as weighty as if the tree itself had knotted her among its roots and grown steadily over her. It didn't matter that she hadn't tied Father Joseph's effigy back onto a branch. In the space between the snip of the scissors and the cloth body landing on the ground, the charm had been broken.

All Caroline could think to do was stand on her toes, trying to see over the heads of the people crowding in the doorway, but she couldn't see Father Joseph or Judith. It was Judith she was looking for. She always sat in the first pew on the left, right in front of where her father had fallen.

That was when the cry went up that the vicar's doll was missing from the tree. Caroline didn't hear who started it, but the news burned its way through the crowd like kindling in a drought.

"Come on," Caroline's mother was saying. "Come on, let's go home." She thought Father Joseph was already dead, Caroline realised, and she didn't want them to see the body brought out.

"Where's Judith?" she asked.

"I didn't see her. Oh, that poor child, she'll be all alone."

"I'm not leaving without Judith," Caroline said. She tried to push her way back inside, but her mother caught her and held her fast.

"I'll fetch her," Caroline's father said, and he made his way back into the church.

He was gone for so long that the ambulance pulled up at the gate while he was still inside, and only once the paramedics had gone in did he reappear with an arm around Judith. She was looking over her shoulder, trying to see what was happening to her father, and her eyes were wet. Some of the people she passed muttered comforting words but she didn't seem to hear them.

She didn't say a thing when they carried the stretcher out. Father Joseph was still alive, but he was pale and his eyes were shut. Caroline held Judith's hand and Judith finally met her gaze. The look in her eyes was the same look she'd had last winter, for days on end after her mother had died.

Judith stayed in Caroline's room that night. They'd gone to see Father Joseph in the hospital that afternoon. He'd been pale and weak and confused, and Judith had barely spoken since then. Now, pressed close together in Caroline's narrow bed, they lay awake and listened to the silence of the sleeping house.

"I understand now," Judith said quietly. She was lying on her back and staring at the ceiling, and Caroline was curled against her side, wishing she knew what to say.

"You understand what?"

"How the tree works."

Caroline watched the minute rise and fall of Judith's chest beneath the duvet.

"How?"

"It isn't a trick. Death knows we're all alive, he wouldn't be fooled by a bunch of dolls. But he likes to make a bargain so he plays by our rules, and if we cheat he punishes us."

"But why would he go along with the ritual if it isn't real?"

Judith shrugged.

"Maybe he's bored. Maybe our lives are pieces in a game to him."

Caroline didn't like that thought at all.

"I hope your dad gets better," she said.

Judith didn't reply. Outside, a light rain pattered against the window, and the two girls lay still in the darkness until the hours became timeless and the morning a distant myth.

───────────────

When Caroline woke up on Monday morning, Judith had gone.

The day before, Caroline's mother had decided they shouldn't have to go to school in case there was a call from the hospital, but the sounds of her brother getting up brought Caroline out of a deep sleep before the sun had risen, and she felt the empty space beside her in the bed, already cold.

She had a drowsy recollection of Judith climbing out of the bed, but she hadn't thought anything of it and had fallen back to sleep. Now she was wide awake, and she sat up and turned on the lamp.

Judith's clothes were no longer draped over the back of Caroline's chair. Caroline scrambled out of bed and went out onto the landing, searching. She could hear her father humming in the bathroom, and downstairs she found her mother and David in the kitchen.

"What are you doing up, poppet?" her mother asked. "Did we wake you?"

"Where's Judith?"

Her mother paused in the act of buttering her toast.

"I thought she was upstairs with you."

Caroline knew then. A creeping dread had been gathering inside her since she'd woken, and when she went out into the hallway she wasn't surprised to find that Judith's shoes and coat were missing and the front door was unlocked.

Her mother had followed her out of the kitchen, and she was looking at the coat rack, too.

"She couldn't have gone to the hospital," she said. "Not without a car. Could she have gone home? Or to the church, to pray?"

"We have to find her," Caroline said.

"Why don't I call her house and see if she answers?"

She picked up the phone, but Caroline grabbed her coat and tugged her boots over her bare feet.

"Carrie, you can't go out like that!" her mother said. "At least get dressed and we can go search together."

"There's no time!"

She fled the house, skidding on the ice, her mother calling after her, and ran along the street. Judith wouldn't be at the church and she wouldn't be at her house. Caroline knew where Judith had gone, and she knew with a bone-deep certainty that something terrible would happen if she didn't find her in time.

The sun was still an hour off rising, and as she turned off the street and entered the woods, she had to slow down. She'd forgotten the torch again in her haste, but nothing could stop her: not the branches catching in her hair, not the tree roots hidden beneath the snow, not the smothering night that clung to the woods and tried to obscure the path.

"Judith," she called, but even though her voice was thin she was terrified that the wrong person would hear her, and she didn't dare call out again.

She thought she'd lost her way by the time she reached the clearing of the old Tom Pit. She stumbled upon it suddenly and then stopped at the edge of the trees as she sensed the open space around her. There was a trickle of pre-dawn light in the sky now, which picked out the edges of things, so that patches of darkness slowly transformed into ghostlike shapes. First the bare, spindly branches of the trees, then the puddled shadows of footprints in the snow, and then the dark mouth of the pit itself, a yawning chasm in the earth.

Caroline couldn't be sure, but she thought she saw a figure standing at the edge of the mine shaft, facing into the hole.

"Judith." It came out as barely a breath, evaporating in a cloud of steam, unheard.

As she stood there, paralysed, willing herself to move, she realised that Judith was talking to someone. Her voice was a low murmur, and Caroline couldn't hear the words. She sounded like the echo they'd heard from the pit, indistinct and not quite right, and Caroline wondered with a shock of terror whether it was really Judith's voice she could hear or someone else's.

The voice fell silent, and there was a moment as full as a drop of water right before it falls. Caroline felt the irresistible force of gravity, and it pulled her three steps further towards the pit and wrenched her voice from her throat.

"Judith, don't go!"

She would never be sure if Judith had heard her. It would haunt her, that vision of Judith's shadow at the threshold, staring into the earth and never once looking back towards Caroline's voice. Somewhere above them in the endless sky, a whisper of daylight hushed over the edge of the world, and Judith stepped into the old Tom Pit and was swallowed by the shaft.

Caroline stood in the twilight and watched her go. She wished she was brave enough to follow, wished she was a hero of old myth who could walk into the underworld and bring back the dead, and maybe she would have become one if she'd dared. But she didn't.

She felt something watching her from the old Tom Pit. Something waiting, with a patience that had seen bones become coal, to know whether she wanted to make a bargain, too.

It was still watching when she turned and walked away.

SARA CENTURY

THE
DEATH OF
A DROP
OF WATER

ROSE'S fingertips slid down the inside of the window, wet with condensation. Through the rain, in the darkness, she saw the smiles of all the women in white, drenched to the bone, moving closer without moving at all. Surrounded by grey trees, half hidden in the tall grass. She had turned the light off to see them better, but she'd seen quite enough. She backed up, and flipped the switch again, illuminating the room and lingering in the doorway. It didn't matter if they saw her. They knew where she was, either way. She could hear them moving towards the house in their strange, blinking way, their bodies still as they slid through the gaps between seconds.

Now, she could only see her reflection in the glass, too thin from months and even years of worry. Losing so much and still waiting for the other shoe to drop. Things had been so bad for so long. From the loss of her mother last year, first her character and then her life, to the way her own symptoms seemed to mirror her mother's. Forgetfulness, anxiety, paranoia. Trying not to notice that her sister, on whom she had always depended, began more and more to pull away from their lives here in their childhood home...

Lightning struck. A woman was pressed against the glass. Thunder roared, covering Rose's scream as she jumped backwards and ran to the kitchen, throwing over the drawers filled with useless tools that would not protect her. She flailed helplessly for only a moment, then worked to calm her breathing. She reminded herself that she needed to keep calm.

Rose started up the stairs. They were everywhere outside. She could see them through the large windows that dotted every side of the house. She ran by the mirror on the wall, but it was a woman in white that passed by on the other side. She paused long enough to throw her palm against the glass, letting out a short, ragged shriek. It shattered. Her hand bled. She looked back. One of them at the bottom of the stairs, and then many of them were, and then just one again. Some of them laughing, some of them crying. They began to climb.

The women had first appeared to her a few days before, in what she supposed was a dream. The day had been hot and humid, and she'd fallen asleep on one of the couches in what was once her grandmother's den. She suddenly found herself in another world, walking through a dying landscape, shuddering from the damp chill soaked through her skin to her bones. It was a strange, petrified forest. Black, spindly trees jutted into the dark grey sky. The moisture of the air seemed to try and bind to her skin as if it were burrowing in through her pores. It left a film on her skin.

As the initial shock faded, she noticed that there was something wrong with the sounds of the forest. She studied them as she walked, a deep dread rising up in her chest. What was it? She listened, baffled by what exactly seemed so wrong. Suddenly, she realized. The sound was backward. From her footsteps to her breathing to the shuffling of the deadened grey grass, the noises were all backward. How was it possible? She tested it, rustled a branch, scraped a shoe across the path, breathed harshly into the air. Backward.

As she neared a great grey lake, she realized that this was her forest, the forest that surrounded her home, the forest she walked through every day of her life with few exceptions since childhood. Only...this place was dead, shadowy, and barren. The trees had no leaves. The sun was absent, leaving a dim haze in its place. That was when she began to suspect that she must be in a nightmare. The thought gave her no moment of comfort, for it was a nightmare that sought to keep her within its clutches indefinitely, until she herself became a part of the dream.

That was when they began climbing up from the water.

The women. All seemingly the same woman, their faces muted and vague in the thick mist. Appearing in slow blinks of time and vanishing again, but always, always moving towards her. It was impossible to tell how many there were. At times, there were none, at times, more than ten. They flashed in and out of existence, but they were all crawling towards her. She stumbled back, trying to grab the branches of the trees to steady herself, but cracked and snapped off, and the women were upon her. They grabbed at her with hands like ice and began to pull her toward the lake.

She awoke in a panic, screaming and thrashing until her sobs turned to ragged coughing fits. Normally, her sister Elizabeth would have come to help her, but she was traveling. Rose was alone. Since her mother had grown weary of all the illness suffering and drowned herself in the lake, Rose had been alone.

Elizabeth had barely been present over the last few weeks of her mother's life. Rose wondered if her sister would be there when the same thing that happened to their mother happened to Rose, or if she'd be at a party somewhere surrounded by strangers and would get a sudden chill and know that Rose was dead.

She thought about Elizabeth, and their mother, and how those two had been so close to one another that she'd felt jealous of them. Later, when her mother took ill, there had been a distance between them that seemed sudden to Rose. Still, she felt she was on the outside looking in, and couldn't understand their sudden animosity.

Rose often thought of when her mother and her sister would go down by the water, and how they would hold hands and whisper and sing things in languages that she didn't understand and they wouldn't teach her. She thought of how Elizabeth had looked at her with some pity when they'd return from the lake, like she was just an ill-fated pawn in a chess match that was played behind doors that were forever closed to her. Maybe Elizabeth had known about the women.

Maybe she'd helped to call them, and that's why she wouldn't come home.

Though Elizabeth had called her later that day, Rose hadn't told her about the nightmare. She didn't want to spoil her trip. The last time they had spoken about anything serious at all, Elizabeth had said that Rose was too needy, that she held Elizabeth back. The words had splattered over Rose's heart like acid, and she'd burst into tears, hanging up. When Elizabeth called back, she'd choked out an excuse and hung up again. Now, as everything around her was fraying and her world felt like it was falling apart, she was still trying desperately to prove her wrong.

More than anything, Elizabeth had seemed almost relieved when their mother had died. Rose wondered if she would be secretly glad that the wraiths that took their mother had finally come for Rose, and the thought was too much to bear. Elizabeth could be so mean, and she knew exactly what to say and do to cut a person to the core. She was charming, funny, and lovely to be around most of the time, but lately, Rose had seen more of her sister's dark side than the light. She wondered what Elizabeth knew about the women but she was afraid to ask.

As the days dragged by, the women began appearing to her during the day as well as the night, always drawing closer and closer. She had no doubt that they were coming from her mother's lake, which had become her lake when her mother had died. She would watch them from the windows while they were still far out in the choppy waters, but when they had gotten closer than that, Rose had shut the curtains. It must have been the rain that finally brought them to the porch. Like pale nightcrawlers, rising up from the mud, they crept closer.

Tonight, they'd come inside, uninvited and unwanted, as if the heavy oak doors did not exist. She pushed all the furniture in the bedroom in front of the door, but she could still hear them outside, speaking backwards. It was impossible to understand what they were saying, but they talked all through the night in their strange, grinding version of language. Rose tried to stay awake, but she had barely slept in all this time. Exhaustion lay on her chest like a heavy brick, and she slowly drifted into sleep, finally falling into a dream of stillness and silence.

When she awoke the next morning, it was to a ringing phone. It took her some time to locate the landline, which she had never used and didn't realize was still in service. She could almost hear Elizabeth's chiding tone. "What a waste of money!"

Rose agreed that it was a waste of money, but nobody told her about it, so she wasn't sure what she could have done. That was how things always were with Elizabeth. She would wait for anything to go wrong and blame it on Rose, but not directly. In a sort of condescending undertone. Rose lifted the receiver, and began to say "hello."

A voice on the other side shrieked, in the same backwards way she had in her dream. Rose slammed the receiver back down, but the sound continued until it filled the house. Rose hid under the bed with her hands over her face and sobbed.

After some time, the noise subsided, and she finally crawled out. She walked to the window, the blinds still drawn closed like they had been the night before. Hesitantly, she reached to the drawstring, and began to pull. The cloth crinkled and rose up, soundless and smooth. She drew it up halfway, then paused, taking a deep breath before her wrist jerked downward. The curtain lifted and revealed the world to her.

Rose gasped. The women were everywhere. She was back in the dead world from her dream. The terror was too much. They could see her. She kicked backwards and fell, head crashing against the floor, and, once again, she was asleep.

When she came to once more, her head was throbbing. She scrambled to stand up. Looking out of her window, everything appeared to be normal. A sunny afternoon, with storm clouds forming at the edge of the horizon. She placed a hand over her mouth to stifle a sob. Not another night of rain. She wanted to pray for help, but there was no one to pray to when the weather started to come down as it did. Not even God could stop the storm.

Rose grabbed her shawl and walked out into the yard, tears streaming down her face. She strode out into the field and yelled at the sky, her voice eaten up by the wind. She put every bit of her misery into her voice and wailed at the clouds, but she still gasped when she felt drops of rain on the back of her hands. She looked at them, and then to the lake. A soft backwards moaning appeared under the wind. Rose's anger shifted, faded, and changed to fear. She turned and ran back up the stairs, bolting the door shut.

She sat at the dining room table, smoking a pack of cigarettes out of her mother's stash. The smokes were stale, but they were complemented by the richly aged whiskey that she'd found next to them. She ashed into a teacup, knowing it would make her mother and her sister absolutely furious to see her now. Not just for the lack of manners. She glanced around. This was a highly flammable house, after all. The long cloth curtains, oversized paintings, expensive rugs, and old wiring made for a dangerous mix. She supposed she didn't have to care about that, now.

Rose had considered calling her sister and begging her to come home, but the condescending tone with which Elizabeth would surely respond was more than she could take. More than anything, she wished her sister could be gentle with herself, and that it might help her be more gentle to others. Elizabeth couldn't come home right now, not in the way that mattered. Rose felt it was futile to drag her into this mess.

That was the problem, after all, Rose thought as the shadows grew and the sunlight faded. The overwhelming sense of futility hanging over her head. If she escaped, she would still be ill, wouldn't she? She'd still just end up like her mother—dead, in a coffin. Elizabeth would leave soon, maybe to get married or maybe just to live in the city like she always said she wanted. Who, then, would be left for Rose to talk to? Who would stay by her side, besides nurses?

She knew she was being defeatist, but she'd seen the face of the woman crawling to her, and the face may have been her mother's, and it may have been her own.

Rose heard a noise outside, took one final drink to fortify herself. Then, she strode to the front door, pushing it open. The women were approaching from far away. This time, with wind and rain and darkness in her eyes, she watched them come.

Once they had gotten nearly to the door, Rose leaped forward and ran outside. She bolted past them, their boney, grabbing hands, through the slick, sharp grass of the field, into the forest. Blades of grass sliced at her legs, and thin ribbons of blood blossomed down her calves. The women screamed in layers, shrieking as she darted through the woods.

The lake was in sight. Her lake. Not the still lake of a dead world but a swaying, living body of water teeming with life even under the grey and black sky. The women were nearly on top of her once more. Rose thought of everything—the pain, feeling inconsequential, needing people who did not need her, and with a final scream, she ran down the dock and leapt with her full body into the dark waters. In the last moment as she fell towards the water, she saw her mother, laughing, her arms stretched out wide to welcome her. She screamed, her body suddenly struggling against its own leap, as she crashed into the lake.

It seemed so sudden that she opened her eyes once more. It was morning. How was that possible? She remembered dying, or at least something like dying. She breathed a sigh of relief to know she had survived the night. Yet, when she looked down, she saw that she was dressed all in white, like the women from the water's edge. Thick black liquid lapped against the walls of her bedroom. She was soaked all the way through, covered in it. The phone rang again. Rose opened her mouth to cry out, but hands rose up from the water, gripping her arms and legs. They pulled her down, under the oily surface, deeper and deeper. Darkness fell over her, and for long, terrible moments, everything was excruciatingly silent.

In another world, rising from a dead lake under a great black sky, she dragged herself to the shore. She collapsed on the sharp rocks, and screamed, and sobbed, and ripped at her own flesh. Through the reflection of the lake, she could see herself on the other side, picking up the phone and calling Elizabeth to come home. She looked away, burying her face in her hands, unwilling to watch any longer. The petrified trees did not move with the breeze. Except for her, there was no sound. In this dead world, she was alone, and every noise she made, it came out backward.

KRISTI DeMEESTER

A
RITUAL
FOR
PLEASURE
AND
ATONEMENT

I STOPPED eating on a Sunday.

It felt right. That most holy of days; the purging of fleshly desire laid bare on an altar of my own making. If there was any God lingering in the holy dust I carried in my lungs, I could taste nothing other than the emptiness I would craft for myself.

So I balanced the final bit on the edge of my knife and pressed it against my tongue, wishing I could pass the serrated blade into my throat again and again and just be done with it. But my fingers were disobedient, clumsy things, and instead I smiled at Michael and chewed like a good boy, all white straight teeth and perfectly combed hair, and made a small sound that was something like appreciation.

Michael drained the last bit of his Bloody Mary and smiled back. Later, he would taste of tomato and pepper, and I would hold my breath when he kissed me because I could never abide either of the flavors coating his tongue. In my mind, I would repeat the prayers I'd learned as an altar boy; the names of the flaming angels who stood watch over the earth tumbling forth as a litany to hold up as our bodies carried on in the act of memorization of the other. Every curve. Every muscle. Every bone. All of it parceled out in the dark, our breath coming heavy and fast. Michael had started to keep his eyes screwed shut tight when he came. I told myself it wasn't because he couldn't bear to look at me anymore or the extra thirty pounds I'd gained over the past six months.

There had been a previous starvation. In college, halfway through my junior year, I spent the winter learning to hate myself, and the solution was so easy. So simple. I'd spent my life denying my body all the things it wanted. The good Catholic son. The finality of that last bit of food was not so different as the clandestine sweat of my carnal desire for muscled, sinful bodies.

Michael and I left whatever new, trendy restaurant it was and walked to our house with the backs of our hands touching. It was something Michael liked. This barest form of intimacy. Our cells dying off and commingling at this surface level. Once, I'd teased him that his form of romance was nothing more than an obsession with the macabre, and he'd bared his teeth at me, a ghoul's moan rattling out of his throat followed by the explosive laughter that had made me fall in love with him.

For six years I'd loved him, and now I'd grown to hate the body I laid down next to him at night. The stinking organs inside of it, how they stuttered through their steps, the necessary operations of drawing blood through my heart, oxygen through my lungs. I'd begun to wake before Michael to watch myself in the mirror, the pale violet and verdant blur of my veins a reminder of the wet slop of my heart. I would close my eyes and hear it, the dull rush of blood, and I would have to turn and quietly vomit into the sink.

I would run the water over my hands until they stopped shaking and then go to the window and watch the trees. How they bent under the weight of the vanishing moon. How there seemed to be things moving beneath them. How they seemed to be the portions of myself I wanted to erase. How I could not hear but knew they whispered their approval of this lightening, and this was how I arrived at my decision. How I knew that it was time again. To end. To stop. To waste as I had once before. There had been a kind of ecstasy at the end of that last time. A beautiful delirium. I could replicate that moment. That feeling. I could.

That afternoon, Michael put on a movie—a worn copy of *The Pillow Book* because Ewan McGregor went full frontal in it—and groaned about the bloat in his stomach, how he'd need to spend extra time on the treadmill, and I nodded along with him.

"I think I'll skip dinner. Too full," I said, and he agreed, and there was no question from Michael. No concern for the beginning of my starvation. We were worried about the appearance of our bodies. About the extra five pounds. About a beer gut. For Michael, purging had everything to do with vanity, and I knew his disgust would mask itself behind support.

I woke again in the early morning and told myself I would not go and stare in the mirror, but of course I did, all the while wishing when I stared into that darkened glass I would see the future of my body. The hollowed cheeks. The sharpened jaw. But there was only the face I'd come to despise, and I pressed my fist to the glass, my teeth bared.

Behind me, the window beckoned, and there were those whispering things in the trees, but I could only focus on the indelicate, ugly machinations of my body. How it was a thing to be spilled in the dirt. Unworthy and hideous. Still, I could not keep myself from turning away from that reflected hatred and looking out.

What had once lain in shadow was now illuminated. Pale, bloated forms drifted, seeming to search for something on the ground. Bent low, they moved slowly; their heads—if that's what they were—twitching side to side as they searched. Whatever they were, they should not have been, and I turned away, my hand clamped over my mouth so I would not cry out. It seemed important that whatever moved out there in the dark did not hear me.

Michael slept on in our bed, and I placed myself beside him, my eyes open so I would not fall into slumber and see those *things* creeping beneath the trees in a dream. And I told myself that was what I'd seen. The vestigial remnants of a dream. Nothing more.

The next morning, I rose and showered without glancing in the mirror—even by accident—and left before Michael could wake up and make us breakfast.

At work, I sat in front of my computer and drifted—the screen blurring and then snapping back into focus—as I thought of the shadows. Of their slow movements and of my fear. How it outweighed the sharp hunger that had already stolen its way into my belly.

I had not stayed at the window long enough to see what the shadows were looking for. If they were even real or if they were only things I had dreamed up. Pareidolia in its finest form.

During an afternoon meeting, I drew the creatures on my notepad, but they were poor approximations. On paper, there was nothing frightening about their mass. It was that slow creeping, the heads twitching without revealing a mouth or a set of eyes that I could not stop envisioning. And always the low susurrus of their whispers and my curiosity. My longing to know what it was they were saying.

As I sat through the remainder of the afternoon, I wondered how long it would take my body to die. I wondered if I would be able to stop myself before anything went too far. I had before, but there had been talk of hospitals. My mother's face drawn up in concern, and my father's visible disappointment filling the room like a heavy vapor.

At home, I sat beside Michael and watched the television without comprehending anything.

"Any thoughts on dinner?" he asked without removing his gaze from whatever bullshit cooking show was on. It was a conversation we were always having. The mundane need of stuffing our bodies and then performing some awful form of penitence later. Squats. Pull ups. A 10K on the treadmill. Our bodies as performance and temptation.

"I think I ate something weird at lunch. Haven't felt right since. But you go ahead," I said, and he nodded but stayed on the couch.

"I've been thinking about intermittent fasting. Nothing from eight p.m. to noon. Jeremy said he lost fifteen pounds in a month."

"That's crazy," I said and pictured what it would look like if my kidneys failed. If they would shrivel. Yellowed or blackened or sludgelike and peeling off proteins into my bloodstream. If it would be my kidneys or my gallbladder that would go first. My body dissected and pinned open, the skin butterflied and exposed to the chilled air of some coroner's examination room as they tried to discover exactly what added up to my end.

Michael pinched his belly and shook it. "I used to have a six pack."

I didn't respond because he didn't expect me to, and there was a part of me that understood that underneath the commentary of his own failings, there was the more obvious subtext of his criticisms of me. The evening wore on, and I imagined Michael fucking Jeremy, their skins flushed with blood, the dark interior of their mouths stinking with rot, their tongues flopping like pink worms as they licked stubbled stomachs. Michael was absorbed in his phone, so he didn't notice when I darted from the couch to the bathroom, the exhaust fan barely covering the retching that brought up only bile and saliva. Outside the window and under the tree, the figures clustered together, bent low as always but unmoving as if in prayer. Like some dark sabbat.

I pressed my forehead against the glass, but there was no coolness there, and I wondered if I had a fever. If what I was seeing was nothing more than my body reacting to my self-imposed starvation. Maybe Jesus never saw the Devil during the forty days and nights of his temptation. Maybe it was only his mind crafting evil out of the earth molded by his own hands. Maybe I was doing the same, and the creatures were devils of my own making.

Perhaps the figures were prostrate out of reverence. Perhaps they worshipped something that lived beneath the trees or was buried inside the earth. Or it was possible their bent shapes were nothing more than a request. Prayers of thanksgiving and prayers of need often fall from the same lips.

I giggled at the inanity of my own thoughts. They weren't real. Those creatures with their bodies flush with the earth. Yet here I was inventing stories for them. Scriptures of obedience outlining their behavior. They weren't real, but I was determined in my hunger to make them so.

Slowly, I pushed the window open. Just a crack. Just to let the air in. Not to listen to the quiet. Not to listen to see if I could discern the meaning of those syllables, those whispers. Never that. But the creatures were silent. There were no whispers, no sounds, and disappointed, I closed the window. Even in its emptiness, my stomach churned, and I thought I would vomit again, but I held my breath and listened for the chatter of the television, and when I looked again at the window, the forms were standing once more. Immediately, my skin prickled.

I could see their faces.

There were no eyes. Only mouths. Dark openings gaping inside mounded flesh. Together, they closed and then opened again, and I scrambled backward and slammed into the sink countertop, my hands fumbling behind me for the door, for anything that would take me away from seeing those mouths opening and opening and opening. Hungry in the way I could never be again.

Behind me, the door rattled, Michael calling my name in concern. "The hell was that? You okay?"

I drew in a ragged breath and forced my eyes away from the window. "I'm fine. Just dropped something," I said. I checked the window again, and the forms had bent back toward the earth, their mouths hidden, their whispers still silent.

I splashed water on my face. Rinsed my mouth and spat, unable to look at the sink to see the blood I imagined would be there. When I opened the door, Michael had already parked himself back in front of the television, and he lifted his head as I approached, but his eyes didn't leave the screen. If he had looked, if he had really seen me, could he have seen the imprints of those things? Could he have seen the small openings in my flesh, the skin flayed and pulsing with their squirming bodies as they pushed further and further into the meat of my wasting organs?

"I'm tired," I said, and Michael grunted, his face uplifted for the expected goodnight kiss, and I bent, passed the tip of my tongue over his lips in the movement that told him everything was fine. Everything was normal. He laughed and drew me closer, but when my body did not respond, he sighed and pulled away.

"Sleep tight," he said, and I turned, willing my body to not tremble until I was behind our bedroom door, my head buried beneath the covers as I had when I was a child and woken from the depth of a nightmare.

I was practicing my death through starvation, but still the monsters had found me.

No amount of playing dead would keep them away.

I slept fitfully, waking as Michael turned over in his sleep, his arm flung around me, my body sweating under the covers. In the morning, I should have felt hollowed out. My body an automaton with darkened skin under its eyes, the whites threaded through with red. Weakened and lethargic with lack of food and sleep. But I rose, and my body bent and stretched, and my heart counted out its beats with health and fervor, and I was thinner, but death had not marked me, and I tore at the thin cage of skin over my ribs and screamed silently behind clenched teeth, understanding then that what the creatures were whispering was not prayer or worship.

It was a ritual.

I left without showering. Even in daylight, I could not go back into the bathroom, could not face that window. As I backed out of the driveway, Michael waved from the front porch, and I pulled my lips back from my teeth, hoping that in the glare of the windshield, he would interpret it as a smile.

Through intersections and red lights and stop signs and then highway traffic, I could see only the creatures—those sightless faces lifted toward the dark of the moon. Even as the hair of my arms lifted, there was a portion of the vision I recognized. As if the scene that had unfolded the night before was something lifted from another point in my life. By the time I climbed out of my car, I could feel the dim outline of it, aware in the back of my mind but fluttering about in the way déjà vu strikes and then evaporates.

Tucked inside my cubicle, I powered up my computer and wished for the enervation I should have had by that point. Three days without food should have left me fatigued and confused, but my body felt lithe and my mind clear as I typed into the search engine already knowing what I would find.

When I was twenty, when I'd last starved myself, I'd studied abroad in London. A single, summer semester filled with droning professors and too many cigarettes to mitigate the hunger. On the weekends, I let myself gobble hash cakes with the other students in my cohort—the only calories I'd allow past my lips—and wandered through the city, high and laughing at how absurd it was that we existed in this moment. That was how we found ourselves stoned out of our minds and standing in the National Gallery. A girl named Martine had declared herself my personal chaperone and dawdled behind me in her dowdy peasant dresses and scuffed combat boots. She had a pale mustache that she touched the tip of her tongue to constantly, and she smelled of melted butter. Her presence made me even more paranoid, but I couldn't tell her to go. It felt like kicking a wounded dog, and I was so wounded myself. It felt good to at least have some form of attention paid to me even though I'd still been fifteen pounds shy of my goal.

She trailed me through the exhibits, and I lurched from painting to painting, trying to peer past the swirls and stiffened acrylics into something deeper, but Martine was a distraction. The deep odor of her seeped in and darkened my high so that by the time I came to the Salvatore Rosa's, it felt as if I was wearing my skin inside out, and every color was blood-tinted.

After, when I was back in the dorms and coming down, I told myself it was the drugs combined with the lack of food; the paranoia of Martine at my back, her fingernails snarled in the loops of my sweater and her breath heavy on the back of my neck. Told myself I had not seen the painting—Rosa's *Witches at Their Incantations*—move, the colors rippling and the forms turning to look out at me with faces that seemed to have no eyes. Told myself the nude, pallid witch seated in the center had not turned her fleshy body toward me, her hands splayed before her as she lifted her head to reveal an empty, cavernous mouth. Told myself the cowled face in the background had not flung itself outward in a quick, skittering motion; that the decayed corpse swaying on its rope had not begun to climb down.

Stumbling backward, I'd knocked Martine to the ground and left her there, blubbering with a bloodied nose, as I fled back to the dorms. When the sun finally rose, I was still terrified but had at least forced myself to somewhat believe that what I'd seen had not been real. But I'd never looked at the painting again. Too afraid that I'd see again what I saw all those years ago even if it had only been a hallucination.

But seated in my office, I waited for the image of the painting to load and curled my fingers against my palm to keep them from trembling. On my screen, the pixels did not bend, did not bloat to become anything other than what was set down in paint so long ago. If there was anything of nightmare in the image, it remained locked in the past.

Still, I was frightened. The pale witch. It was her body I'd recalled—the dim subconscious calling it forth. Those creatures in the backyard looked so much like broken versions of her hunched form. It had taken their movement, the revelation of their amorphous faces, for me to understand the sharpened edge of my breathless fear. Those faces had turned. And they had seen me. The same ones that had stared out from the painting when I was in college when my starvation had reached its apex. I'd dismissed the vision then, but I understood as I stared at my computer that I shouldn't have.

I pressed my face to the screen until the colors bled together and then closed my eyes. Around me, the air grew hotter, but I could not open my eyes. Knew that if I did, I would turn to see the witch behind me, her fingers trailing over the carpet as she traced sigils and signs into fibers, and looming over her, the cowled form with its arms outstretched before it fell upon me, mouth open and tongue worming damply over my neck and jaw.

I grew up believing in the Devil. In the possibilities of demons possessing the unsuspecting and wayward sinner. How their arms and legs would contort, their throats bulging with obscenity. I grew up believing that fasting was a way of purging the body for greater spiritual transcendence. Daniel had done it. Christ himself had done it.

But this was not what I was doing. I had not gone seeking any kind of spiritual rebirth either then or now. It was the messy churning of my organs, the slippery meat of me that I could no longer abide. I had not drawn the creatures forth with prayer or piety, yet they had appeared once more.

Through lunch, I kept my face close to the computer screen and my hand cupped against my ribs as I followed the painted lines of the witches' bodies. No one bothered me. No one offered anything other than silence. I wondered if that was how my body was feeding itself. On the silence of so many unasked and unanswered questions and the ease with which people see only what they want to see. How wasting away was something worthy of either admiration or apathy, and where the people around me passed me over, the creatures—these witches—had followed me into this second famine.

Perhaps they saw something in me worth paying attention to. Perhaps in my wasting, they could sense something more. Only those whose poverty starved them were worthy of burning. So much of history taught us that.

I left work early and drove home where Michael was not and likely would not be for the duration of the night.

Happy Hour at Salted Pig. Wanna come?

He'd texted while I was driving, and I ignored it. Figured he would forget the lack of my presence after his next gin and tonic and come stumbling home in the early morning with the ghost of an apology on his lips.

Instead, I drove home and waited for the sun to set.

Outside, I sat at the base of the tree, my back pressing into the bark, my legs planted in the earth as I formed and then dismissed the questions I wanted to ask the witches.

Why had they come? Why was I not hungry like I had been before? Why was I not dying when that was what I had gone seeking?

But they did not come that night. The night fell around me, the damp creeping up from the ground, and I sat alone. If I breathed in their remainders, it did not sit in my lungs as a slow, aching rot. Before Michael was home, I was inside and tucked under the covers, drifting in and out dreams I would never remember.

———

"You were whispering last night." Michael was pouring coffee into the green, chipped mug he always used, the sugar bowl defiantly ignored because he'd overindulged the night before and was determined it wasn't going to throw off his diet. "You want me to make you a cup?" he said, and I shook my head, my hand over my chest.

"Heartburn. What was I whispering?"

"Just a bunch of random words. Didn't make any sense."

"Like what?"

"You said something about tongues. Like...about tongues being useless muscles? And then something about trees. I dunno. Must have been some weird-ass dreams."

"Yeah. Must have been," I said, and he kissed me with the corner of his mouth. Noncommittal. Absentminded. An afterthought of love. How long had I been gathering these mediocre scraps, telling myself they were a feast?

Michael showered, did his hair, spritzed his Tom Ford cologne three times into the air and then walked through it, and I dressed without letting him see my body. Inside the closet, I bent over at the waist and breathed in deeply and erratically, filling my lungs until I thought they might burst, and then stood up with a jerk, waiting for the dark spots on the edge of my vision, waiting for the rush of blood to leave my head, waiting for an indication that the portions of myself that had gone without food were beginning the inevitable process of shutting down, but nothing happened.

I did not go to work but parked twenty minutes away at a chain coffee shop that smelled too much of heated breakfast sandwiches and too little of coffee. My stomach should have been lurching inside of me; my body responding without regard for my will in the face of the greased scent of bacon and eggs and carbohydrates. But it was still. Dead. I pressed a palm against my chest to be certain my heart was still beating. It was, but it was a dull flutter, as if an insect had crawled into my chest and become trapped there, calcifying into an approximation of a heart and pushing what little blood remained up to my stuttering brain. I took my hand away and drew a breath and pushed it out and then turned the car around and drove back home.

I didn't think the creatures, the witches, whatever they were, would appear during the day, but I wanted to sit again where they had sat, to breathe in what they had breathed, to press my body to the earth where they had supplicated themselves. Perhaps there would be some remainder, some portion of their ritual they had left behind, and I could catch it, burning and bright, up in my hands and examine it until they revealed themselves to me. Stepping out of the ether to gather me to their bloated breasts, to feed me with their mouths until everything else had flooded out of me, voided into the air to stink and become corruption in a way that had nothing to do with their blessed acts of cleansing.

Beneath the tree, I lay prostrate, my face pressed into the grass and rocks and exposed roots, and closed my eyes.

My throat. My stomach. My organs. My blood. Empty. Empty. Empty.

This was my own incantation. My own ritual. Without an altar. Without a living sacrifice other than what should have been my own failing body fumbling through the motions of existence.

If the appearance of the witches was supposed to be a harbinger, I was impatient for the personal apocalypse it should have heralded. My heart turned to ash, my blood immolated and scattered as so many seeds. If I pressed myself hard enough, would the earth open its maw and devour me whole? Would the witches take my limited body and transmute it into something worthy? As I sat, the want—the *need*—for them to come, to make me anew grew larger until it was a warped kind of pain.

I did not open my eyes when the whispering began. It could have been only the wind, and I did not want to open them and see only disappointment. There were no discernible words, only the small, glottal clicks of consonants followed by small sighs and then inhalations.

Time passed, but I wasn't sure how much. The light seemed to fade and then darken even though not enough time had passed for night to fall. I opened my mouth and tore at the earth with my teeth. Swallowed and ate. Perhaps this was some form of communion. Some form of acceptance.

It burned going down and dropped heavily into my belly, anchoring me there, holding me with a tenderness and fierceness I'd only ever felt on the brink of orgasm. Was it possible for the body to die without experiencing weakness? Without the gradual slowing of the heart and the final, shuddering moments as everything shut down, blinked off, cut out piece by piece until there were only the still animate nerves causing twitching fingers?

If magic was a force that fruited hidden desire, was that what the witches had felt in me? The fevered burning of my body a beacon and then this second, more absolute resolution of starvation the very thing that finally set the final step of their ritual into motion. If I were to open my eyes, would I see a full, heavy moon set too low in the sky? Would I see pale, amorphous forms drifting through the air, their horrible mouths open in silent screams as they went hunting for something to gnash between their teeth?

Michael would come home and go inside and never think to look for me beneath the tree. There had never been any significance to that rough bark, to that scattering of leaves on the grass. Outside, I would grow lighter until the witches, the creatures, could cradle me in their arms as their whispers dripped over my emaciated form like honey and only then would I gather enough strength to rise as something new. Perhaps I would return to Michael and press my mouth to his and pour into him everything I had learned. Beneath me, he would choke and gibber under the weight of those transformative syllables, and when the tears fell down his cheeks, the water would taste only of gratitude and nothing of fear or confusion or regret or hunger.

Above me, something creaked. A limb bent under weight. I envisioned one of the witches creeping through the branches, her fingers spread wide as she dropped lower and lower toward the earth. Thought of her coming to stand over me and then crouching to taste what little my wasted flesh could provide. Such an inconsequential, foul offering.

But I had done what I could to cleanse myself even if I hadn't understood at first that was what I was doing, and I hoped for at most their forgiveness and at least their repulsion.

"Take me. Take me," I said, and something settled next to me and exhaled. Still, I could not open my eyes. Still, I could not bring myself to look upon what I had called forth with my self-fashioned deprivation.

When they parted my lips with fingers cool and smooth as the stones at the bottom of a lake, I let them push past my teeth, my tongue. Let them reach deeper until they scraped the back of my throat. They smelled, tasted, of nothing or of an early morning wind in the winter when the ice has not yet cracked under the weight of the waking world.

With their hands, they fed me portions of themselves. I kept my eyes closed. It was the only thing I could imagine.

The witches neatly drawing themselves open and then offering me the communion of their blood. Perhaps this was what I'd been approaching my entire life. This disgust with my body leading me toward a new kind of satiation that could only be delivered once they'd seen me emptied of the physical.

They whispered, but the words carried no meaning. There was only the eating. The rough stroke of their hands. The ache in my jaw. I would have nothing else. Let it all be obliterated. Let it all crumble. The witches had seen me once and had bided their time, but I could not wait any longer now that I understood. I gasped and swallowed and waited for a command, wishing I had known to listen for it. Wishing I had begun my starvation so much sooner. So many years wasted as I fought against my need. Against my nature. But no more.

I cried out. I lifted my hands. I willed my flesh to fall away. To rise and take the place the witches had made for me. To become more than the limitations I'd been born into. More than the altar boy. The shamed son. The excommunicate. The failed, cuckolded lover. The starved.

The whispers dropped away. The hands withdrew.

I opened my eyes.

There was the tree. The earth. But there was nothing more.

I ran my tongue over my gums, hoping to find their taste, a lingering scent, anything that would prove they'd been with me, but there was nothing.

I did not scream but waited under the tree until I heard Michael's car out front and then drifted inside, accepting his kiss but feeling nothing, hearing nothing, until he left again. I wasn't sure for where.

For five nights I waited for Michael to sleep and then slipped outside to sit beneath the tree, my eyes closed as the wind played over my naked body. But the witches did not come. The air held no whispers. The nocturnal creatures shrieked to one another, but there was no absolution in their sounds.

Still, I took no food. In the shower, my hair had begun to fall out, and my hips appeared bruised, but I felt none of

206 ★ KRISTI DEMEESTER

the typical effects of hunger. Michael told me he was jealous. He'd never seen me look better. He'd never wanted me more.

Would it have been enough before the witches came to me? Would Michael's frenzied rutting, his need laid so raw and bare, been enough to sate me?

Ten nights. Eleven. I slept but there was not even the comfort of a dream where the witches finally came to me.

On the twelfth morning, Michael rose early and kissed me goodbye, his hands exploring the new angles of my body. He marveled. He groaned. There were too many hours to get through before he could touch me again. I smiled, my tongue pushing against an incisor that had begun to come loose.

"Not much longer now," I said, and he kissed me again, swearing that if he was late to work it was my fault. How could he be expected to do anything productive when I had a body like that?

But he did leave, and I listened to the thick silence of the house. Wandered from room to room until I no longer recognized the items that sat inside of them.

It hadn't been difficult to gather what I would need. A single trip to the hardware store. Payment in cash. A crumpled ten-dollar bill pushed across the counter. The plastic bag not even hidden but resting on the kitchen table, the receipt folded beside it. Michael had not noticed. Had not asked. Later, I knew he would not remember seeing the bag or what it held.

Outside, I stood beneath the tree and closed my eyes for the last time. Should I have prayed then? Would the witches have even responded if I had? For a count of thirty I waited, and when there were no whispers, I opened my eyes and went back into the house.

The chair was light but sturdy. One of the four from the dining set I'd brought with me when we moved into the house.

Around me, a nimbus of heat blossomed, but I had forgotten the singular dominion of my physical body—how it fights, how it longs to not be extinguished!—and there was only the symbolic cord about my neck, and the hanging tree, and the leaves skittering as I took a breath and then another.

It was only right to do this. To join the witches in their filial death. To hope they would see and understand what I was willing to give.

Did they fear before the fall? Did they wonder at the dark expanse that opened under their feet, at the Reverend's promised hell licking upward to swallow them up?

I feared my body would be too light, but there was the rush of air, the momentary sensation of weightlessness as the ground rushed upward.

In the moments before darkness, I waited for the whispers.

As the rope caught, as it held as it had held for every other witch, for every other person prepared to shed the weight of the body, the silence had never felt so infinite.

TIM MAJOR

THE
SLOW
KING

CAMPBELL'S

dad watched him from beyond the cordon, through the gap between catering vans. Reluctantly, Campbell raised his hand—a motionless salute rather than a wave—but his dad's eyes continued to scan from side to side.

Campbell jammed his hands in the pockets of the padded gilet he had been forced to wear. He surveyed the collection of makeshift tents. Their interiors glowed red with light from large electric bar heaters.

"Excuse me," he said to a middle-aged woman hurrying in the other direction, "do you know where Laine is?"

"Kid, I don't know where anyone is." The woman brandished a folded sheet of paper. "But if I don't get these new lines to Kier's trailer in the next few minutes then I'll be taking a turn up there myself." She nodded at the two metal cages that hung from the tree at the foot of the hill. They were the shapes of birdcages but each big enough to hold a person. A stepladder had been placed below one of them and a man in a day-glo tabard was testing the metal bars of the cage.

Campbell trudged across the space between tents, where boardwalks with raised treads had been placed over the wet grass. He wondered how long he'd have to stay before he could legitimately return to his dad and say that he hadn't been needed after all. His dad wouldn't be happy. This was a big opportunity, he had said.

"Is there anything I can do to help?"

Campbell turned in the direction of the voice. This woman was young but the lines on her forehead suggested she was a

212 & TIM MAJOR

natural worrier. Her wide eyes made Campbell imagine her as a burrowing creature unused to direct light.

"I was looking for Laine," he replied. "Laine Owen?"

The woman laughed, though not unkindly. "You do realise how in demand he is right now?"

Campbell shrugged.

"Sorry," she said. "Why would you know that? Stupid Ruth. I don't talk to children often." She held out her hand. "I'm stupid Ruth."

"I'm Campbell." He shook her hand, enjoying the maturity of the action.

She tilted her head. "Really? How appropriate. Anyway, you'll have your work cut out if you want to speak to Laine—he's got folks lined up to get his approval on any number of decisions. And directors just love making people wait. It's all a power trip. What do you need him for? He's not your dad, is he?"

"He came to my school. Him and a woman, but I don't know her name. He asked if any of us wanted to be in his film and then he ended up picking me."

Her face lit up. "Really? That's pretty cool. I was told I could be in it, too, but the only thing on offer was 'flirtatious wench' and I told them it just wasn't me. But I'm hoping I'll end up at the back of a crowd scene at some point. Is that what you'll be doing, too? Or is it a *part* part?"

Campbell felt his cheeks glow. "It'll sound like a big thing when I say it, but it isn't. I don't have to speak. I've never acted before, except in the school Nativity."

"Hit me."

"Apparently I'm going to be the 'Slow King'."

Ruth's wide eyes became even wider. "Serious?"

"That's what Laine Owen said."

"You're the eponymous Slow King?"

Campbell grimaced. His dad used long words like that, then got crabby when Campbell didn't follow. "What does that mean?"

"Shit. Sorry, I'm just demonstrating my ineptness with kids, aren't I? And sorry for saying 'shit', too. You're too young for that sort of language."

"I'm twelve."

"Yeah." She sucked her cheeks. "'Eponymous' means giving your name to something. I'm guessing you haven't been told the title of the film yet?"

"I wasn't told anything. They got in touch with my parents and my dad sorted it all out."

"The film's called *The Slow King*."

They looked at each other for a while.

"Don't go quiet on me, kid," Ruth said. "You're my only friend here."

Campbell blinked. "I was just wondering whether maybe it was the title that got Dad interested. He always says that films are rubbish these days. But 'slow king' is sort of our joke because it's what we call chess."

"That's not much of a joke."

"All right, not a joke. But I called chess 'slow king' back when my dad taught me how to play, because the king can only take one step at a time. I was only maybe four, though."

"He taught you to play chess when you were four?" Ruth said with a smirk.

Campbell nodded and thrust his hands back into his pockets. "Dad thinks it's important to learn new skills and get really good at them. He says life demands a lot and you have to be prepared."

The way Ruth was looking at him made him feel uncomfortable. He blew on his hands and folded his arms.

"We'd best announce you," she said, turning. "Hey! Anita! I present to you the Slow King."

A woman in a nearby tent, who was sitting on a canvas chair and leafing through a stack of papers, looked up. Her eyes travelled over Ruth and then Campbell without interest. "Didn't you hear? Everything's delayed. Laine woke up this morning with a thunderclap of an idea which I've no no doubt must be evidence of artistic genius, but which also means everything's been back-to-front from the off. We're not doing the Slow King scene 'til one at the earliest."

Campbell looked at his watch. It was only half past ten.

Ruth rolled her eyes. She gave the woman a half-hearted thumbs-up, then put an arm around Campbell. "You brought your parents along with you, I suppose?"

"My dad. Even though he said he can't imagine anything worse than hanging around on a film set."

"Sounds like a riot, your dad. Let's go find him."

When they returned to the cordon, Campbell could see no sign of his dad. The car was gone, too.

"Don't fret," Ruth said. "He'll have popped into town, assuming you'd be busy for a while."

Campbell nodded uncertainly.

"How about you and I hang out while we're waiting for your big scene?" she said.

"Don't you have things you need to do?"

Ruth gave a hollow laugh. "Hardly. I've been given the grand title of Historical Adviser, but from day one it's been clear that an accurate depiction of eleventh-century society isn't precisely what floats Laine's boat. There are three stunt coordinators on set, for goodness' sake. The most dramatic sort of event in Yorkshire in 1020 would have been, I don't know, a fight over a pig. Commoners weren't all performing parkour in their spare time. Anyway, I'm being paid to hang around on set but I swear nobody's asked my opinion even once—so a little company is more than welcome, Campbell."

A thought occurred to him. "Why did you say my name was appropriate, before?"

Ruth grinned. "Come on, Slow King. I'll show you."

The metal boardwalks continued beyond the tents and trailers, leading to the foot of the hill. The man in the day-glo tabard was now standing at the foot of the stepladder, holding it steady as another person climbed up. The climber shrugged off his long duffel coat. Underneath he wore only a tattered loincloth and his body was covered in lesions and mud. He hunkered inside the metal birdcage, pulled the door to, shuffled on his haunches a little and then gave a double-thumbs-up to the man standing below.

Further along, Campbell saw the roofs of shacks. As he and Ruth climbed the hill a group of people came into view, standing in the centre of the ring of tumbledown huts. They wore rough, dark outfits and their boots sunk into the thick mud. A cameraperson weaved in and out of the crowd, followed by a gaggle of people wearing wellington boots, thick jackets and woollen hats. A tall man holding a long pole with a microphone attached to its end reached over the heads of the other crew members, glancing down every few seconds to avoid losing his footing.

Ruth pointed at two people in the middle of the group of pretend villagers. "What did I tell you? They've both got fucking swords, for pity's sake. Sorry again for swearing."

"And that isn't how it would have been in the year 1020?"

"There'd have been no need for them. Farm tools, yes. Swords? No chance. And I've seen those things up close, at the props tent. They both look like Excalibur or the Sword of Grayskull or something. Worth more than everything else in the village combined. Un-bloody-believable."

But she was grinning, all the same. Campbell decided that he liked her very much.

"Anyway," she said. "Don't pop your head up again, otherwise you'll be in shot and we'll be in trouble. Over here's what I wanted to show you."

Further around the base of the hillock the slope became more pronounced, forming a natural passageway between the hillside and an area of sparse woodland. Campbell wondered whether the cart tracks on the ground had been made naturally, or whether the production team had created them for the film.

"They've been using this bit of track for filler scenes of journeys," Ruth said. She pointed at the side of the path. "There, take a look at that."

A large shard of stone protruded from the ground, a marker stone for travellers. Campbell bent to read the place names inscribed upon it.

A violent shudder passed through his body.

He reached out a finger to trace the letters. It wasn't real stone—perhaps fibreglass.

"You okay?" Ruth said. "I thought you'd get a kick out of it."

Campbell rose. He turned to her but couldn't speak.

Ruth pointed in the direction from which they had come. "See, that village is modelled after Campbell—or rather, the village that would later be known as Campbell. The sign's inaccurate because the settlement was so tiny it didn't even have a name in 1020, though that's the least of the historical facts that have been ignored on this film. Anyway, so you'll be Campbell the Slow King, in *The Slow King*, set in Campbell. Neat."

"But what about the other place?" Campbell said. His throat was dry and his voice didn't sound like his own.

Ruth frowned and looked at the two place names written on the fake marker stone. "They only built one of the villages for the film. Coombes is the next town along."

Campbell shook his head. "But it's my name."

Ruth stared at him as though he were an idiot.

Campbell gestured helplessly at the marker stone, indicating the top place name and then the bottom one. "Campbell Coombes. That's my name."

Ruth laughed, then stopped abruptly. "Really?"

"Really."

"That's...wow. I can't begin to imagine what the chances might be. You don't have links with Yorkshire, do you? Ever been to the East Riding, or have any family up there?"

Campbell shook his head. "I don't think so."

Ruth exhaled and rubbed her chin. "Weird, huh?"

"Yeah. Weird."

"You said your dad—"

"Yeah. Maybe my dad knew. Maybe he already told me. I don't always listen properly. My dad says sometimes it's like I'm just not there."

Ruth nudged his elbow. "Hey. You seem all right to me. And nobody listens to everything their parents say. What are you interested in?"

"I play lots of chess, and I'm having piano lessons—"

"That wasn't what I asked."

Campbell puffed his cheeks. "I like stories."

"Let me guess. Your dad doesn't approve?"

"He buys me information books. How the world works. He says I have to be prepared to be an expert in everything, if I want to make a success of my life. He says if I get myself properly ready there's nothing to stop me ruling the world."

"Hmm. What kind of stories?"

"Old ones. Stories about way back. Myths and legends."

"All *right*. Now you're talking my language."

"But I've never heard about the Slow King. Is it real?"

"It's a real story, which I suppose is what you mean. It's mentioned in hardly any books, to be fair. That makes these coincidences even stranger..." She trailed off, then shook her head. "My guess is that with this boom in Folk Horror films, they'll scour the history books for every last superstitious ritual Britain has to offer. Your man Laine thinks he's the next Piers Haggard."

Campbell nodded, though he barely understood what she had said. "Then what's the story?"

Ruth linked arms with him and pointed along the path. "Let's keep walking. The story of the Slow King is barely anything at all, but compelling all the same. A thousand years ago—it'll be literally one thousand years next year, when this stupid film will be thrust upon the cinema-going public—the residents of the-village-that-would-be-Campbell and the surrounding settlements suffered what I guess you might call a shared hallucination, a mass hysteria...Sorry, no, that's my analytical brain speaking. The actual story is that for whatever reason the population believed that one person among them

218 ≈ TIM MAJOR

was special—so special and so strange that he shouldn't be forced to live among them, or even live in the same era as them. They weren't idiots—they knew that their lives were close to meaningless, little more than basic survival. It seems they couldn't bear the thought that this special one among them would be forced to eke out the same kind of existence."

"What was special about the boy?"

Ruth smiled. "You're way ahead of me. Yes, this person was a boy. And it wasn't recorded quite what was so unusual about him. There are hints, though my Old English isn't too hot. I suppose nowadays you'd phrase it as the boy being ahead of his time."

"And they called him the Slow King."

"The name came later. Myths are created by the accrual of details and elaborations. The villagers didn't necessarily call him anything at all, when they conducted the ceremony."

Something registered in the periphery of Campbell's vision. He strode ahead, past tall metal poles topped with chunky unlit lamps. A bright yellow JCB blocked the path, the scoop on the end of its long arm lowered towards the hillside. Campbell thought it looked like a brontosaurus grazing.

"The team were way behind schedule digging it out," Ruth said. "They finished during the night, hence the floodlights."

Campbell kept walking until he stood facing the hillside where the digger's scoop touched. It had taken bites out of the earth, creating a hollow that was head height at its outer part, but became lower the further back it went. Campbell crouched but couldn't see all the way in.

"Is this where they did the ceremony?" he said.

Ruth's voice seemed to come from far away. "Sure. This is the recreation of the location. You can visit the real thing in the East Riding. I did try to explain that to Laine, but he was taken with the idea of all the location work being in this one spot. Probably there are a ton of financial reasons for that."

"And they put the boy in here?" Campbell said. Everything seemed to be growing darker, the longer he looked into the hollow. "Why?"

"Because the world wasn't ready for him yet."

"Because he was the Slow King." Campbell swallowed. His throat hurt, as though it was scalded. "What were they hoping would happen?"

"That he would be preserved ready for his right time."

"He'd get up and walk out of there?"

"It was more convoluted than that. They expressed it in strange ways. It wasn't so much as him rising, like Jesus after the Crucifixion. They said the boy himself would 'bring him into life'. Does that make sense?"

Campbell didn't turn from the hollow. "He would make himself alive again, just using his mind?"

Ruth hesitated before replying. "I suspect that this boy—whoever he was—his specialness may have been his ability to describe unusual things. Back then, sages were essentially storytellers. That would explain this assumed ability to simply imagine himself into being, when the time came."

Seconds passed in silence.

"But Campbell, none of that means—Oh hell."

Campbell rose and turned. "What? What's wrong?"

Ruth was staring up at the sky, her hands shielding her eyes. It was only now that Campbell realised that clouds had covered the sky and that it was raining. He shivered.

"The forecast was clear all week," Ruth said. She groaned. "This'll set things back. Let's dash back to the tents and see what the damage to the schedule will be."

Campbell glanced at the hollow.

Ruth was hopping from foot to foot, her body hunched. Her mousy brown hair had already turned black with wetness.

"You go," Campbell said. "I'll be along in a sec. I don't mind rain."

"Sure?"

"Yeah."

She hesitated. "Aren't I *in loco parentis* right now, or something? I'm sort of responsible for you."

Campbell put his hand on her shoulder and squeezed it. "I'll catch up with you. I promise."

Ruth frowned at his hand, but nodded slowly. "Okay then. Don't be an idiot and catch hypothermia, because then they'll pick another boy to bury."

With that, she turned and scurried back along the path.

Campbell crouched once more before the hollow and ignored the rain.

———————————————

He barely remembered the long walk home. His dad's car hadn't reappeared. Campbell didn't have a mobile phone and had never memorised either of his parents' numbers.

He was shivering from the cold as he trudged into the cul-de-sac. Rainwater made rivers that snuck under his shining gilet, his jeans were stiff with wetness and his feet squelched every time his shoes made contact with the pavement.

Both of his parents' cars were parked in the driveway to Number 12. Even if his dad had been shopping in town, why had he returned here rather than the film set?

He plodded up the steep driveway and onto the doorstep. He tried the handle but the door was locked. He had never been trusted with a key.

He pushed the doorbell. He waited twenty seconds, then pressed it again.

There were lights on in the sitting room.

The rain was too loud for him to hear the chime of the doorbell. Maybe the battery was flat. He rapped on the glass panel of the door, then again, louder.

He padded around the porch and into a narrow flowerbed, then pushed himself onto his tiptoes to peer through the window. His house was at the top of a rise, and from this low angle he could only see lampshades and the top of the wall-mounted flatscreen TV. He jumped into the air and landed with a nauseating slapping sound, his trainers sinking into the soil of the flowerbed.

In that brief glimpse he had seen figures. They were in the conservatory which adjoined the sitting room.

Sighing, he tramped to the wooden gate at the side of the house. It was locked, too. With some difficulty he scrambled up the sheer surface, using the hinge brackets as footholds. The upper edge of the gate was rough; splinters dug into his hands. He dropped down on the other side, landing badly and falling to the wet concrete. He tasted blood in his mouth—he had bitten his tongue. Wincing at the stinging sensation in his mouth and in the palms of his hands, he limped along the side of the building.

The back garden was impossible to make out in the growing gloom. Wasn't it only early afternoon? There must be a storm coming. He should get inside as soon as possible.

The light coming from the conservatory made a yellow halo on the surrounding paving stones. Through the glass walls Campbell could see three figures. His mother stood in the archway that led to the sitting room. Her arms were folded and she was watching two people who were seated opposite one another in wicker chairs, both looking down at a chess board on the coffee table between them.

At the far side was Campbell's dad. His hands were raised in a prayer pose. His index fingers smoothed his moustache again and again. It was his thinking posture.

Campbell couldn't tell who the other player might be. From the rear it appeared he was male, with short, fair hair. He was shorter than Campbell's dad, and leaner. The stranger reached forward and moved one of the chess pieces.

Campbell stumbled forwards. He rapped on the glass just as thunder sounded overhead. Inside the conservatory, the heads of his mum and dad and the stranger all shifted to glance at the roof. Campbell still couldn't see the stranger's face.

He knocked again. Nobody inside reacted and he couldn't hear the sound himself.

He waved his arms, trying to get the attention of his mother and father, both of whom were facing more or less in his direction. Neither responded.

Campbell strode onto the lawn. Now he stood perpendicular to the chess players and directly opposite his mother. The unknown chess player was a child, perhaps around Campbell's age. His head was bowed to the chess board.

"Mum!" Campbell yelled. But her eyes continued moving between her husband and the boy.

"Dad!"

His father tapped his lips twice, reached out to move a chess piece, then sat back in apparent satisfaction.

Campbell squinted at the boy. Was it one of his friends from school? He tried to think who might have called for him. He was shocked to realise that no names came to mind—of anyone in his class, let alone any of his friends. Getting drenched must have made him ill. He should be in bed.

Suddenly he felt very afraid.

He launched himself at the glass wall of the conservatory, battering on it with a fist.

His dad looked up again. Then he turned to Campbell's mum and said something that Campbell couldn't hear. His mum nodded and shielded her eyes to stare at the sky, shaking her head.

The boy seemed unaffected. He reached out a thin arm and moved one of the black chess pieces, then plucked one of the white ones from the board. Campbell was surprised to see that only the black king now remained.

Then, without any particular show of satisfaction, the boy turned from the chess board and looked out into the garden.

Where the boy's face ought to be was only a blurred streak, as though he were staring at Campbell from behind a rushing waterfall.

━━━━━━━━━━━━━━━

The woman gripped Campbell's neck, forcing him to look up at her.

Campbell stopped struggling and allowed her to continue dabbing at his face. She must be nearly finished. If Laine had explained that he would have to undergo all this time in make-up, Campbell would never have agreed to take the part.

"When will—"

The woman hushed him. He had forgotten to ask her name. Like Ruth, she must have been offered a part in the film. Her hair was matted and her face was plastered with fake grime.

He waited for her to finish. "When will it be time for my scene?"

She nodded patiently.

Campbell looked up at the black sky. "It was supposed to be one o'clock. Wasn't it supposed to be a daytime scene? Wasn't that what the director wanted?"

The woman only frowned at him.

The canopy that had been erected at the foot of the hillside was doing nothing to keep out the chill wind. Campbell wished that he had been offered one of the padded coats that reached to your feet, or at the very least the silver survival blankets that he seen the principal actors wearing around their shoulders between takes. His ragged shirt and hessian trousers weren't lined for warmth, and goosebumps had sprung up on every part of his body.

"Where's Ruth?"

The woman shrugged.

"Laine?"

The woman pointed over Campbell's shoulder. He turned, but the path was in total darkness.

"But I haven't been told what I should do."

The woman produced a cup and lifted it to his lips. He realised that he was very thirsty. He took a sip, but immediately spluttered and shook his head wildly until she took the cup away. The liquid wasn't hot but it had scalded his mouth and throat and left an awful, bitter taste.

He saw movement and looked up to see moving sources of light. What he had taken to be floodlights were actually flaming torches.

The make-up woman backed away into the darkness.

Campbell reached up to touch his face surreptitiously, not wanting to ruin the effect and have to endure the application of make-up all over again. His fingers came away sticky and dark. He rubbed the substance between his fingertips, then raised them to his nose. They smelled like blood.

Figures descended the hillside, stumbling on the slippery grass.

The torches they carried illuminated other people, who surrounded Campbell. How long had they been standing there in silence? They all appeared to be extras—at least, Campbell didn't see any of the lead actors: not Kier Franklin, who people said was a famous West End actor, and not Janice Eddington, who apparently had had a small part in one of the *Harry Potter* adaptations. He could see no crew members either, and no cameras.

One man strode forward at the front of the dozen or so new arrivals. He had a tangled beard and he held a heavy-looking wooden staff.

"Is he prepared?" he said in a deep, scratchy voice. Campbell was struck by the odd idea that these weren't the man's precise words, but only the sense of them.

"He is ready."

"I don't know if I'm ready, though," Campbell said. "I don't really know what I'm supposed to do. Nobody's spoken to me at all."

"You have spoken and we have listened," the man replied in his strange flat tone. "That is all that is necessary."

"But I'm not even a speaking part," Campbell said, his arms wide. "My dad said all I had to do was show up and be the Slow King. And I think he should probably be here right now, but his car's gone and I…" A vision came into his mind. He saw himself returning to his house only to find himself replaced with another boy. When had he fallen asleep, to dream that dream? In a quieter voice he said, "I'd like to see Ruth, please. She said something about *loco parentis*."

The circle of extras shuffled inwards.

The man with the beard held his flickering torch at arm's length. It shone on the hollow cut into the steep hillside. Where the JCB had stood was a tall tree. Its bent branches mimicked the arm and scoop of the machine.

The extras continued shuffling. Campbell moved, too, in order to remain in the centre of the ring. The idea of allowing any of them to touch him seemed unbearable.

"Laine Owen came to my school," Campbell said weakly. "He said I'd be taken care of. My mum and dad wouldn't have agreed to this if they knew I'd be left here without a...a..." A word he had heard on school trips occurred to him, though he was startled to find that he had no mental image of any school trip in particular, or the school building, or his teachers. "Chaperone."

The bearded man's lips parted to reveal filthy-looking teeth. "We do not understand your words, but we will fulfil our duties."

Campbell's eyes darted. Was it possible that the cameras were just beyond the circle, just beyond the firelight? Was it possible that this was the Slow King scene, right now? He had heard of filmmakers who sprung scenes on their actors at odd moments, to make the reactions seem less rehearsed.

But even if that was the case, this was surely wrong. He was only twelve years old.

"I shouldn't be left here alone," he said.

The man hesitated, then said, "These are your own wishes."

"I don't want this."

"In your tales you spoke of the need for this act. We are your servants." The man gestured with the torch, casting firelight onto the faces of the assembled people. Their faces were pockmarked. Amid the muck, Campbell saw scars and open wounds.

"We are your servants," they all said together.

"I shouldn't be left here alone," Campbell said again, helplessly.

An idea seemed to occur to the bearded man. "You will not be alone, my lord."

The words triggered something within Campbell. He began to cry.

The circle of people drew tighter around him.

The man with the tangled beard held up the torch to guide Campbell towards the hollow.

Campbell looked around at the actors. Their faces were harder to discern now, streaked through his tears.

He bowed his head.

He took a step backwards into the hollow, pressing himself against the damp earth. He crouched and then stretched his legs into the narrow part of the opening. His stomach dragged against the soil. He pushed himself into the dark.

The light of the torches diminished as the first handful of earth was thrown into the opening. Campbell heard singing or perhaps moaning.

He dropped his face to the black soil.

He prepared himself for the long wait.

TRACY FAHEY

DEARG-AN -DAOL

MEMORY is a place of shadows. It's a complex thing of sights and sounds and smells. I stand in the old kitchen, softly touching the pitted surface of the worktop. Everything is as I remember it—the dim red glow of the Sacred Heart painting, the lingering smell of smoky turf from the open fireplace, the pile of yellowed newspapers on the armchair, pages curling upwards like petals. A beetle runs over my foot, quick and oil-black. Then a second one darts across the floor, burying itself behind the gap in the skirting board. *Aithníonn ciaróg ciaróg eile.* One beetle recognises another beetle. I see it vividly, that poster of Irish proverbs in my old school classroom. But more than that, I recall the shape and feel of the memory. The primary colours of the poster; two jolly beetles facing each other over a table set for tea. I see it from the low vantage point of a tiny brown plastic chair, its back bolted to the metal frame with yellow plastic nuts. If I close my eyes, there's the smell of chalk; the feel of the cold sweat of condensation on the old walls…

I shake my head and turn on the light, dousing the kitchen in a hard glare. It seems to flinch, stains and cracks exposed. The old wall behind the cooker is tobacco-stained with the residue of a thousand meals. There's a faint smell of drains, and a dull, damp rot deep in the walls. I flip off the light, disconcerted. Outside the window, weeds grow high and wild. Between them is the rise of the old mound, the shimmer of the stream winding its way back into the woods behind the house. I touch the letter in my pocket, that poor, untidy scrawl that drew me back here. Memories rise again, blurred and incomplete; the stream glinting in the sun, the soft darkness of the trees, the tiny well, half-invisible with the rag-tree blooming over it. There's a queer emotion I can't identify; when I look too hard at it, it's gone. It's something like disquiet, a little fear, a sense of dismay at life coming full circle. I'm here again, in the one place I never dreamed of returning to.

Out of the corner of my eye I see a black flicker on the draining board. Another beetle. The sight tickles my memory. *Dearg-an-daol*, Uncle Sean used to call them.

———————————————

I sit by his bedside. It's morning, but in the intensive care unit, they relax the rules. The weak spring sun washes the windows. Sean is asleep. In the pale light, he looks smaller, shrunken. One hand trails outside the covers, blue-worm veins standing out against the spotted skin. The room is filled with his raspy wheeze. Next time I'll bring a book.

I sit on the lumpy hospital chair. The metal pokes up between the burst plastic covering. I think of that bright summer, so long ago. My mother, mysteriously sick, me staying with Uncle Sean. There's vague images of long grass, tall trees, the dark water of the well. He took me to a circus, I remember. There were tigers there, their faces an angry roar, and clowns with smeared faces.

Sean's hand twitches—once, twice—on the white sheet. I touch it because I feel I should. It's chilled and frail; it falls to one side under the press of my fingers.

My face is reflected in the polished steel of the machine. Dark hair, pale face, forehead bisected by a pink scar. Out of habit, I touch the puckered seam of the old wound. I see him then, clear in my memory; Uncle Sean looking down at me, his blonde hair ruffled in the breeze. We're in the woods. My clothes are wet.

His eyes are bright and clear in the sunlight. "Well, boy, you've gotten yourself in trouble here."

I blink and rewind the image, but no more memories surface.

———

Tonight the glass rattles in the old windowpane. The fire sputters into a kind of half-life; logs sparking and spitting in a shower of green stars. I stretch my hands out and feel the slow spread of heat around the kitchen.

Tomorrow, I think, *tomorrow I'll tidy up a bit*. The sink is full of half-washed dishes, the food remnants dried to a hard crust. The floors are streaked with mud I've tracked in from the woodpile. I remember the quiet evenings here, from that summer long ago. Me playing with my Dinky cars, Uncle Sean's face sunk behind the paper. The rustle as he put it down to check on me, the smile as he watched me scoot the cars around in complicated traffic patterns on the stone flags. If I concentrate I can almost believe I smell a pot of stew on the gas cooker, fragrant with slow-cooked beef, a scent thick with herbs from the garden.

I'm so absorbed in the memory that the sharp *rat-tat* of the knocker makes me jump.

"Anne." It's my sister. The biting wind lifts her hair, whips it around her head like snakes.

"Mark." She doesn't wait for an invitation, just pushes past. I step back and let her in. She pulls a chair over to the stove and sits there, hunched. Her back makes a sharp, angry angle.

"Hey. How are you?"

She doesn't answer for a moment. She picks up the poker and stirs the fire. The logs spark and hiss.

"What are you doing here?"

I shrug and sit down opposite her. "Sean wrote to me. He asked me to come and stay here. Come in to see him in hospital."

Her face is older, he realises. The lines around her eyes and mouth are sharp-etched in the firelight. "And that's why you're here." It doesn't sound like a question, but it is.

"Yeah. I should have come sooner, I know…I didn't realize he was so ill."

She clicks her tongue against the roof of her mouth—a hard, exasperated sound. "He's been sick for a long time. We've had to be in and out to him a lot this last year."

"Right." I don't know what I'm meant to say. A black beetle scurries across the floor, perilously near the grate.

"Remember Sean used to call them *dearg-an-daol?* What did that even mean? Red devils? Makes no sense. He used to tell me stories about them, the summer I spent here. Said they were cursed because they betrayed Jesus to the soldiers in the Garden of Gethsemane." I know I'm babbling nervously, but I can't stop. The memory is flooding back. "He told me that if you see one, you should stamp on them before they turn up their tail, and wish on them the curse of the seven deadly sins."

She lets my voice peter out, and then sits forward. "You needn't think there's any money.'"

It's so unexpected I can only stare. "What?'

"There's no money. There's only this place. This patch of land. And my Joe has been helping him on it this last ten years."

I feel a surge of anger. "I'm not here because of money."

She cocks her head. "Really, now? You just happen to be here when he's on his last legs? And me here, doing for him, cooking for him, looking after him all this time?"

I can't resist it. I look around at the dirty kitchen, the unwashed plates, the stained walls. "Looking after him?" I don't bother to hide the sneer in my voice.

She gets up then and stalks to the door. "It'll do you no good, sucking up to him at the last minute. You'll see." Her face is alive with spite.

"Don't let the door hit you on the way out."

She doesn't.

The machines hum and tick. Sean is still asleep. I look at his hair, pale and fine as a baby's. His limbs jerk and settle under the white covers. I feel that rush of unreality again; that such a tall, strong man can shrink down into such a small bundle of flesh and bone.

"Are you awake?"

At first there's no reaction. Then his waxen eyelids flutter. He blinks once, twice. His eyes are still the blue I remember, but the whites are yellowed, like those of an old horse.

"Mark." His voice is a breath.

I bend over him. "It's me, Uncle Sean. I've come down from Dublin like you asked." It sounds nobler than it is. I'm between jobs; it suited me fine.

"The house..."

I understand it's a question. "It's grand." I feel a flicker of guilt and promise myself I'll *definitely* tidy up when I get home. At least wash the dishes. "Just a few creepy crawlies. Nothing to write home about."

His eyes fix on me. "The *dearg-an-daol?*"

"Just a few in the kitchen." My voice is soothing.

"Watch them." His voice is a shade stronger now. "And watch...out the back."

I'm puzzled. "What about the back of the house?"

"Make sure...make sure you do all the things...the dirty water..."

I remember this from my summer with him. "Throw the dirty water outside the house?"

He stretches his mouth in a short, terrible smile.

"Keeps the Good Folk away, doesn't it, Uncle Sean?" I can hear that tone in my voice, that jolly, brisk tone that the nurses use.

"Do it...and if there's trouble...fire will bind them." He closes his eyes.

I'm happy to humor him. "Of course." His breathing evens out. I sit back on the lumpy chair and open my book.

"Mark." It's so quiet, I almost miss it. "Bring me water...the well...drank it every day...keeps me safe."

I put a finger in my book and close it over. "Water from the well. Sure. I'll bring it tomorrow."

"You're a good boy." He sinks back into the white nest of a bed. His raspy breaths become a snore.

I sit there, finger still in the book, lost in thought. Memory is a strange thing. It's so fleeting, so untrustworthy. I remember reading that each time we remember something, we're actually recalling the last time we remembered it. Or at least that's how I remember remembering the article. But the gist of it was that we dilute things when we bring them to mind, each summoning of the old event steps back further and further from the reality that was. And yet sometimes, unprompted, they come up, fresh and unexpected. Memories.

You're a good boy. His words stir an echo in me.

I see Uncle Sean, his face looming over me.

"Well, boy, you've gotten yourself in trouble here." A black beetle scurries across the mossy ground. I pull at my soaked clothes. My toy car is in my pocket, a reassuring lump of metal. I feel an unpleasant warmth trickle down my forehead.

"We won't tell anyone about this. You're a good boy." His face is huge, blotting out the blue sky, the green leaves.

I follow the quick-running stream through the overgrown field. The cold spring wind billows my coat around me. *Should have brought wellies,* I think, as my boots sink into the sludgy mud. *Perhaps there's a pair somewhere in the house?* I feel it again, that sense of acute amazement that I could fit into tall Uncle Sean's wellingtons. Maybe they'd even be too small for me? I'm still carrying the plastic dish from the kitchen—yes, I finally did the washing up. I empty it out on the grass, smiling to myself at his superstitious ways and leave it to collect on my way back.

I reach the dark shelter of the trees, and as the branches close overhead, the bitter wind dissipates. It's quiet in here. I can hear the burble of the stream as it rushes among the stones, the hoarse *caw* of a bird somewhere above me. My feet make no sound on the mossy carpet. I push against the bushes that grow along the banks of the stream. It should be here somewhere...ah, there it is. The rag-tree. It's smaller than I remembered, a bush, really. Faded ribbons cling to the stripped branches; baby-blue, ice-cream-pink, a cream that was once yellow. Below it, there's the well. The holy well. The rag-tree and the well are all connected; the waters from a holy well are believed to have healing properties. When I was a child, I remember the occasional person wandering out around the back of the house, bottle in hand, to collect water. The rags on the tree look like faded party favors, but each one signifies a wish that was once granted, a healing that took place. The well itself is unimpressive; it's a tiny, whitewashed basin, sunk into the ground, a layer of silt covering the bottom.

I hesitate. Would he know if I took the water from the stream? This well-water looks soiled, dank. Still, it's what he wants. I take the empty plastic bottle out of my pocket and dip it in, balancing carefully on the rim of the well.

Hahahaha. A trill of laughter bubbles up, sweet and silvery. I swing around, startled. There's no-one there. I shake my head to dislodge the sound, and dip the bottle again. The brackish, brown water mirrors me as I bend over.

The bottle breaks the surface of the water. My reflection shimmers. For a moment, in the half-light I see myself, smaller, younger, forehead marked with an ugly cut.

Here. It happened here.

I stand back sharply. My heart pounds low and quick in my ears. As I screw the cap on the bottle, I see them. Beetles. A coal-black line of them, swarming over the edge.

Aithníonn ciaróg ciaróg eile. One beetle recognises another beetle.

I bring my foot down on them, time and time again, until their shining bodies are crushed to ink and smears.

The next day, I'm back on my seat in the intensive care unit. The curtains are drawn around Sean's bed. He's asleep again. I take my book out and read a few chapters, but I'm finding it hard to concentrate. Doors open and shut, voices murmur through the plastic curtains. I put the book down and day-dream of running streams and pale grey skies and my fractured, uncertain reflection in the brown water.

We sit together in silence till the nurse comes and checks the humming machines.

"Ach, poor fella." Her voice is soft. "It's good you're here."

"Has my sister been in?"

"Is she the girl with the long, dark hair? She was in earlier, but she left. Didn't seem best pleased with the way we were treating him."

"That's Anne, alright." I smile at her ruefully. "Sorry about that."

The nurse smooths the bedclothes with a practiced hand. "Ah, we're used to that here. People get very emotional at this time." She pauses and looks at me, and her voice drops to a whisper. "You know it's coming? It's anytime now."

I knew it was coming, but I'm jolted. "Sean?"

She nods. "It won't be long. You get to know the signs. If you want to talk to him, today would be the day." Her green eyes are the colour of crushed grass.

———————————

It's evening by the time Sean wakes. I watch him tremble into life; a series of tiny spasms, eyes flickering open.

"The water…" His voice is barely there. I pour the water carefully into a disposable beaker. I've tried to separate the silt out, but a few stubborn particles swirl and eddy, refracted in the plastic. His lips tremble on the brim as I hold the glass to his mouth. He manages a sip, then another. The excess water glazes his chin.

"I'm…going." Beads of moisture glitter on his stubble. "The water…kept me…can't do…any longer." I put the beaker down and fold my hands over his cold ones. It feels strange to do so, womanly, but no-one can see me here behind the curtain.

There's a long silence. His eyes close, his breathing is hoarse and laboured. Then his head jerks upwards, his eyelids open. "Lay me out at home." His eyes are fierce and blue, startling in his shrunken face.

I don't insult him by pretending he's going to survive this. "I promise." I've been to many wakes as a child; ham sandwiches, walls sweating with steam from boiling kettles, the good dishes out, the coffin lid peeled back to display a rigid corpse. I'm not sure how I'll organise it, but I can't refuse him.

"And the water…"

"The holy water?' As far as I remember, it's tradition to sprinkle it on the dead. "Sure. Of course."

"I have…"

I lean closer. "What's that, Uncle Sean? I didn't catch it."

"I have…"

"I have a darkness inside me." His face is clenched now, a mass of moving lines. His worn hands tighten on mine.

"I'm here,' I say, but as I do so, his grip loosens. The harsh breaths stop. All at once, there's only one of us in the room.

I'm a man. I don't cry. But there's a wetness on my face, a slickness I rub off roughly with my sleeve.

———

The wake is as wearisome as I expected. Neighbours who hadn't been to visit in years call by, eating their way solidly through sandwiches and cake, stretching out hands for the cups of tea, for whiskey glasses. In the good room, in a cheap coffin, Sean is stretched out in his Sunday suit, shiny with wear, and a clean white shirt. Thank God the undertakers dressed him. I just supplied the clothes. His fingers are knotted in a pair of brown rosary beads. His face has settled in hard, pale lines. He looks, well, he looks *dead*. Not just dead, but like he'd never lived, as if he'd always been this strange, motionless statue of himself.

Anne stands by the coffin, wearing a black dress and jacket. I'm just surprised she hasn't added a mantilla. She took up the position as soon as she arrived; it suits her to stand there as the official family representative to shake hands, to accept condolences, and to tell people over and over again how kind they are. Her husband Joe has the decency to take a back seat. He's drinking whiskey in the hallway with some of his cronies. Anne's black hair shines in the lamplight. From time to time she touches the corner of her eye lightly, as if to brush away an imaginary tear.

"Aren't you very good to come?"

"Ah, I'm sorry for your loss. God bless him, he was a decent oul' skin, the same Sean."

"Thanks now, he'd be happy to see you here."

I listen to as much of their meaningless remarks as I can before I use the excuse of food to move periodically back into the kitchen. I boil the kettle, butter bread, cut cake. The rhythm is comforting.

"Mark. They need more sandwiches out here." Anne stands in the doorway, cheeks flushed with heat and importance.

I close my hand over the knife. "In a minute." I hack into the bread with a savagery that's almost enjoyable.

———————————

It seems like the guests want to stay forever. My head rings with the noise of their chatter. I wander through their ranks, half-listening to snatches of conversation. A few people are telling stories about Sean as a young man.

"He was a big strong fella, he'd pitch more hay than anyone in the course of a day."

"He could have made the county team."

"No better man for the dances when he was a gossoon." I feel my memory of the younger Sean fleshing out, growing more solid with every word. Over the last week or so, it feels like I only dreamed that tall man once stooped over me, in the woods behind the house. Anne is still shaking hands, her head bowed to one side, her expression carefully regretful. I boil the kettle again.

You're a good boy.

The stories continue, relentless. Sean hadn't mixed much in years, not since the summer I'd been there. Some of them weren't even stories, just the kind of banalities people trot out on such occasions.

"I hadn't seen him in a long time, and then I happened to be passing by the house not so long ago. I thought he looked fierce shook." Heads shake, wise looks are exchanged. One old man even sang *On the banks of my own lovely Lee* in a quavering voice, which made no sense. Sean wasn't from anywhere near the river Lee, or from Cork. I cut more cake, a smile fixed on my face.

And then finally, blessedly, they're gone. I stack up the dirty dishes and carry them out to the kitchen. Joe gives me a hand. He's not a bad guy. He just never stands up to Anne.

"Mark?" And there she is. *Think of the Devil, and he'll appear,* as Sean would say. She stands in front of me, hands on her hips. "When is the will being read?"

"No idea," I say truthfully. "Maybe ask whoever this solicitor is?"

"As if you don't know!"

I shrug and keep clearing up. Mind you, I wouldn't object if Sean has remembered me in his will, but it's not the reason I came down to spend time here. The reason I…I frown, head blurred. I don't quite know why I've come down. I can't remember.

"He knows who looked after him. Doesn't matter how much you fussed over him in the last while. Sure all you did was spend the summer here as a boy." Her eyes are hard and spiteful.

I've had enough. I open the door. "Isn't it time you were going?"

The washing-up is done. Anne and Joe have long gone. I pour the water outside, as Sean would have wanted me to do. It must be almost midnight, but I'm not sleepy.

I go back into the good room. Anne swept and polished it earlier, so we wouldn't be shown up in the eyes of the neighbours. It's the best room in the house, but unused, so under the air-freshener and the beeswax is a low, disagreeable odour of must and rot. I pull a chair up to the coffin and sit. It feels like the right thing to do, to sit with Sean on his last night in the house.

It's been a long night. The room is still warm with the press of bodies, the heat of the teapots. I close my eyes for a moment. Images rise up, blurred at first, then more focused.

It's a bright summer's day. I'm playing outside, but I've lost one of my Dinky cars. I look under the tussocks of grass and peer into the clear water of the stream. I can't find it.

It's my favourite one! The red car. Maybe I dropped it by the well? Carefully I wade through the long grass, towards the trees. If I follow the stream, I'll find the well...

My hand tickles. My eyes snap open. There's a beetle climbing industriously over my fingers.

"Ah!" I fling it to the ground, disgusted. It scurries off before I can crush it under my boot. I sit up straighter, dazed. I'm not sure if I've been asleep or not.

"I did my best," I say aloud. I tried. I came down when he asked. I went to the hospital. I got him his well-water...

Damn it. I knew I'd forget something. The holy water for the wake. I sigh and go to the kitchen. The remnants of the dirty water are still in the plastic bottle in my coat pocket.

"Right," I say. "The last thing you wanted." I pour some water on my fingers and sprinkle it over Sean's stern face, his Sunday-best suit.

The front door slams shut. It makes me jump. Then the windows rattle.

What the hell?

I hear it again, that light, silvery laughter.

"Who is it?" I stand up, and as I do, the coffin moves slowly on the trestles. I'm paralysed with a breathless, ice-cold fear. Sean still lies there, eyes closed. But his skin…his skin bubbles as if something's moving under the pale, hard flesh. His shirt ripples on his chest.

And then they come, pouring out of his nose, from between his lips, forced apart by pressure. A glistening horde of fat, black beetles, slick with saliva and juices.

I have a darkness inside me

I scream and jump back. They pour out of the coffin and onto the floor, relentless, a hideous, shining shoal of movement.

The years peel away, I see myself. I see Sean. I remember.

If I follow the stream I'll find the well. I walk into the forest. It's dark here, darker than it seemed when I went there before with Uncle Sean to get the water from the well. It's dark and lonely here, and I feel a bit scared. But I want to find my car, so I keep going.

I can hear someone laughing. That's better. At least someone's here. I take a few more steps, and then see a flash of colour. The ribbons on the rag-tree. Nearly there.

And then I see it, on the lip of the well. Red and shiny and precious. "My car!" I run to pick it up, then slip, trip slowly, then faster. My head bangs off the well, and I'm falling. I'm falling and all I can hear is laughing as I hit the water.

I open my eyes. I see Uncle Sean, his face looming over me.

"Well boy, you've gotten yourself in trouble here." A black beetle scurries across the mossy ground. I pull at my soaked clothes. My toy car is in my pocket, a reassuring lump of metal. I feel an unpleasant warmth trickle down my forehead.

"We won't tell anyone about this. You're a good boy." His face is huge, blotting out the blue sky, the green leaves. "You hear me?' he shouts at the trees, at whoever is still laughing in the deep woods. "He's a good boy. If you're trying to take someone, take me instead."

The laughing stops, and he picks me up. "We'll get you home now," he says. His voice is a deep rumble in his chest.

"But before I do…" He brings his heel down neatly on the black beetle, grinding it to a black paste. *"The curse of the seven deadly sins on you."*

I touch the scar on my forehead, feel it bloom under my touch. Sean. Uncle Sean. *I owe you.* I stand in the flood of beetles, and know what I have to do.

It ends here.

The old house goes up like dry tinder. The beetles pour out of the doors and windows, but it's too late. Their bodies crisp, curl up, burn like matches. As the orange flames leap higher, the shadows pull back.

Water is good, but fire is better. Fire binds them, after all.

I see Sean's face loom over me, bright in the sunlight; his hands reach out and pull me upwards into against his warm chest.

I stand in the orange glow and feel the memories return. They spill forth, clear and bright and beautiful, as the fire licks the night sky.

FINIS

BIOGRAPHIES

SARA CENTURY is a queer writer who specializes in short stories, articles about comics and film, and who has written many, many zines. She knows a lot about comics, movies, and history. She is an artist, comic creator, filmmaker, and podcaster, and she used to be a musician. She can found online at www.saracentury.com.

KRISTI DeMEESTER is the author of *Beneath*, a novel published by Word Horde and *Everything That's Underneath*, a short fiction collection published by Apex Books. Her writing has been included in Ellen Datlow's *The Best Horror of the Year* volumes 9, 11, and 12, *Year's Best Weird Fiction* volumes 1, 3, and 5, in addition to publications such as *Black Static, Pseudopod, The Dark,* and several others. Find her online at www.kristidemeester.com.

TRACY FAHEY is an Irish writer of Gothic fiction. In 2017, her debut collection *The Unheimlich Manoeuvre* was shortlisted for a British Fantasy Award for Best Collection. In 2019, her short story, 'That Thing I Did' received an Honourable Mention by Ellen Datlow in her *The Best Horror of the*

Year Volume 11, with five stories on Datlow's Recommended Reading list for 2019. Her short fiction is published in over twenty-five Irish, US and UK anthologies. She holds a PhD on the Gothic in visual arts, and her non-fiction writing has been published in edited collections and journals. She has been awarded residencies in Ireland and Greece. Her first novel, *The Girl in the Fort*, was released in 2017. Her second collection, *New Music For Old Rituals*, collects together her folk horror stories and was released in 2018 by Black Shuck Books.

COY HALL lives in West Virginia with his wife and a handsome green-eyed cat named Locksley. He splits time as an associate professor of history and as a writer of horror and mystery stories, nearly all of which are set in the distant past.

ALYS HOBBS lives in Derbyshire, where she divides her time between writing, gardening, and exchanging slow blinks with cats. Her work has been published in literary journals such as *Popshot*, *The Ghastling Magazine* and the Kandisha Press *2020 Women of Horror* anthology.

ANDREW MICHAEL HURLEY lives in Lancashire, where he teaches English literature and creative writing. He has published two short story collections. His first novel, *The Loney* (2014), won the Costa First Novel Award, was short-listed for the James Herbert Award, and was published in twenty territories. His second novel, *Devil's Day* (2017), jointly won the Royal Society of Literature's Encore Award in 2018. His third novel, *Starve Acre* (2019), has continued his darkly atmospheric explorations of English folk horror.

HAZEL KING lives in Oxford, England. She holds an MA in Creative Writing from the University of Manchester and currently works in a university library to fund her writing habit. This is her first publication.

JACK LOTHIAN is a screenwriter for film and television and currently works as the showrunner on the HBO/Cinemax series *Strike Back.*

His short fiction has appeared in a number of publications, including *Weirdbook, Hinnom Magazine,* the *Necronomicon Memorial Book, The New Flesh: A Literary Tribute to David Cronenberg,* and *The Best Horror of the Year Volume 12.* His graphic novel *Tomorrow,* illustrated by Garry Mac, was nominated for a 2018 British Fantasy Award.

TIM MAJOR's recent books include SF novel *Snakeskins,* short story collection *And the House Lights Dim* and a nonfiction book about the 1915 silent crime film, *Les Vampires,* which was shortlisted for a British Fantasy Award. His latest novel is *Hope Island* (2020, Titan Books). His short stories have appeared in *Interzone, Not One of Us* and have been selected for *Best of British Science Fiction* and *Best Horror of the Year.* Find out more at www.cosycatastrophes.com

NEIL McROBERT wrote a PhD thesis on Gothic Literature before fleeing the halls of academia. He now lives in an old, haunted village in the north of England, where he spends his nights writing about things the polite folks don't mention. He has written for *The Guardian* and reviews for numerous other publications. "A Well-Fed Man" is his second published story.

ELIZABETH TWIST writes speculative fiction, some of it dark, some of it dreamy. She loves the wobbly line that separates the known from the unknown. Sometimes what she writes is funny, sometimes on purpose. Her work has appeared in *NonBinary Review, AE: The Canadian Science Fiction Review, Daily Science Fiction,* and elsewhere. Find her on Twitter @elizabethtwist.

SHAWN WALLACE lives and breathes folk horror in the Boston metro area, where he works. He enjoys traveling throughout New England when he gets the chance, particularly in the autumn months. He is haunted by abandoned buildings, and tries to photograph them when they're not looking. "The Binding Tide" is his first published short story, although he's got a number of other folk horror short stories written, and plans to write many more. Find him online at folkhorrific.com.

COPYRIGHTS

EDITORS' NOTE

In an effort to maintain the spirit of the authors' intent and their use of the English language as an expression of Folk Horror, Nosetouch Press has retained English spellings from the writers who used them.

A NOTE ON THE TYPE

The text of this book is set in Adobe Caslon Pro, and is based upon the typeface first created by English typefounder, William Caslon I (c. 1692–1766).

The distinction and legibility of his type secured him the patronage of the leading printers of the day in England and on the continent. His typefaces transformed English type design and first established an English national typographic style.

Caslon worked as an engraver of punches, the masters used to stamp the moulds or matrices used to cast metal type. He worked in the tradition of what is now called old-style serif letter design, that produced letters with a relatively organic structure resembling handwriting with a pen. Caslon established a tradition of engraving type in London—which previously had not been common—and was influenced by the imported Dutch Baroque typefaces that were popular in England at the time. His typefaces established a strong reputation for their quality and their attractive appearance, suitable for extended passages of text.

Caslon's typefaces were popular in his lifetime and beyond, and after a brief period of eclipse in the early nineteenth century, they returned to popularity, particularly for setting printed body text and books.

Adobe Caslon is a popular revival designed by American designer, Carol Twombly. It is based on Caslon's own specimen pages printed between 1734 and 1770 and is a member of the Adobe Originals program. It added many features now standard in high-quality digital fonts, such as small caps, old style figures, swash letters, ligatures, alternate letters, fractions, subscripts and superscripts, and matching ornaments.

Composed by Clever Crow Consulting and Design,
Pittsburgh, Pennsylvania

NOSETOUCH PRESS™

Nosetouch Press is an independent book publisher
tandemly-based in Chicago and Pittsburgh.
We are dedicated to bringing some of today's most
energizing fiction to readers around the world.

Our commitment to classic book design in a digital
environment brings an innovative and authentic approach
to the traditions of literary excellence.

NOSETOUCHPRESS.COM
We're Out There

Science Fiction | Fantasy | Horror | Gothic | Supernatural | Weird

YOU MAY ALSO ENJOY

THE FIENDS IN THE FURROWS I
An Anthology of Folk Horror

THE FIENDS IN THE FURROWS III
Final Harvest